DARE YOU TO *Love*

OAK SPRINGS BOOK ONE

MINA COLE

Edited by Kelly Zaledonis
Cover by Kate Farlow with Y'all. That Graphic
Proofread by VB Proofreads

ISBN: 9798839242340

www.minacoleauthor.com

For Tony.

Thank you for believing in me, encouraging me,

and helping to make my dreams come true.

Forever & Always.

Chapter 1

KATE

SUNSHINE SPILLED THROUGH the second-story window of my home and seeped into my skin. The heat, mixed with the smell of coffee, woke me from a peaceful sleep. Was there ever a better invention than a timer on a coffee pot? Not any I knew of.

Normally I used those quick-brew pods, but the brewer was already packed in one of the many kitchen boxes. Moving was a pain in the ass. I was ready for the next phase in my life, though. Ready to close this chapter and open a new one. Maybe even a whole new book.

Stretching out with my arms above my head, lengthening out my spine, I closed my eyes and counted to five. I sat up and put my feet flat on the floor and stretched my neck, five seconds on each side. Then I took a few deep, calming breaths before standing up.

It was the same routine every day. Stretching and deep breathing. It's what helped to center me before starting the day. My alarm hadn't gone off yet, which meant I had thirty extra minutes to get ready for work.

After a quick shower, I made my way down to the main floor of the house. I cinched my robe a little tighter as I walked down the carpeted stairs. I rounded the banister and stopped in the living room. This was the room I'd miss the most.

My best friend, Mindy, and I had spent a lot of time watching movies and curling up by the stone fireplace. A few open boxes were in the room awaiting their final contents before I sealed them up. I had to remind myself that selling this house was a good thing. It was too large for one person, and the bad memories in the house outweighed the good ones.

The smell of fresh brewed coffee wrapped around me like a warm blanket when I entered the kitchen. It was my second favorite room in the house. I'd taken a few cooking classes over the past few weeks and was really starting to love it.

Cooking for one was always a challenge, and lots of food went to waste until a few months ago when I discovered a local food bank close to the house. They were always happy to take any leftovers I had. It only encouraged me to cook more. Most times I didn't even eat the food, I just drove it to the food bank and dropped it off. Serving there a few times a month brought me great joy, especially since I was able to meet the people who ate my food.

Stepping around the obstacle course of boxes, I grabbed my favorite mug from beside the sink and poured the steaming liquid in. As I added cream and sugar, I looked out the kitchen window over the large backyard.

The parties I wanted to host back there died along with my dreams for this house when my ex-boyfriend, Vincent Bradbury, walked into this very room eight months ago and told me he was cheating on me. For the second time.

After I threatened to tell his mother if he didn't leave—he was a mommy's boy through and through—he packed his things and left. He transferred the house to my name shortly after. Hush money in the form of a half-a-million-dollar home that was too large for me to handle on my own. That, coupled with the expensive-as-hell mortgage I couldn't afford, was reason enough to sell.

The house still belonged to him, no matter how much I renovated it. He had it constructed for us a year and a half into our relationship. I was so excited to pick out flooring and paint colors. To decorate the inside and fill it with things we loved. Except none of that happened.

Vincent became a different person. Not the same man I met and fell in love with, if you could even really call it love. I was so enamored with the life he was promising me, I confused it all with love. It was just the hope of a different life, not that my life was terrible or anything. Far from it. It was just… boring.

I wasn't one to leave the nest on my own, and Vincent was the push I needed. We met when he was on a business trip in my hometown in Pennsylvania. I fell in what was clearly lust and followed him to Bellport, North Carolina.

For the first year, we lived together in his fancy three-bedroom condo while I attended college. I was lucky to be able to transfer mid-semester. I think it had something to do with the school being Vincent's alma mater. He always managed to pull strings. I could see now that it wasn't luck or connections, but rather the specific strings that allowed him to control me.

Vincent didn't want me in school. He held to the old-school and sexist belief that many women had fought against: the woman's place is in the kitchen. Vincent wanted control, though, and the only way for him to have that over me was in the home. Everything in our relationship was always his way, and the young girl in me didn't argue.

It wasn't how my parents were with one another and wasn't how I was raised. Looking back, I couldn't figure out why I went along with it for so long.

After forcing me to drop out of school, he got me a job at a company owned by a friend of the family because I insisted on working. I was hired on as a secretary, where I remained for six years before they promoted me a year ago. A promotion I earned thanks to my hard work and dedication. Not because of Vincent and his connections.

The secondary alarm on my phone went off, indicating I had twenty minutes before I needed to be out the door. Thankfully, I only had to change. On my way to the master bedroom, I stopped in the hallway and stared into the spare bedroom just beside it.

Vincent and I had talked about marriage and kids. It was three years into our relationship and a happier time. Vincent started acting like the man I fell for again, and we started trying to have a baby. This room was meant for the baby, and I had started taping paint swatches on the wall.

This was also the room that changed our relationship for good. After a year and a half of trying, and a few doctor's visits where Vincent was told he couldn't have kids, he changed. It started with ugly comments aimed my way. Then it escalated into personal digs that chipped away at my self-esteem and self-worth. Six months after that, he stopped coming home at night, claiming he was working late.

It took another six months before I found out he was cheating on me with his secretary. They were having late nights at the office, but not a lot of work was getting done. I left him and went to live with my best friend. He begged me to come home and promised he'd change. And he did, for almost a year. Until a woman I didn't know approached me with pictures, claiming she was pregnant with his child.

Turns out she was wrong. Vincent was still shooting blanks, and she was having someone else's kid. But I'd had enough and kicked him out. He tried to lie and manipulate his way back home, but I stuck to my guns. Unfortunately, I was still dealing with his bullshit. Calling every day, showing up at my work unannounced, and coming by the house often.

Speaking of work. Shit, I was going to be late. I was never late. I ran to the bedroom and threw on the pencil skirt and blazer I had picked out the night before. Flats were the shoe of choice today since I was going to be in and out of meetings all day, some outside the office.

My hair was in pretty good shape. I sprayed some dry shampoo on my roots and rubbed it in, then ran the warmed-up straightener through it, smoothing it out, and ran for the door.

"YOU'RE LATE," BONNIE, the assistant my boss and I shared, sang out.

"I know, but only by five minutes."

"Mm hmm."

I rolled my eyes at her and headed for my corner office. The door clicked shut behind me, and my feet shuffled quietly on the carpeted floor. I unloaded my bags from my shoulders and sat down at my desk. My computer was already on, which I found a little odd, but it made things easier since I was already late.

My eyes nearly fell out of my head at the number of e-mails in my inbox. How the hell did I have three hundred overnight? It was a weekday. I was going to need more coffee to deal with those.

I headed for the small break room. Only a handful of employees worked on the top floor. A year ago, they promoted me from the ground to the top. It felt good to skip the middle. I now worked directly for the owner himself, Mr. Trent Lawrence.

Overall, he was a decent boss. A little sexist but he covered the comments well, and they were never aimed at myself or Bonnie. The only issue I had was that he was friends with Vincent and his father. Which meant that they both dropped in whenever they wanted, and Mr. Lawrence never told them to leave.

"Head's up," I heard Bonnie call out. I turned to see if she was talking to me, and my blood ran cold. Speak of the devil. Vincent strolled through the door.

"There you are," he said, opening his arms to me for a hug.

When I didn't move, he smiled bigger and opened them a little wider. I still didn't move. I raised an eyebrow at him and continued to stir my coffee.

"Come on, Katherine. I thought we were past all this," he said, dropping his arms.

"It's Kate, and yes, we are past all this. Because we're over."

He sighed and stepped closer to me. "Still holding a grudge, I see. I had no idea you could be so stubborn."

"I'm not holding a grudge against you, and I'm not being stubborn. It's called a break-up."

He chuckled. "Still playing that game, are we?"

"There's no game," I gritted out. He was maddening.

"Come to lunch with me," he said, taking another step toward me. My back dug into the countertop behind me, causing me to wince. "I just got here. I have a busy day with lots of meetings. Besides, we're not together anymore. It's been eight months, Vincent. Get a clue. We're through."

"Katherine, one of these days you're going to run back to me, and because I'm such a nice guy, I'll be there with open arms."

I took a step toward him now. "The only way I'll be back in your arms is if I fall and you have to catch me."

"You fell for me once, sweetheart. It'll happen again. You'll see."

I let out a frustrated growl and pushed past him. On my way back to my office, I almost ran into Mr. Lawrence's sons. They were about as dumb as a box of rocks. Another downside of working here was that I had to work closely with the two of them.

My job differed from anything I'd ever heard of, and part of me wondered if Mr. Lawrence made it up because it fit what he needed. I was what he called a *closer*. When a large offer for development was on the table and the client needed a little push to accept, they sent me in.

I'd closed sixteen offers in the year since I'd been promoted to this position. I was damn good at my job, and I actually liked what I did. Especially because Lawrence Development Company was one of the top retail and housing developers in the southeast. Small-town expansions were our specialty and also my favorite.

Small towns were so charming. Every time I went to one, I collected a small trinket as a memento. They were always homemade items, not something you'd get at a big retailer which made them special. I loved that.

I had barely made it back to my office when Vincent strolled in. He unbuttoned his suit coat and sat down in the lone chair in front of my desk. I resisted the urge to stab him with my pen and sat down in my office chair.

"What do you want?" I asked.

The corners of his mouth lifted in a smile, and he casually crossed his ankle over his knee. "I want to get lunch with you."

"I already told you, I'm busy. It's nine in the morning, anyway. Don't you have to be at work?"

I clicked on several e-mails that I wanted to delete and sipped my perfect coffee. It made my taste buds sing when I got the blend of coffee, cream, and sugar just right.

"I don't need to be in the office today. I've got a meeting with a client at three, but other than that, I'm all yours."

I looked up at him and scowled. Or at least I attempted to scowl, but it didn't seem to have any effect on him.

"Vincent, you've got to stop this."

"Stop what?"

"This." I gestured between us with both hands. "This following me around, at work, at the house, to the gym. Calling and texting. It all has to stop. We're through."

He frowned and leaned forward, dropping his foot to the ground. "You're serious?"

"Yes, I'm serious! Did you think I was joking all this time? That this was some stupid game?"

"Partially, yes. I thought maybe you just needed time, and you'd come to your senses, but I see now that I need to try more aggressive tactics."

"What does that mean?" I asked. My voice shook a little, like it used to, and it pissed me off. I was turning into the scared little girl around him again. In all fairness, though, his tone and words really scared me. What more could he do? He was basically stalking me already.

"It means that you need more convincing. I have just the thing." He smiled and stood up, buttoning his suit coat before walking out.

"Tell your dad our tee time is at eight. Don't be late," Mr. Lawrence called out as Vincent walked toward the elevators. I hadn't realized he was standing near my door.

"We won't. Thanks again for your help today, Trent. I think good things are coming our way," Vincent called back.

Mr. Lawrence chuckled and waved to him before popping his head into my office.

"Kate, nice of you to finally show up."

"I was only five—"

He cut me off. "Meet me in my office in ten to go over the Perkins deal. You've got a meeting with Mr. Perkins at eleven." He tapped the door with his knuckles before walking away.

I let out a breath and pulled up the file. Before printing everything out for the case, I wrote *find a new job* on a sticky note. If I was going to make a clean break from Vincent, then I needed to get out of this place. The relationship Vincent had with my boss was not healthy for me.

THE DAY FLEW BY, and I was more than ready for it to be over. We had a lot of new projects. Some that were in the development stages, a few which were in proposal stage, and two that were in the scouting stage.

I worked as a scout for six months before Mr. Lawrence promoted me. If I were being honest, I enjoyed scouting much more. Scouts went to the locations for the developments and checked them out. If it was a small town, they stayed somewhere local and checked out the area. Ate at local restaurants and talked to owners of small businesses to get a feel for how the town was doing.

Then Mr. Lawrence sent in his sales team. It was made up of four employees plus his two idiot sons. His sons usually took the simple jobs. The ones that basically sold themselves. If a client was dragging their feet, then I went in and pushed their hand using my skill and charm.

Every project followed the same protocol, and every project went through to completion. My first two meetings today went well, and both clients signed on the dotted line. Then I met with a building owner who was ready to dump an apartment complex.

Mr. Lawrence wanted to purchase the building for a development idea he had. I went down to give the man our offer. He needed time to think about it, so next week sometime I'd follow up with him and give him a little nudge.

"Ready to go, dear?" a familiar voice that grated on my every nerve said from the doorway.

"Vincent," I said on an exasperated exhale.

"C'mon, let me at least buy you dinner. I wanted to talk to you about something."

"Tell me now. I want to go home and soak my feet."

He scrunched up his nose, and then quickly smiled when I caught him. He'd never approved of my nightly ritual. It wasn't every night. Just when I'd been running around all day. I deserved a glass of wine and a foot bath.

"We won't be all night. Just a quick dinner at that little bistro you like, and then I'll have you home right after."

I wanted to scream. Why wasn't this man getting it? I didn't want to have to file a restraining order, but things were headed in that direction. It would make things really awkward with my boss, considering they were friends. Vincent was sort of the reason I had this job. He helped me get my feet in the door. The rest was all me.

"Fine. One dinner. Consider it your goodbye dinner."

He laughed. "You're funny. I didn't know you had such a good sense of humor."

I shook my head and waited for him to exit my office so I could lock up behind him. He put his hand on the small of my back as we walked to the elevators, and I sidestepped away from him.

"No touching me."

He put his hands up. "Okay. No touching."

"I mean it, Vincent."

He crossed his finger over his chest. "Cross my heart."

A muffled growl escaped me as we got into the elevator. We rode down in silence, and when we got to the car garage, he tried to persuade me to ride with him. I refused four times before he finally gave up and settled on me following him.

It only took two minutes to drive to the bistro. I could have walked, but I needed a few minutes alone to think of my next move. This was not part of my plan. Giving in to Vincent was only going to spur things on further. I should have just gone home.

Vincent tapped on my window, letting me know I was stalling. I could hear him yelling it on the other side of the glass. I quickly texted Mindy to let her know where I was and to send help if she didn't hear from me in half an hour, then I got out and followed Vincent inside.

This restaurant was our little spot. Even when times were bad, we'd come here, and time seemed to stop. All the anger and fighting stopped, all the mean words disappeared. The tension between us drained away when we were here. We'd just sit and enjoy our meal as two civilized adults, almost like friends. It was peaceful.

I hadn't been in here since we broke up. Vincent asked for our usual table, which happened to be open. I slid into the booth and placed my napkin on my lap. Vincent did the same and took a sip of the water that was already at the table.

"This is nice, huh?" he asked, looking around.

"Sure."

"Have you been in here since we…" his voice trailed off.

"Since we broke up? No."

I thought I saw him wince, but he covered it with another sip of his water.

"Vincent, can you just cut to the chase?"

"Relax, we'll get there. Let's just enjoy our dinner like we used to. Surely you can be civilized for one meal?"

"Yes. Can you?"

He chuckled. "Of course."

Vincent ordered expensive wine and an appetizer. I nibbled at a slice of bread while we waited. The server brought out our wine, and a few minutes later, the appetizer came out.

We had almost finished with our meals when Vincent finally got to the point of our dinner.

"Katherine, I'm not sure if you heard, but my Grandmother Violet passed away recently."

"Oh no, I'm so sorry." I lifted my hand and reached for his before I realized what I was doing and put it back in my lap.

He nodded. "Thank you. The family is holding a memorial service on Saturday, and I'd love it if you'd attend. You know how much that would have meant to my grandmother. She always liked you." He smiled. It wasn't forced or fake, and it threw me a little.

It was true, his grandmother did like me, and she made it a point to tell me so every time she saw me. Which was often since Vincent and I had attended many family dinners.

"I'll be there," I mumbled. "For Violet," I added.

"Yes, of course."

Vincent paid the bill, and I finished off my glass of wine.

"What time should I pick you up on Saturday?"

I looked up at him and, for the first time since our breakup, felt bad about turning him down. It could have been my own sorrow about his grandmother passing away or the sad look on his face. Still, I wasn't going to ride with him and get stuck there. Especially since his family would be there.

"No need. I'll drive myself."

He raised an eyebrow. "You'll drive there? Do you remember how to get there? I was always the one that drove us."

"I remember. I'm not an idiot."

"I never said that you were. I was merely implying that you might not remember since you were always a passenger."

I rolled my eyes. Tired of this conversation and the back and forth with him. "I'll be fine, Vincent."

"All right then. I'll see you there at three."

"Yes. See you at three."

We walked out to our cars in awkward silence, having already said goodbye in a way. I slid behind the wheel and quickly shut the door before he could say anything else. He hesitated beside his car before getting in and driving away.

What had I just agreed to? I found myself connected to Vincent more and more lately. Here I was trying to sell the house to make a clean break, and I had just agreed to spend an afternoon with Vincent and his family.

Chapter 2

PETER

"LET'S TAKE A VOTE," Tom Tracy suggested from the front row. "All in favor?"

I held my breath. For once, I was the one they were voting on, or rather my choice in clothing. As the mayor, I was expected to dress a certain way. It wasn't like I was trying to change things completely, just a little. Instead of wearing a suit and tie every day, I'd only wear them when there was official town business or when I had a meeting.

No hands went up, and my hope of changing things deflated like a leaky balloon.

"All opposed," Tom called out.

All hands in the room went up. I shook my head.

"Really?" I asked Frank. He was my best friend, or at least he was supposed to be. Now I wasn't so sure. The smirk on his face told me he was messing with me. "Payback's a bitch."

Tom coughed, and I shot him a look. He was grating on my last nerve with his formalities.

"I move to add a 'Daily Happenings' column to our newspaper," Beverly Anderson said.

I rolled my eyes, as did Frank, Sid, and Tom. Beverly and her friends, Ethel, Mary Ann, and Rose, were always trying to add a gossip page to the town's paper. The paper was online and only reported actual town news, but it didn't stop the group of gabby women from asking for us to vote on one every meeting.

"Beverly, the paper is online, and we already report the daily news."

"It's boring," Ethel called out.

"It's a newspaper," Tom replied.

"It *used* to be a newspaper," Ethel pointed out. "It used to be easy to find, too, but now it's on that fancy internet and it's hard for us old folk to keep up."

Frank scoffed, and Rose shot him a look of disdain. I covered my laugh with a cough.

"Ladies, we've gone through this a number of times. Last year we voted to change the paper to digital form. We're not going to change it back."

"I wasn't here," Mary Ann piped up. "I wouldn't have voted for it."

"It would have taken more than one vote against it for us to keep it in paper form," I explained.

"I move to a vote," Ethel shouted.

"What exactly are we voting on?" Sid asked. He had a point; this was getting a little out of hand.

"I vote we get rid of the old-school deputy hats we've been forced to wear," Frank said.

"Oh, for the love of..." I rubbed at my forehead. I was losing control of this meeting. Which wasn't a surprise; I normally lost control at least once during each meeting. An hour and a half—on a good night—each week that I could never get back.

"We're not voting on that again," I said through gritted teeth.

Frank smirked at me. "All in favor?" He lifted his hand high in the air.

When he noticed Sid wasn't raising his hand, he nudged him in the side. Sid's hand slowly went up. Frank's smirk quickly turned to a frown when he looked around and saw they were the only two with their hands up.

"Seriously? Tom, c'mon man. You know the hat thing is dumb," Frank said.

"I think it makes you look sophisticated," Tom replied with a shrug. Ken nodded. Ken and Tom were best friends and owned stores next to one another.

"Sophisticated?" Frank scoffed. "Try dumb."

"That's no way to get votes, young man," Rose chided.

"Okay, that's enough. All opposed?" I asked.

All the other hands in the room went up. Frank looked around, threw his hands up in exasperation and frowned. I caught his eye and made sure to smirk the same way he did to me earlier while I slowly lifted my hand. Frank glared at me, and I laughed. I'd warned him.

"That's bullshit," he muttered under his breath. Sid chuckled quietly beside him. "Don't know why you're laughing. You have to wear them, too."

"I'm not the one who has a problem with it," Sid replied.

"Suck up."

"You're such a child," Sid said.

Before Frank could respond, I addressed the other subject up for discussion, "Beverly, what exactly did you ladies want to vote on?"

"To change the name of the paper from *Oak Springs Tribune* to *The Daily Happenings*," Mary Ann said quietly. She was the most timid of the four.

"No, that wasn't it, Mary Ann," Rose scolded. "Although I don't care much for the name of the paper right now, either."

"It was to add a 'Daily Happenings' column in the paper. We don't care whether it's online or in paper form," Beverly said.

"Although it would make it easier for us to read if it weren't on that fancy online thing," Ethel added.

"You mean the computer?" Frank snipped.

"Quiet, you! Your time is up," Rose chided again, tossing a wadded-up piece of paper at his head. It could have been a used tissue; that thought caused me to laugh out loud. Sid and Tom laughed too. Frank crossed his arms over his chest and pouted.

"Okay, there seems to be a lot that you want to vote on. We can vote on them all separately or all at once. Any thoughts?" I asked.

"I think we should vote on each one individually," Laney finally piped up. She had been busy typing on her phone, keeping notes for the meeting. Like she did every meeting.

"This isn't fair. They want to change the name of the paper, make it paper form again, and add a gossip column. I vote no!" Frank said.

"Hush," Rose said throwing something else at his head.

"What are you throwing at me, and where are you getting it?" Frank asked as he turned around to face her. She was sitting a few rows behind and over to the side of him. I was honestly impressed with her aim.

"Things from my purse. You'd better quit before I get to the heavy items," she warned.

He muttered something under his breath and turned around to face the front.

"Enough. Let's vote and get this over with. Tom, call out each item up for vote, and I'll take count. Laney, you keep track." She nodded.

"All in favor of the name changing?" Tom called out.

A slew of hands went up, which was surprising. I counted quickly. "Fifteen."

Laney's eyebrows went up as she typed on her phone.

"All opposed?" Tom asked.

"Five," I said.

"All in favor of keeping it digital?"

Quite a few hands went up, but not as many as I thought there would be. "Seven."

"All opposed, which means we move back to print?" Tom called out.

"Thirteen," I mumbled.

"What?" Laney asked. I wasn't sure if she was asking because she was as shocked as I was or because she didn't hear me.

"Thirteen," I repeated.

She nodded and rolled her eyes as she typed on her phone. It meant more work for her. She and Tom were the ones who worked on the paper, which meant they were the ones who had to get it printed again.

"I move for an addendum to that," Laney said.

"Okay, what's the addendum?" I asked.

"It wouldn't be weekly anymore; it would be bi-weekly or monthly. It's too difficult to print weekly, and if you want your gossip page or happenings page in there, then you should keep it online because it would be easier to have it appear daily as you requested."

This was why I loved Laney Walters. She was quiet when she needed to be, and spoke up when she had something important to say. She was articulate and my voice of reason. We were usually on the same page.

"Okay. I change my vote," Ethel said.

"Me too," Mary Ann agreed.

Before the other two ladies chimed in, I spoke up, "Ah hell, let's have a recount."

"All in favor of digital form?" Tom called out.

All hands went up.

"Unanimous."

Laney smiled and recorded the number on her phone.

"All in favor of adding the daily gossip…er…happenings page?" Tom asked.

Sixteen hands went up. The head count for the evening had been twenty. Laney would put the items up for vote in the paper the next day and allow an online vote, open for only twenty-four hours, for those who were unable to attend. So our actual count would come in later in the week.

"Okay. To recap, 'no' to the mayor wearing plain clothes during normal business hours," Laney said, and I cleared my throat because I was still feeling a little bitter about that one. "'No' to the deputies getting rid of their hats. 'Yes' to keeping the paper digital and 'yes' to the new 'Daily Happenings' column. Anything else?"

"Vote on a name change for the paper," Ethel called out.

I rolled my eyes. "It will take too long for us to come up with new names and vote on them tonight."

"What if we did an online poll?" Laney asked.

"That could work," I said. "Who will come up with the names?"

"We could do two polls. One that's open for name suggestions, then we'll collect the top three, and the second poll will be the actual vote on the name."

"I like that," Frank said, pointing at Laney.

"Okay, do we need to vote on that idea?" I asked while crossing my fingers. This meeting needed to end. Thankfully, everyone shook their heads.

"I like it. Let's do it. One of you youngsters can help us older ladies vote," Ethel said. Rose eyed Frank, who was trying to shrink down in his seat.

"One more order of business before we close. I'll be out of town for family business this upcoming weekend. If you need to get a hold of me, please contact Elaine, or if you have my number, leave me a message and I'll get back to you. If there's no other business, then I officially end this meeting." I waited, and after a minute of silence, I slammed my gavel down on the small desk I always sat behind and breathed out a sigh of relief that the meeting was finally over.

THE DRIVE BACK TO my house was slow and quiet. Not many people were out on Main Street since they were all still at the meeting or heading home for the night. The meeting had taken three hours, and it felt like it sucked the life out of me.

Kind of like on *The Princess Bride,* when they used that machine to suck the life out of Westley. That's what the meetings did to me. It was the only part I truly despised about being mayor. Everything else was fairly easy.

After losing what felt like a year of my life to the meeting, I was about to lose many more on the upcoming trip I had to take. My grandmother, who never judged me, passed away, and her memorial service was Saturday. I wanted to go because I adored my grandmother. It was the other people in attendance I couldn't stand.

To say I didn't get along with my family would be the understatement of the century. I detested them, and the feeling was mutual. Six years. That's how long I'd avoided them. They had no idea that I was the mayor of a small town, or that all the "crap"—as my mother called the furniture in my grandmother's house—was handmade by me.

They only cared that I wasn't a doctor or a lawyer like my older brothers. Or that I hadn't settled down yet. In fact, when my mother called to tell me of my grandmother's passing, she asked if I was going to bring a date. Who brings a date to a memorial service?

I sighed and let myself into my house. Luckily, there were still a few days before I had to leave, and if things went south, I could always drive right back home. It was a three-and-a-half-hour drive, but I'd gladly do a turn and burn if it meant I didn't have to suffer through listening to my obnoxious and self-righteous family.

I was only going for two reasons: to pay my respects and say goodbye to my grandmother, and also to collect all the furniture I made for her. If my family got their hands on the items, they'd throw them away, or worse, burn them. My parents didn't understand or care about the talent and time that went into making a piece of furniture.

My grandmother did, though, and she was always supportive and encouraging of my professions. She was the only one who had known I was the mayor of Oak Springs, and she took my secret to the grave. Literally.

I saw her a few months ago when I brought her a new piece of furniture. We sat and talked and walked her property. That's when she found out about my job. She was so proud of me. My chest had swelled with pride. It was a moment I'll treasure forever.

My parents would never be proud of me like that. They shamed me every chance they got, hoping I'd change course and get a job worth being talked about. I despised being associated with them, so I was perfectly fine with not being talked about.

They were everything I wasn't. Ruthless, materialistic, rude, and haughty. My mother was so consumed with her social status that she turned her nose up at anything that didn't have an expensive designer label. Thus the reason my furniture was crap. She tried to keep up with the rich people around her and tried to get ahead of them every chance she got, which never seemed to be effective.

My father had been born rich. My grandfather owned a jewelry store that did very well. He was also excellent in investing. Naturally, my father inherited the store, but he sold it to a large chain for twice what it was worth and retired early to travel the world and play on his big yacht.

My mother, on the other hand, came from humble beginnings. She'd been born in the small town where I resided. She hated it now. It was because of that deep hatred for the town that I didn't tell her about becoming the mayor. It would just be one more black mark against me.

I felt as if I could never measure up to my parents' expectations. My father and I never saw eye to eye, and he sent me away as often as he could when I was growing up. The best thing he ever did was force me to spend summers with my mother's parents in Oak Springs. I sort of owed part of who I was today to him, though I'd never admit it.

Both of my parents berated me, but my father was far worse. He'd always hoped I'd get into something having to do with finance. He wanted me to take care of his bookkeeping and then hopefully his investments. He obviously didn't know me well. I'd rather jab a hot poker in my eye than look at numbers all day. I looked at enough numbers since I owned my own business.

I had a falling-out with my father about ten years ago, and I hadn't talked to him since, even when I did see him. My mother still attempted to keep in contact with me, but it usually ended in an argument and her crying. I wasn't sure why I continued to put myself through it.

This wasn't about them, though. This was about my grandmother. I didn't have to stay long, I told myself as I threw clothes into the washer. I went through my closet to find the suit I wanted to wear to make sure it was clean and ready to go. My shoes were shined and ready along with a nice tie.

I was exhausted, and instead of warming up something to eat, I peeled off my clothes and collapsed into my bed. Everything else could wait until morning, including a meal.

Chapter 3

KATE

A COLD CHILL SWEPT through my body, making me shiver. Had the temperature dropped, or was it just all the cold-hearted people who filled the room? I glanced around at all the faces that used to feel so familiar and felt nothing but sadness and regret. That last one was an emotion I felt often when it came to Vincent. Regret.

I regretted allowing him to manipulate me into the meal earlier in the week and then convincing me to come here. I also regretted not putting my foot down more when he visited my office every day. The only thing I felt good about was rejecting him repeatedly when he asked me to lunch or dinner.

Vincent, with his smug smile and conniving ways, was a pain in my ass. This wasn't how I wanted to cut ties with the man. This was only making things worse. Muddying up the waters between us and making my intentions of removing myself from anything having to do with him unclear.

A shrill sound rang out from the corner of the room, causing me to jump. Vincent's overly dramatic mother, Mary, clutched her chest. Always the actress. His father, Edward, fawned over her, trying to figure out what could possibly be the matter this time. News flash: it was probably nothing, just like always.

I rolled my eyes and finished my glass of wine. I checked the time on my phone, wondering how much longer this was going to take. It was supposed to be a simple memorial service. I had to continue to remind myself that I was here for Violet.

I would miss Violet and her theatrics. She'd made the mandatory family dinners I attended while dating her uptight grandson bearable. Her family was nothing like her. Instead of warmth and kindness, they radiated hatred and ice. They were a bunch of money hungry assholes who only cared about their social status and how much crap they had. The complete opposite of my family, and another reason I was thankful Vincent and I hadn't worked out.

I suppressed a groan; it was only four thirty. The whole "paying respects" thing lasted an hour before Mary and Edward shuffled us into the library to wait for the staff to clear the dining room.

Edward had a letter his lawyer had given him. Apparently, it was from Violet. He felt that today would be a good time to read it since we were all gathered together. It wasn't a bad idea, except I had no idea why I was included.

Seconds ticked by, which turned into minutes, and then an hour had passed. I had finally finished the glass of wine I'd been milking when I really wanted to toss back a whole bottle, and we were still waiting. I was itching to leave. The whole thing was annoying as hell.

I wasn't sure why we couldn't just read the letter here in the library where everyone was already gathered. My only thought was that Vincent's parents wanted it to be a formal affair. They loved attention and drama. Thrived on it.

I shivered again. Goosebumps ran down my arms and legs. Vincent took a seat in the chair beside me, scaring the crap out of me. It was like my own personal demon sprouted up from hell and manifested itself in the form of Vincent. Conniving smile and all.

"Hello, Katherine. Thanks for coming," he said.

"It was for your grandmother."

He ignored me and looked around the room, smiling and waving to someone I didn't know. "I'm sorry I wasn't able to greet you when you arrived; there were so many people I had to speak with. Can I get you a refill on your wine?" Without waiting for an answer, he grabbed my glass and headed for the sideboard.

I made a mental note to check to make sure he hadn't poisoned it. How would one go about doing that? I looked around for a plant that I could toss a little into just to see what would happen. I guessed that if the plant shriveled up or died, then I'd have my answer.

To pass the time while I waited, I stood and walked over to one of the three mahogany floor to ceiling shelves that surrounded the library. Perusing the books seemed like a good way to keep busy. Each bookcase was filled to the max with books of all different genres. They were all organized by subject, then alphabetized by author last name. If I had a library, I'd do the same. It made finding your favorites easy.

I always wanted to get lost in a book whenever I wandered into this room. It had a large bench seat that overlooked the breathtaking backyard and pond. The plush seat with matching pillows always drew me in. One night, I spent an hour in this room before anyone noticed I was missing. I read a quarter of *The Catcher in the Rye*. Was it possible to inherit a room? If so, I wanted the library.

Vincent returned and shoved the wineglass into my hand. "Here."

"Thanks," I muttered. As I took a sip, I noticed he was seething.

"They finally cleared out the dining room for us. Took them long enough," he scoffed.

"This is your grandmother's memorial service. I'm sure the guests just wanted to pay their respects. The food was in that room," I reminded him.

He turned to face me. "Yes. I'm aware. I'm just ready to get this over with so we can leave."

His lack of respect irritated me. Why had I stayed with him for so long? Oh, that's right, because I was weak. Not anymore. I refused to play the part of the naïve, shy girl. Someone easily broken and manipulated. It took a lot of work with a therapist to get to where I was now, and I'd be a damn fool if I let Vincent drag me right back to where I started.

Vincent put his hand on my lower back and steered me out of the library. My skin crawled. I wanted to shake him off but let him guide me into the dining room anyway. My heels clicked on the marble flooring as we walked down the hall. We passed the drool-worthy kitchen as we went. That would be the second room I'd want to inherit, and it was second only because I wasn't a good enough cook to fully enjoy it. The kitchen was made for chefs, and I was no chef.

We entered the dining room, and I held in a gasp. It had been over a year since I'd been here, and it never ceased to amaze me. The long, dark oak dining table was so large it spanned the whole width of the room. The matching chairs were intricately carved. The table had three large leaves, and I wondered whether it took more than one man to lift them. They looked massive.

Vincent pulled a chair out for me at the table, and I reluctantly sat down. He helped scoot me in, and then placed another full glass of wine in front of me, taking the still full one out of my hand. Looking around the room, I thought about the horrible dinners that took place in this beautiful room and cringed.

Double doors opened to a terrace that overlooked the expansive backyard with rolling hills. Soft lighting from not one, but two large chandeliers gave a nice ambient feel. But even with the most elegant china and mood lighting, the family still managed to make the room feel cold and miserable.

The things they said to one another were awful; words that should never be uttered to those you love. Personal attacks and angry words laced with hatred. I'd always ignored most of it and stayed quiet. More like Vincent's prop than a true guest.

During one of the dinners, my mind drifted off. Violet's crystal, displayed in large cabinets in the corners of the room, drew me in. Violet leaned over to me amid all the bickering and asked if I liked her china. I nearly laughed at the woman. How could she be going on about china when her family was verbally hurling daggers at one another?

When my eyes met hers, though, they were filled with warmth and kindness, and her glowing smile put me at ease. She nodded, as if to prompt me to answer her question.

"Yes. The china is lovely."

She smiled again and proceeded to tell me a story about each piece. How she acquired them and what they meant to her. Some were wedding gifts, some were from travel abroad with her husband, and a few pieces were from her children and grandchildren.

My favorite story was how she found a vase in Italy and had to fight for it. Her stories were interesting and kept me distracted from the hate that swirled around us. It almost felt like we were in the middle of the storm where it was calm.

A tear escaped my eye, and I swiped it away. I looked around, thankful that not a single person was paying attention to me. I gulped my wine and thought about how I would rearrange my kitchen to house the elegant crystal and display cases if they were mine.

I wouldn't mind the large oak coffee table in the family room with the ornate carvings. It was my favorite. I'd eyed it many times before. The first time was when the family argued about finances, and I'd slipped away into the room.

The room alone took my breath away with its large floor to ceiling windows that overlooked a large landscaped yard. A mantle above the fireplace matched the other dark oak furniture in the house. My eyes had landed on the table, and I'd spent a half hour thinking of ways to slip it out of the house.

When I came through the front double doors today, I'd quickly checked the room. The table was still here, but Mary would likely use it for kindling when tonight was over. The thought of something so beautiful being destroyed was painful.

Vincent, his brother Thomas, and his mother started an argument, which drew me back to the situation I had gotten myself into. Elizabeth, Thomas's wife, rubbed a hand over her large pregnant belly and smiled at me. I returned the smile and tossed back my glass of wine and looked around for someone to refill it. I had a long night ahead, and I needed a good buzz to get through it.

Chapter 4

PETER

MUD SPLASHED UP ONTO my windshield from the road. It was raining so hard I couldn't see in front of the truck. It was like a bad omen. I was already running late, which wasn't like me unless it was intentional. Which, of course, this was. I'd been dragging my feet. My stalling caused me to be really late, and now I was kicking myself.

I'd gotten great at avoiding my family, but this was something I couldn't back out of, and the anxiety of seeing them again ate away at me most of the drive.

The black iron gates that stood at the end of my grandmother's long driveway appeared out of nowhere. I hit the brakes a little too hard and almost slid past them, my back-end fishtailing in the mud. I didn't remember my grandmother's road being so terrible. It was riddled with massive potholes and so thick with mud my tires sank down into. I was amazed I hadn't gotten stuck.

I managed to turn into the small space in front of the gates and hit the call button to get buzzed through. The gates were locked, which seemed strange since the memorial service was open to anyone who knew my grandmother.

The gates unlatched with a clank and slowly creaked open. If I didn't know better, I'd think the place was haunted. The whole scene was like something out of a black and white horror film, complete with lightning strikes.

I pulled in and made my way up one side of the long half-circle drive to the front of the house. It was monstrous, with nine bedrooms, six and a half bathrooms, a library, living room, sitting room, and dining room. My favorite part of the house was the industrial-sized kitchen on the main floor. It's where I spent a lot of my time. Our cook, Francine, and nanny, Adaline, always spent time together there, and I hung around for the delicious baked goods.

I stopped just in front of the door. A gentleman holding an umbrella ran out and stopped at my window.

"Hello, Sir. May I walk you in and park your car for you?" the man asked. He smiled when he recognized me, and I did the same.

"Oh, Peter! We haven't seen you in years. It's me, Benjamin Froth, your grandmother's groundskeeper. Tonight I'm the valet," he said as he smoothed his hands over his vest. "Go on inside; your parents will be thrilled you're here."

"I doubt that Benjamin, but it's so nice to see you again. They'd better be paying you well." I grabbed my suit jacket from the passenger side before exiting the vehicle.

Benjamin chuckled, which told me they weren't. He handed me the umbrella before sliding in behind the wheel. I ran up the steps, careful not to splash too much water onto my pants. Under the small overhang above the front door, I lowered the umbrella and shook it off.

Before I could reach for the door handle, one side of the large double doors opened, and a tall man ushered me inside. My parents were taking advantage of my grandmother's staff, which shouldn't have surprised me.

"Good evening, may I take your umbrella?" the man asked.

"Sure."

I dried off my shoes as best I could on a white, fluffy mat just inside the door and shrugged on my suit coat. I wanted to look presentable for my grandmother, even though she wouldn't be here. Also, my mother would cause a scene if I looked anything less than perfect.

Stepping to the left, I looked myself over in the mirror that hung above a small wooden table. *My* wooden table. I was taking inventory of everything I had given to my grandmother. Careful not to leave anything behind.

I had brought a packet of small sticky notes with me. They were bright yellow, so I'd be sure to see them. I tagged the table in the back where no one else would see it unless they were looking for it. Then I checked my hair in the mirror.

The rain had done a number on it. Combing my fingers through the long strands on top and tousling it was the best I could do. I adjusted my tie and took a deep breath before turning back around and heading to the right of the stairs to find everyone.

The hallway was empty. I checked some rooms as I passed. The library was first, and it was empty. The kitchen? Also empty, except for the staff. It was too quiet in the house for a memorial service. Was it already over? My dress shoes squeaked on the floor as I walked. Bickering floated out of the dining room and hit me in the chest like an actual fist, stopping me dead in my tracks.

I tried to think of an exit strategy. My brothers were most likely arguing with my parents. Maybe it would be best if I didn't attend. I could sneak around the house and load up my furniture. The only thing was, I wanted to wait until the rain died down. I didn't want all that wood to get ruined after all of this. Some pieces I wanted for myself.

I inhaled and slowly let it out as I slipped into the room. Just as I suspected, my mother and brothers were fighting about something. My father was talking to one of his brothers and a few cousins. There were a number of other people I didn't recognize seated around the table.

I gazed around at them, and my eyes fell on a gorgeous brunette I didn't recognize. Was she a friend of the family? Perhaps my grandmother's caretaker? She seemed uncomfortable, fidgeting with the stem of the wineglass in front of her. Her eyes were locked on the table.

Unable to tear my eyes off her, I continued to stare. Her hair was curled and pulled half up, held by a silver clip that shimmered in the chandelier's light. The rest of her beautiful hair cascaded down her shoulders and back.

She looked up, and her eyes locked with mine. My heart stopped, and time stood still. Her cheeks turned pink, and she glanced away. She had beautiful eyes. A bright blue that sparkled like my favorite ocean off the coast of Greece. Mesmerized, I took a step toward her.

My mother shrieked out my name at an octave only dogs should have been able to hear and ran over to me, throwing her arms around me.

"Darling, where have you been? Come sit down, we've been waiting for you."

She was always putting on a good show for everyone. Even if the audience was only family. She had a smile plastered on her face, and she smelled of whiskey.

"You're late as usual," she hissed into my ear as she led me to the table.

She stopped at the chair across from the brunette. I was about to introduce myself when my brother, Vincent, sat down next to her. She must have been the girlfriend my mother was always telling me about. Apparently, they were still together. There wasn't a ring on her finger though. I checked. How the hell my brother got a girl like her was beyond me.

"Katherine, this is my brother, Peter. You haven't met him before because he doesn't like to come to family things," Vincent quipped. He turned toward me. "Peter, this is Katherine Miller, my—"

"His ex," she blurted out before he could finish.

"Pleasure to meet you, Katherine." I extended my hand to her across the large table.

"Please, call me Kate. And it's a pleasure to meet you, too."

She placed her small hand in mine, and a shock of electricity raced up my arm. I almost pulled away. A small gasp escaped her lips, and I knew she felt it too. I squeezed her hand and smiled. She pulled her hand back and took a sip of her wine, eyes glued on the table again. She looked adorable with the pink hue still on her cheeks. A shy smile crossed her face before she quickly hid it.

My mother, dressed to the nines, complete with an oversized black hat and veil, tapped a wineglass with a knife to get everyone's attention. I winced at the thought of my grandmother's favorite crystal breaking. My father ran over and took it out of her hand, then helped her back to her seat. I shook my head. *Same old shit.*

"Shall we start, everyone? Your grandmother left us a letter," my father announced proudly. I knew he was really only concerned with what he would inherit. He had tried to talk my grandmother and grandfather into just leaving everything to my mother and him.

I wrangled myself a glass of scotch, took a sip, and sat back for the show. There was no way my family would not argue every part of that letter. I glanced at Kate. She threw her wine back and signaled for another. I chuckled. She was having about as good a time as I was.

But why was she here if she wasn't dating my brother anymore? Had Vincent forced her to come? Maybe she took care of my grandmother before she passed away. I knew nothing about what had gone on around here for the past six years.

The table blocked most of my view of her, so my imagination was running wild. Visions of a tight pencil skirt that hugged her curves was enough to make me shift in my seat. The casual blouse she was wearing did nothing to hide the fullness of her breasts. I avoided looking in that direction so I wouldn't look like a shallow ass. Plus, she was obviously here with my brother even though they weren't together any longer.

My dad stood at the head of the table and cleared his throat. He took the documents out of the large envelope and laid them out on the table. Then he took a deep breath and looked around the room, smiling at everyone. I smiled as well, but not for the same reasons. My grandmother couldn't go without getting the last word in, and it would no doubt be very entertaining.

The letter was nothing more than my grandmother telling us each what she left to us. Normally that would be done in a will, and she had one of those, too, but my grandmother knew us well, and she knew that my parents and their siblings would fight it every step of the way.

She was smart by setting up a letter so she could say what she wanted and why she left people the things she did. Vincent got the books from the library. That made me laugh. She also left him some money and outed his gambling addiction, which I already knew about. It appeared Kate also knew his "secret" judging by her pinched lips and coy smile. My father seemed surprised and glared at Vincent.

Thomas and Elizabeth got nothing important. Love and kisses, blah, blah, blah and a few things no one would fight them for.

My dad quietly read the letter before his eyes flew to mine. Rage and murder in them.

"She left him the house!" he screamed.

My eyes widened, and my jaw dropped. The scotch in my hand almost fell to the floor. No, that couldn't be right. What the hell was I going to do with this monstrosity? My father dropped the letter and was up and out of his chair screaming, his anger directed at me.

"This is an outrage. That boy doesn't even come around. How will he take care of this house without a serious solid job?" my father went on. And he wondered why I never came around anymore. I shook my head. Nothing had changed. I would have avoided coming here altogether if it wasn't for my grandmother and what she meant to me.

"Keep reading, Edward. There has to be an explanation," my mother said.

My father read out loud, *"Quiet down, everyone; I was only kidding. He wouldn't want to take care of a large house like this, anyway. I left the house to my three sons to split up. Peter, take with you all the things you've built for me so your mother doesn't throw them away. Pick whatever else you want. I know whatever you choose, it will be because it means something to you. Never lose that precious heart of yours."*

"We'll be sure to call the lawyer first thing on Monday," my father said with a nod in my uncle's direction. I held my breath for a rude comment about being a carpenter or all of the "crap" I've made my grandmother over the years, but it never came. Instead, he continued reading.

Kate got the china, and I was happy to hear it was going to someone who would appreciate it. I had briefly considered taking it all home. I didn't know where I'd put it, but it felt wrong leaving it behind. It meant a lot to my grandmother.

My father had an envelope in his hand, and he hesitated before giving it to me.

"Be good to one another and try not to kill each other when this is over. I love you all despite your flaws. Until we see each other again, Violet."

I stuffed the envelope into the pocket on the inside of my suit coat and escaped outside. The house erupted into chaos, and I wanted to be as far away as possible.

Chapter 5

KATE

THE ENTIRE HOUSE BROKE out into an uproar. Vincent's mother was out of her chair screaming, his father was arguing with Thomas, and Vincent was storming toward them. They were all going crazy over a letter that honestly meant nothing unless it was in the will.

I looked around the room at everyone, thinking about the kind of hell it would be to be married into this ridiculous family and feeling glad that it hadn't happened. During the reading of Violet's letter, my mind kept wandering to Vincent's brother. *His brother.* I was shocked. How had we never met before?

He was gorgeous and tall. I tried to avert my eyes from him, but they kept finding their way back. The suit he wore fit him like a second skin. It looked like it was made to fit his wide frame and sculpted body. He seemed comfortable in the suit, and I wondered what kind of job he had. Was he a CEO of a business? A lawyer like Vincent? He had to have some fancy job since he belonged to *this* family.

Before Edward had begun reading Violet's letter, I snuck a peek at Peter. His chiseled jaw, with a dusting of whiskers, clenched and unclenched as he scanned the room anxiously. The rain had really done a number on his hair, but it only added to his appeal.

The shouting from the corner of the room drew my attention back to the present. My eyes landed on Vincent. Compared with Peter, Vincent looked old. He had aged a lot over the years I had known him. His black hair had a lot of silver in it now, and the laugh lines around his eyes really showed his age.

There was a six-year age difference between us, but thirty-two was still young in my opinion. Life had done a number on him. Probably from all his scheming and lies. I would imagine that would take a toll.

Vincent was skinny and shorter than both of his younger brothers. He had hazel eyes and looked more like his father. The middle brother, Thomas, looked a lot like Peter. They both had dark hair and a more muscular build. Both had green eyes—different shades though. Peter's were more vibrant and stunning. He was the most attractive of the brothers. In fact, he was the most attractive man I had ever seen.

The volume of the shouting increased, and it seemed like the perfect opportunity to escape. I gulped down the rest of my wine and slipped out onto the terrace. Peter was there sipping on a drink he'd been smart enough to bring with him. It was too late to chance going back for more wine. I needed to get out of there anyway.

"Some family, huh? My grandma knew us all well. She never once passed judgment, just rolled on as if our fighting was normal, or as if she didn't even realize it was happening. I miss her already," he muttered.

The crisp night air was blowing my hair around. Rain was still coming down in every direction, soaking us as we stood. I kept my gaze straight ahead and didn't respond, too busy trying to think of an exit strategy.

I wasn't sure how I would get to my car out front. Sneaking through the backyard would work, except my heels would sink into the grass, and I'd get soaked. Right now, that seemed like a small price to pay for freedom.

Problem was, I didn't know where they had put my car. Even if I took my shoes off, it wouldn't help. Also, I needed to leave my address so they could ship the china to me. I was stuck.

"I'm sorry about what your dad said about you. That must hurt," I finally said.

"Thanks, but I'm used to it, so it doesn't bother me much anymore. Like everyone already pointed out, I don't come around much, so I don't have to hear it all the time. Did you get everything you wanted?" he asked.

I felt bad for him. It must hurt a little to not be close to your family. I couldn't relate.

"I did. Well, except for that beautiful dark oak coffee table in the living room. It kind of has a special place in my heart. There was this terrible dinner one year, and I wandered into the living room. The beautiful craftsmanship of the table distracted me from how awful the evening was. I hope nothing bad happens to it."

I looked up at him and startled. He was standing much closer than I had thought. His tall stature blocked some of the rain from me. The smile on his face confused me. It was as if I'd given him a compliment.

A familiar shiver ran down my spine, and I glanced over my shoulder. Vincent's icy gaze felt as if it was slicing through my midsection. I clutched at it as I watched him push off the table he'd been leaning against to make his way toward us.

"Shit," I whispered.

Peter turned around, and then took a huge step away. The cold rain hit me, and I missed his warmth. It felt good to have him standing there, not only blocking the rain, but also as a protection against Vincent.

"There you are. I've been looking for you. Can you believe it? Books. Like I even have the time to read now. What the hell am I going to do with all of those?" Vincent stopped in front of me, and then smiled. "Do you want to get out of here, sweetheart?"

I winced. I wasn't his anymore, and I needed to end this whole thing. There was no use in avoiding it or dragging it out much longer.

"Vincent, I'm glad I came here tonight. It's like closure for us." I patted his chest. "You should be grateful for those books. If you decide to pass on them, you have my address. I'd love to take them off your hands. I was thinking of renovating one of the upstairs bedrooms into a library. If you'll excuse me, I'll be taking off now. Alone." Most of what I had just said was a lie. I was selling the house. I'd still take the books off his hands, but I'd have to store them in a basement instead of a nice room.

I turned toward Peter, "It was nice to meet you."

Just as I took a step, a hand clasped around my wrist. I whirled around and tried to pull myself free, but Vincent tightened his grip.

"Katherine, I know things between us are strained, and I know that some of it is my fault. I was hoping you'd come to the cemetery tomorrow. We're all staying here tonight, and in the morning, we'll drive over there to say our final goodbyes. Will you come?" he asked. And then added before I could respond, "It would have meant a lot to Grandma Violet."

Vincent was pretending to be so nice, but it wasn't fooling me. He knew how to manipulate me and get me to do what he wanted. I tried to pull my wrist free, but he tightened his grip again. I had to twist my body to keep it from hurting with the way he held onto it.

"Fine, but only for Violet. Let go of my wrist. You're hurting me!" I shouted.

I tried to twist and pull it away, but Vincent yanked on my wrist and pulled me closer to him. I was panicking now, and I had a history of panic attacks. The walls were closing in around me. I slammed my eyes shut and willed it to go away.

Looking weak in front of him would only spur him on more. He'd feel like he'd won. His grip was so tight my wrist started to burn. Bending at a very awkward angle, I tried to ease the pain.

"Let her go, Vincent," Peter commanded.

My eyes flew open at the sound of his voice. He was standing very close to Vincent now, almost in his face. Vincent had a crazed look in his eyes, one that I'd never seen before, as he stared into Peter's face. His grip tightened on my wrist. The look on his face was menacing, and it scared me.

"Ow! You're hurting me!" I screamed.

Peter grabbed Vincent by the shirt collar and pulled him up, so they were now eye to eye. "Let her go now!"

"Or what!? You'll do what?" Vincent spat out.

"Vincent, let go of me," I pleaded. I wiggled and pulled, but he held on tight. He had never laid a hand on me before.

"You have one more chance to let her go, or else," Peter warned.

"Or else what?" Vincent laughed. It was manic and terrifying. "You can't do anything to me. This is none of your business anyway, so butt out!"

He pushed off Peter and turned his gaze on me, yanking my wrist. I jerked to the side and started to fall. Someone caught me before I hit the ground, freeing my wrist from Vincent's grasp. When I was standing upright again, my eyes fluttered open. Vincent was bent over holding his nose. I didn't know what had happened.

The panic attack was setting in, and the darkness was creeping into my vision. I knew what was coming. I would pass out. Peter's strong arms caught me as I slumped backward. I looked up. His eyes were dark and stormy, and his jaw was working back and forth.

If he were a cartoon character, steam would have been coming out of his nose. That thought helped me to relax a little, and my vision cleared. My breathing was still labored, but I was free. I took a few steps away and started counting backward from ten, focusing on my breathing. It was a technique I'd learned at a young age to help ease the panic.

"You idiot! You broke my nose. I can't believe you just hit me," Vincent screamed. Blood dripped down his hand and onto the pavement. "And for her? You don't even know her."

Before Peter could speak, Edward ran out and pulled him back. Mary threw her arms around Vincent and cuddled him to her chest. Laughter came from behind me, I looked over my shoulder. Thomas was bent over with his hand on his stomach.

"What the hell were you thinking, Peter?" Edward asked. "Why would you hit your brother?"

"He probably said something stupid."

"Stay out of it, Thomas," Mary hissed. Blood covered her dress. "Peter, what the hell is your problem? What has Vincent ever done to you?"

"Not to me, mother. To Kate. He grabbed her wrist so tight she was begging for him to let her go. Look at it; it's all red. I warned him to let her go, and he wouldn't listen."

Peter's face was twisted in a grimace. He held my wrist out so his mother could see. I could feel the anger rolling off him in waves, yet his touch was gentle.

"I bet she was trying to run out on him again. She's a tramp. She slept around and lied to our Vincent about it," Mary shouted.

Red filled my vision. The panic disappeared in a cloud of smoke to be replaced by anger and rage. I didn't give a shit what this family thought of me, but I would not let him tell the world that I was a cheater.

"*I* slept around? Is that what you told everyone, Vincent? I think it's time you tell your family what actually happened before I hit you myself," I threatened, moving toward him.

Adrenaline coursed through me, and I was ready to beat him. He pushed himself away from his mother and scowled at me, his jaw working back and forth. I knew my threat was weak, but I also knew he didn't want his mother to think badly about him. He straightened up and lifted his chin.

"I cheated, mother, not Katherine. But I've begged for her forgiveness, and I'm willing to do whatever it takes to win her back." He turned toward me. "I love you."

It was the same old game. He'd beg for forgiveness and promise to never do it again. One time I got a new phone, the other time a new Apple watch. This time it was dinners and shows. Flowers at the office and even a diamond necklace. I declined the meals and shows, made sure to throw the flowers away in front of him, and mailed the necklace back.

Yet here we were again, this time in front of his family, so I looked like the fool if I didn't take him back. He had some nerve. Vincent took a step forward, and I took a step back. Putting his hands up in surrender, which I knew was all for show, he stopped advancing on me.

"Katherine, can we just go somewhere and talk about all of this? We don't need everyone involved in our business."

"I think you've done enough talking, and if you think I'm going to let her go anywhere with you alone when you physically assaulted her, you're a bigger idiot than I thought," Peter warned.

"Why are you even involved? You don't know her or our situation!"

"I don't have to know the situation. I know you, and that's enough." Peter's jaw ticked in anger, but he remained in control.

Vincent turned toward me and tried again. "Katherine, please just give me a chance."

"I don't see why you two can't work this out. He apologized," Mary said, standing and smoothing out her dress.

My mouth hung open as I gaped at her. She believed him? Of course she did. He was the golden child. The one who could do no wrong. And even when he did something wrong, if he apologized and put on a good face, she believed him.

"He cheated on me, and just now he grabbed my wrist and left marks," I said, showing her my arm.

She waved a hand in front of her face. "It was just a misunderstanding. I'm sure he didn't really grab it that hard. You probably tripped, causing him to squeeze tighter to keep you up."

"Is that what you think?" Peter's voice boomed, causing me to jump. "That your precious son couldn't have hurt her? That he isn't capable of being a disgusting human being? If the cheating and the lying aren't enough to make you believe that he's not the son you think he is, Kate's red wrist should. And if that still isn't enough, then you will never see him for who he truly is."

Vincent let out a laugh that sent shivers down my spine. He started to slow clap and stepped into Peter's space. "Oh, baby brother. You haven't been around for six years to know anything that goes on in this family. It's best that you just go back to your simple life and build things. Stay out of things that are none of your business."

Peter took a step forward. His hands clenched at his side. Edward stepped in and put his arms between the two, separating them.

"That's enough. Mary, help Katherine inside. It's time for her to go. Peter, get your things and get out. I've had enough of this behavior from you. Every time you come around, it's the same thing."

Without a word, Peter turned and headed inside. Mary looped her arm through mine and held my wrist in her hands as she walked me inside. She treated me with more kindness in that moment than she ever had in the six years I'd known her. I would never understand this family, and I was more than happy to get the hell out of there.

They could forget about me attending the funeral. Vincent was lucky I wasn't heading to the police station to file charges. I left my name and address with Mary—it'd be a miracle if I ever saw the china again—and then ran down the hallway.

I hurried toward the front doors like the house was on fire. I didn't know where Peter had gone, but it didn't matter. I wanted to sever all ties with the Bradburys. He seemed more than capable of handling his dysfunctional family all on his own. Right now, I needed to escape before Vincent found me again.

The man by the front door handed me my coat as I ran by. Freezing rain hit me as soon as I stepped outside and soaked me to the bone. The cool spring air blew my hair in every direction. I was free, and that was all I cared about.

"Madam, allow me to get your car. Take my umbrella until I can fetch it," an older gentleman said. He handed me the umbrella.

I chewed on my thumbnail while I waited for my car. When it arrived, I hurried around to the front and slipped behind the wheel, practically tossing the umbrella at the man in my haste to escape. Foot slammed on the gas, I left without looking back.

I was driving too fast on the dirt road, and my car slid in the mud, but my wrist still hurt, and I was mad as hell. The rain was coming down in sheets, fast and heavy, and I couldn't see the road ahead of me. Once I put some distance between myself and that house, I'd slow down.

Thunder cracked, and lightning lit up the sky. A fallen tree appeared in the road ahead, illuminated by the lightning show. I jerked the wheel to the side while I hit the brakes. My tires slid in the mud and spun me sideways. I screamed and put my hands over my face.

The car slammed into the tree on the driver's side, which flung my body around like a rag doll before my head hit the window. Hard. Everything went dark.

I WOKE UP IN A FOG. The airbag had pushed my head into the window. I maneuvered my way around it and sat back against the seat. My head throbbed and there was blood on my hand.

Tiny shards of glass covered my lap, and there were minor cuts on my legs. It was raining on me. When I looked up, I saw the passenger side window had shattered. The rain was strong, hitting me in the face. The driver's side window had shattered and was against the tree. The center console was pressing into my body, and I realized it was because the tree pressed my door against my other side.

The car was still running, but I knew it wasn't going anywhere. My pulse picked up as I looked around, trying to figure out what to do next. Wincing from the pain that jolted through my body, I climbed over the center console, which was a feat.

My body screamed at me in protest and tears clouded my vision, but I pressed on. Thankfully, my legs were free, and I could fling myself into the passenger seat. I needed a few minutes before I could get out of the car. One of my heels had come off, and I left it. Taking the other one off to join it.

My cell phone was in my purse, which was on the floor of the car, but its contents were all over. Whimpering as I bent down, I dug around under the seat and found my phone. I attempted to call for help. No service.

Defeated, I looked into the mirror and tried to get a look at the wound on my head. I couldn't see anything except blood, which made me feel a little woozy. It dripped down my face, so I dug some napkins out of the glove box and did my best to mop up the blood.

Tossing the napkins on the ground, I sat back against the seat, feeling on the verge of panic. What was I going to do? The only idea that came to mind was to walk back toward the house for help. It couldn't have been that far. I hadn't been driving for long.

After a few minutes, I mustered up the courage to get out. The rain was cold and felt like little shards of ice on my skin as I walked. My bare feet, covered in mud, ached. The adrenaline was wearing off, and I felt a little light-headed. Blood dripped down my face and into my eyes. I stopped and leaned against a tree for support while I checked my phone again. Still no service.

The house seemed so far away, and I couldn't see it from where I was standing. Was I even going in the right direction? I whimpered and rested my head on my arm. If I called for help, would anyone hear me? My phone flashed a low battery alert. I was running out of time.

I contemplated going back to the car and waiting for help to come. There was a car charger inside, and I could call for help. Except there wasn't any service. I whimpered again and then pushed off the tree. I would not survive by staying put. There was help somewhere, and I needed to find it.

Chapter 6

PETER

AS I STOOD ON THE second-floor balcony of my room looking out over the backyard, anger rolling off me in waves, I thought about how the evening had unfolded. My mother talked to my father and begged him to let me stay to attend the funeral. Reluctantly, my father agreed as long as I apologized to Vincent. I agreed but didn't follow through, and Vincent wasn't coward enough to tell on me.

I was only staying for my furniture. I had planned on taking my grandfather's trailer. No one had used it in years, so I'd have to dig it out of the garage he kept it in. It was dark, and I didn't want to load the furniture in this rain. Plus, I needed an extra set of hands carrying stuff out.

My fist was an angry shade of red and it hurt like hell, but the whiskey was helping to dull the pain. I wasn't sure why I'd reacted the way

I did. I had just met Kate, and clearly she was here with my brother. I shouldn't have cared about what was going on between them.

One of the reasons that I had been appointed mayor was because of my strong desire to do the right thing. Even though Kate and I had just met, what my brother did to her by grabbing her wrist was wrong. I could see the distress on her face. She needed help, and for the first time, I felt a little nervous about what my brother might do. He seemed slightly unhinged.

To clear my mind, I walked out in the rain toward my grandfather's garage, where he kept his vintage cars, in search of the trailer I needed to take all my furniture home. A row of cars came into view on the grass next to the garage. My truck was there, but it was blocked in. Guess I wouldn't be leaving even if I wanted to. And I really wanted to.

I entered the garage and a wave of nostalgia washed over me as I looked at my grandfather's vintage cars. I was the only one of us three boys who took an interest in them. Unfortunately, my grandfather wasn't loving like my grandmother and ignored my interest. I shook off the feeling of sadness that rushed over me and moved further into the garage. The trailer I needed to haul my stuff home was buried in the back and covered in boxes. I'd have to dig it out in the morning when I had more time and Thomas could help me.

I walked back through the rain toward the house, pausing on the front porch to remove my suit coat and shake it out. It was soaked and would need to be laid out to dry. Just as I stepped inside the front door, a page came in over the intercom from the front gate.

"Hello? Is anyone there?" a shaky feminine voice asked. "I need some help. Can someone please let me in?"

I frowned. There were cameras for the gate, but I couldn't figure out how to make them work. The intercom was fancy and had way too many features for me to even attempt. I hit the one button I knew, which was the call button, and responded. "This is Peter. Who is this?"

"Kate. I crashed my car and I need some help. Could you buzz me in?"

Panic washed over me. She needed help. Was she hurt? I fumbled with a few buttons before I found the one that opened the front gate, then I took off running down the driveway. The gate opened enough for her to stumble through. She looked like she was about to collapse, so I ran harder. Her legs gave out just as I reached her, and I scooped her up into my arms.

Cradling her against my body to shield her from the rain, I carried her up the driveway. I didn't stop until I was in my room. There, I gently laid her down on the bed and looked her over.

Blood dripped down her forehead, and she had one eye pinched shut. "Are you alright? I see blood. Where are you hurt?"

I couldn't tell if her eye was injured or if she was closing it so blood wouldn't get in. There were small cuts all over her arms and legs. She had burn marks on her face and arms, possibly from the air bag. Her dress was torn at the bottom of one side, and she was barefoot. I walked into the adjoining bathroom and wet a washcloth.

"What happened?" I asked, coming back into the room.

"A tree was down in the road and I didn't see it until it was too late. I swerved enough that I hit it with the side of my car instead of head on. The driver's side window shattered and the door almost pinned me against the center console, but I wiggled out. I lost a shoe and my cell phone didn't have service, so I couldn't call for help. That's why I walked back here. Everything is pretty fuzzy, and I had to stop a few times. My dress snagged on a tree branch," she said, pulling at the hem of her torn dress.

I sat down on the edge of the bed and tried to figure out what to do next. Would she be okay with me touching her? She seemed shaken up still, so I took control of the situation. She was hurt and needed help. Gently moving her hair to the side, I saw where she was bleeding from. A laceration on her head. It was matted and covered in blood.

Placing the towel on her wound, I pressed lightly. She winced. I wasn't sure if there was any glass in the wound, so I tried not to press too hard. She would need someone to look at it. Taking her to the hospital would probably be a good idea. What if she had a concussion? She said she'd passed out.

"Kate, your head is pretty bad, and there are burn marks on your face and arms from the air bag. I think we better take you to a hospital."

"No. I don't want to go. If I can just get cleaned up, I'll be fine. I can call my friend, Mindy, for a ride," she said, trying to sit upright. She collapsed back down. "I really just need to rest."

She closed her eyes, and I freaked out. "Not a good idea. You have a head injury." I lifted her up and propped some pillows behind her so she was sitting up straight. "Do you think you can sit here and not fall asleep while I go look for a first aid kit?" She nodded. "Okay, good. I'll be right back."

I ran down the stairs as fast I could without falling and headed straight for the mud room off the kitchen. When I was younger, I fell and my grandmother had patched me up in here. I opened cabinet after cabinet and came up empty. I stood there for a few seconds thinking of where else my grandmother would have kept the first aid kit.

The half bath off the mud room seemed like a reasonable spot. I flung open the cabinet under the sink and breathed a sigh of relief. I grabbed the kit and some extra towels and ran back up the stairs, taking them two at a time.

When I opened the door, my blood ran cold. Kate had her eyes closed again.

"Kate."

Nothing.

"Kate!" I shouted, giving her a gentle shake.

"Yes?" Her pretty blue eyes fluttered open, and she looked confused.

My head hung down in relief, but it was brief. I checked her eyes, not fully sure what I was looking for. "What's your name?"

She gave me a funny look before answering, "Katherine Louise Miller."

"Good. You fell asleep while I was getting the first aid kit. Are you sure you don't want me to take you to the hospital?"

She grabbed my hand. "No. I don't want to go."

I looked down at her hand and then back up into her frightened eyes. Nodding, I grabbed the first aid kit and opened it up, looking to see what I could use to help her. I poured some peroxide onto a cotton swab and gently dabbed at the open wound on her head.

She winced but remained still. I used rubbing alcohol to clean up the blood. The wound was still bleeding, so I put a few gauze pads on it and had Kate hold them there. I had no idea how to bandage her head or if I even should, so I didn't.

"Thank you," she said quietly.

Her eyes were heavy, and she looked dazed but still beautiful. My brother was a fool to let her go. Under any other circumstance, I'd make a move. But this was my brother's ex-girlfriend and that made her off limits. Not to mention my brother had a tendency to come a little unglued when he didn't get his way. I didn't want to step in the middle of that. Also, she was hurt and needed help, not someone hitting on her.

I swallowed hard and backed away from her. "You're welcome."

Her eyes fluttered closed again, and I knew I needed some help. Wasn't that the benefit of having a doctor in the family? To help in times like this? I woke her up again before rushing out of the room and down the hall to where my brother, Thomas, and his wife were staying.

Chapter 7

KATE

I WOKE UP WITH PAIN shooting through my skull and an aching body. My eyes fluttered open, and I felt confused. The night before was kind of a blur. Mostly because I kept slipping in and out of consciousness. It probably would have been better if I'd gone to the hospital.

I slowly reached up and felt my head. There was a thick bandage wrapped around it. I was laying on my side, and there was a heavy arm wrapped around me. A large body pressed against my back. It felt nice and warm, and I almost slipped back to sleep, except I wanted to know who the body belonged to.

My pulse started to race. Was it Vincent? I turned very slowly from my side to my back. The small movements were painful and caused me to wince and grit my teeth to keep from whimpering.

Relief poured through me when I saw Peter's handsome face. His eyes were closed, and I took a minute to really look at him. With the sharp angled line of his jaw and slope of his nose, he was perfect. It was a shame he was Vincent's brother. This was the closest I'd ever be to him.

He started to stir, and my pulse picked up again.

"Good morning," he mumbled, his voice raspy with sleep. "You made it."

His eyes opened, and the gorgeous green color took my breath away. That coupled with his smile had me melting into the bed. I was suddenly mad because Vincent was taking another thing away from me: a chance at getting to know this attractive, wonderful, caring man.

Peter was a stranger, and yet he took care of me and made sure I made it through the night. I couldn't help but swoon. He was going to make some woman very happy, if he wasn't already. Oh god, what if he was dating someone? I was lying in his arms when he could be taken.

Peter rolled onto his back and stretched, oblivious to my worry. "Why don't I see if I can get us some coffee and food? What do you say? Breakfast in bed sound good to you?" He stood up and turned toward me, and I averted my eyes to the spot in the bed he just vacated. "Kate?"

"Hmm?"

"Breakfast in bed?" he asked again with a chuckle.

I looked up and then cursed myself for it. He was delicious, and I would much rather have him for breakfast. He was still dressed in his slacks from the night before, but they did nothing to disguise his well-defined thighs and something else that was prominently on display. My eyes moved up, and that wasn't any better since he didn't have a shirt on.

He was lean and toned. I wanted to trace the well-defined ridges and planes of his chest and abs with my hands and tongue. His broad, muscular chest flexed as he stretched his arms over his head. I swallowed hard as I took him in, unable to tear my eyes off him and not sure I wanted to.

A lion's head was tattooed in black and white on the left side of his chest. I caught a glimpse of another tattoo on his right forearm, but he rotated his arm before I could get a good look at what it was, and I was too shy to ask.

He walked to the bathroom, breaking the trance I was in. I pushed my head back into the pillow, and then let out a low whimper. The small movement caused my head to throb and my neck to ache. I moved my legs and frowned. Peeking under the covers, I saw I was wearing a t-shirt and some very baggy sweatpants.

Did I change? I couldn't remember. Whose clothes was I wearing? The last thing I could recall was Peter cleaning up my head wound. After that, the details were fuzzy.

Peter came out of the bathroom wearing a pair of black gym shorts and a gray hoodie. His feet were bare. The light scruff I'd noticed on his jaw yesterday was longer now. His hair was combed over to the side. My pulse quickened, and I nearly drooled.

We would never work in the real world. We were polar opposites. I was the plain jane, girl next door. Quiet and reserved. He was attractive and probably had some hot model girlfriend at home waiting for him.

I reached up to touch my head and groaned. My mind was running away from me, and I blamed it on the head wound. I did have some questions that I needed answers to, though. Starting with whose clothes I was wearing. "Peter, did I change last night?"

"No, you didn't do much last night. My brother Thomas is a doctor, so I had him check you out. He was concerned about a concussion, so he had me keep an eye on you. He cleaned the glass out of the wound on your head and stitched it up. You hardly even flinched as he put the stitches in. His wife, Elizabeth, changed you into my sweats and t-shirt. Then they left. You wanted to sleep, so I stayed awake as long as I could to make sure you were okay. After that, I set an alarm and woke you up every few hours."

"I don't remember you waking me up."

He ran a hand through his hair. "Yeah. You were pretty out of it from the pain medication Thomas gave you. How are you feeling right now?"

"I'm okay. I think. I haven't gotten up yet," I said with a half-smile.

He nodded and looked away. "There's a toothbrush on the bathroom counter for you. I'm going to go down and get your dress from the laundry and see if I can't find us some breakfast."

"Thanks."

He nodded.

My stomach fluttered. He did all that for me? We were practically strangers. No one other than my parents had ever taken care of me like that. Especially not Vincent. My blood ran cold at the thought of him. "What about Vincent?"

"I snuck around as best I could last night; I don't think he knows you're here. His door stayed shut the entire time. Getting out of here should be easy since everyone will be leaving for the funeral around ten."

I felt a little better. If Vincent didn't know I was here, then we could keep it a secret and I could sneak out without him finding out. "What about my car? What if he sees it?"

"What way did you turn last night?"

"Left."

"You're safe. They'll turn right to head to the funeral. Your phone is charged. Elizabeth let you borrow her charger," he said, nodding toward the nightstand.

"Thank you," I said, picking it up. I'd call Mindy for a ride, and then wait until everyone left for the funeral to sneak out.

I sat forward and turned sideways, attempting to get out of bed. I felt a little wobbly.

"Peter, one more thing."

He paused with his hand on the door handle and looked over his shoulder at me. "Sure, anything."

"Could you help me to the bathroom? I feel a little unsteady."

He smiled and stood in front of me. I placed my hands on his shoulders, and he helped me to stand. We walked slowly to the bathroom. I hurt everywhere; even in muscles I'd never realized I had. So this must be what people meant when they said they felt like they'd been hit by a car.

I was so weak, I leaned into Peter, using him as a crutch. "Can you see if you can find me any pain medication?"

"Yes. Sorry, I should have done that before," he said, holding onto me.

"That's okay. I didn't need it until now. I think I've got it from here; thank you." I grabbed onto the bathroom door frame.

Letting go, I took one small step forward and swayed. Peter grabbed me around the waist. My body tingled under his touch, but it also hurt. I didn't even want to see the kind of bruising I had. He helped me ease down onto the toilet seat, then left the room. I was alone, trying to figure out how to stand up and sit back down to relieve myself. Too embarrassed to ask for help with that, I brushed my teeth first while I figured it out.

Chapter 8

PETER

I DECIDED TO WAIT outside the bathroom in case Kate needed me. She seemed really unsteady, and I didn't want her to fall in there without someone to help her. I should have taken her to the hospital. She probably needed more care than I'd provided for her. What if she had internal injuries?

Even though Thomas looked her over and told me she was okay, I still didn't feel confident in our decision to stay here. I wasn't a doctor, and Thomas didn't stay with her overnight. My anxiety was through the roof all night.

My arm draped over her body last night had probably hurt her more than she was letting on. I was such an idiot for laying down beside her. I just wanted to make sure she was okay, that she didn't die in her sleep. She looked so broken, and I just wanted to wrap her up in my arms. When I first put my arm around her, she didn't move. I waited a few seconds for any sign of pain, and when she scooted against me, I took that as a sign that she was okay.

It had been a long time since I cuddled someone in my sleep. A long time since anyone had been in my bed period. It felt amazing, and I slept better than I had in a long time, even with all the alarms and waking Kate up. Every time she'd snuggle back into me, I would fall back into a deep sleep.

I'd gotten up to pace and heard Kate throwing up.

"Kate?" I asked, rapping my knuckles on the closed door. "Can I come in?"

I could barely hear the muffled reply that came from the other side of the door. I hesitated, and then slowly opened the door. Kate was seated on the floor facing the toilet with her head in her hands.

"Are you okay?" I asked, squatting beside her.

"Not really. Everything started to spin, and I got sick. I think I need to lie back down. Could you help me brush my teeth again and get back in bed?"

"Of course." I handed her the toothbrush with a swipe of paste on it and waited until she was done, then helped her to the sink to spit and rinse.

Scooping her up into my arms, I carried her back to the bed. She didn't protest, instead she laid her head on my shoulder as I walked. It twisted me up inside to see her in so much pain. Even though I didn't know her well, it was still hard to watch. She was vulnerable and trusted me to help her.

After tucking her in, I turned for the door. She reached out and grabbed my wrist gently. "Stay with me?"

"I still need to get us food, and you need some water to take your medication."

A pained look crossed her face.

"I can wait until you fall asleep," I said.

"Please. I just… I don't want to be alone right now."

I climbed into bed beside her and wrapped my arm around her shoulders. She snuggled into me, resting her head against my chest, and closed her eyes. I inhaled deeply. Hints of vanilla filled my nose, and I knew that I'd always remember Kate when I smelled vanilla. I closed my eyes, feeling content.

I'd never felt an instant connection to anyone before, and I didn't really believe in that type of thing, but I had a deep urge to hold her forever. To protect her and keep her safe. I knew that we'd never be together, but it didn't stop my heart from beating like a drum around her or my fingers itching to touch her delicate skin. She was mine for right now, and I needed this as much as she needed me.

A FEW HOURS LATER, Kate finally woke up. It was probably the smell of coffee and bacon. I had fallen asleep with my arms wrapped around her yet again. After carefully slipping out of her hold a little while ago, I went in search of food. It was quiet in the house, which I was thankful for.

Kate's eyes met mine, and I smiled, holding out water and two pain pills Thomas had given me. "I have something for you."

"Thank you," she said, slowly easing up in the bed and resting against the headboard. "Does Vincent know I'm here?"

Before I could answer she said, "Stupid question. If he knew, he'd have barged in here already."

I scoffed. "Yeah, and he'd kick my ass, too."

She looked up at me with a frown on her face. "I don't belong to him."

I sat down on the bed beside her. "Hey, I know that."

"It just feels like I do sometimes. My life is so entangled with his right now, and it's taking me a long time to fully get away."

I rubbed my fingers over the back of her hand and remained quiet in case she wanted to continue. When she didn't, I stood up and walked over to the tray on the dresser. "I wasn't sure how you took your coffee, so I brought you cream and sugar."

"Perfect. Thank you," she said, adding two scoops of sugar and some cream. I committed it to memory. Just in case. "What am I going to do about my car?"

"I already took care of that. I called a tow truck. They'll be here in an hour. I'll take you down there while they're towing it and then drive you home if you'd like."

"Oh that's all right. You don't have to do that. You've already done so much."

"Kate, I want to," I said, reaching for her hand. There was a knock on the door, and we froze.

Walking over the door, I pressed my ear against it and quietly asked, "Who's there?"

"Elizabeth. Open up, will ya?"

I opened the door just enough for Elizabeth and her big belly to squeeze in. She was eight months pregnant with the first baby of the family. Thomas walked in behind her carrying a plate of food and a cup of coffee. A brown paper bag hung from his fingers around the cup.

"Is there a code word we should work out?" Elizabeth joked as she walked to the bed, a hand pressed to her lower back.

"What's the plan?" Thomas asked, handing his wife the plate of food and then sitting down beside Kate.

He leaned back against the headboard and crossed his feet at his ankles. He looked relaxed as he blew on his coffee and waited for us to answer. Thomas was the calm one in the family. It took a lot to ruffle his feathers. Unless you were Vincent. The two of them bickered constantly.

I explained the plan to them while Thomas checked Kate out. He shined a flashlight into her eyes and had her follow his finger. Then checked her head wound, applied some ointment, and then put fresh bandages on it.

"Kate, the wound looks good. Take the bandage off when you get home and let it air out. You have four stitches that need to come out in about seven to ten days, so you'll have to see a doctor. I wrote up a report for you last night, and here's a sheet detailing how to care for the wound," he said, handing Kate a piece of paper. "You'll be sore for a few more days. If you notice significant bruising and pain, see a doctor immediately."

Kate nodded.

"I called in a favor and had the pharmacy in town fill a script for pain medication. Benjamin went and picked it up for us. If you have any other issues, follow up with your primary care doctor." He handed Kate a brown paper bag. "The medication is in there along with extra gauze in case you need it."

"Thank you so much, Thomas," Kate said with a smile.

"You're welcome. Come on, honey, let's get ready to go and leave these two alone." He winked at me.

Thomas opened the door, and Elizabeth let out a startled, "Oh!" Vincent stood in the doorway. The room was silent. It reminded me of a horror flick when the killer shows up.

"What's going on in here?" he asked with a scowl. His eyes traveled around the room and landed on Kate. I had a fierce urge to jump in front of her and protect her, but before I could move a muscle, Vincent was beside the bed. "Katherine? What happened? Are you okay?"

"I'm fine, Vincent," she gritted out with an eye roll.

He grabbed her hand and held it between his. "You don't look fine." He looked at Thomas. "Is she okay?"

"She's fine. Just a little bump," he said before sliding from the room, pulling his wife with him.

"What happened?" Vincent asked. He took a seat on my bed, still holding Kate's hand between his.

She pulled her hand free and scooted over. "Nothing."

"It doesn't look like nothing, Katherine."

Another eye roll. "I got into a car accident when I left here."

"What?!" he shrieked, and I let out a sigh. He was just as dramatic as our mother. "A car accident? After you left... last night?"

Oh shit. He was piecing it together. I took a step back, just in case he decided to react irrationally.

"Where did you stay, Katherine?"

"That is none of your business. Thomas, Elizabeth, and Peter took care of me."

Vincent's head swung to me, murder in his eyes. "They did, did they? And what exactly did the three of them do?"

An exasperated sigh fell from Kate's mouth, drawing Vincent's and my attention to her. "Vincent, Peter helped me to this room, and Thomas looked me over to make sure I was all right. Elizabeth helped settle me in, and I stayed here until they checked on me this morning."

"You stayed in my brother's room alone?" Vincent asked. His tone was accusatory.

"Yes," she gritted out. "Alone. Peter gave me his room to recover in."

Vincent stood and looked around the room while he paced, then he flashed me a glare and went back to Kate's side. "Let's go to the hospital and get you checked out."

"I'm fine. I was already checked out by a doctor, and he stitched me up. I'm free to go home and follow up with my doctor in Bellport."

"Stiches?" His voice pitched high and squeaked. He cleared his throat and said, "Then let me take you home."

"Vincent, that's unnecessary. Plus, you have Violet's funeral. You should go. I'm going to call my friend."

"Are you feeling well enough to attend?"

"What?" Kate asked, looking shocked by his question. I was equally taken back.

"Vincent, she just got into an accident. She needs to go home and rest."

"I wasn't asking you," he snipped. "You said you were feeling all right, so come to the funeral."

It was a test. The asshole was testing her to see if she was lying to him. He had no right, and it was time I stepped in.

"This is ridiculous. You can see she's fine. Let her go. It's time for us to go anyway. Mom will pitch a fit if we're late."

On cue, my mother's shrill voice rang up the stairwell, "Boys! Let's go!"

"Coming," Vincent called out to her. "Katherine, I really want to see that you're okay."

"I'll be fine. If you want, I'll text you once I'm settled."

"A text will suffice, I guess. I'd love to bring you dinner later."

I balled a fist at my side. Reason five hundred why we couldn't be together; my brother would never leave her alone.

"Mindy will be at my house." A small ghost of a smile crossed her face.

Vincent scrunched his nose up and shivered. "Very well. Text me when you're settled; I'll check in on you later, and tomorrow I'll come over and bring you food."

"Vincent, please—"

"It's nothing. I want to do this," he said, completely missing the point and steamrolling over her like he did everyone else.

He leaned forward and placed a kiss on her cheek before turning for the door. "Peter, after you."

I looked at Kate, who looked a little panicked.

"I have to get ready," I said looking down at my hoodie and shorts.

"I'll wait here," he said, taking a seat in my vacated chair.

I hesitated and then grabbed the garment bag containing my suit and headed for the bathroom.

Chapter 9

PETER

THE FUNERAL WAS SHORT and sweet, but the burial took longer, and every time I tried to leave, Vincent was right there blocking my way. Since I didn't have Kate's number, he was the one checking in on her. She hadn't left the house yet, and I was eager to get back and help her home.

A half hour passed, and we were finally on our way back. Kate was just getting into the car when we arrived. Vincent was by her side before I could even get out of the car. The three of us had played rock, paper, scissors just like the old days to decide who had to sit in the middle. I lost.

A petite redhead with long curls snarled at Vincent, and he backed up. I bit back a laugh as I made my way over to them.

"She's fine, Vincent. I've got her," the redhead said.

"I'm sure you do, but I'd still like to help her."

"Back off."

"Vincent, just let her get into the car," I said.

Vincent whirled around and took a step into me. "Stay out of this, or you'll regret it."

I chuckled. "Is that a threat? I'd love to see what you're made of again, although I don't think your nose will hold up a second time."

"Fuck you, Peter."

The redhead rolled her eyes at Vincent and stuck her hand out to me. "Hi. I'm Mindy."

I shook her hand. "Peter."

"Nice to meet you. Thanks for taking care of my girl here."

"My pleasure."

Mindy helped lower Kate into the front seat, and then closed the door. She jogged in front of the car and paused at her door. "If you come by her house, Vincent, I'll call the police." She slammed her door and then hit the gas.

"Happy?" Vincent asked.

"Boys, let's go!" our mother called from the porch. Family and a few close friends were gathering for another meal. One I tried like hell to get out of and couldn't. My truck was still blocked in, and I still needed to load furniture.

"You'll still help me, right?" I asked Thomas, slapping him on the back.

"Yeah. We're leaving tomorrow, though. Mom wants to go over the shower arrangements with Elizabeth."

I rolled my eyes. "Fine. We can load stuff up tonight, then, while they're doing that. I'm leaving first thing in the morning, though."

Staying another night here with sheets that smelled like Kate was going to be hell, but it was the price I had to pay to get all of my stuff back home.

IT WAS EARLY, THE SUN just starting to rise, when I checked the straps on the trailer again. Thomas and Elizabeth were already up since she couldn't sleep and he wanted to get home. They had a long drive ahead of them as well. Not as long as the three and a half hours I was facing, though.

I thought about trying to get Kate's address and stopping by on the way home, but what was the point? Torturing myself when we couldn't pursue anything wasn't worth it. Mindy was taking care of her, and Vincent had insisted he'd stop in.

Before I hit the expressway, I stopped for a breakfast sandwich and a cup of coffee. I also shot an e-mail off to my secretary, Elaine, letting her know I'd be out of the office and to call me if she needed me. Even though I'd be home before lunchtime, I'd be too tired to head into the office, plus I had a trailer to unload.

For most of the drive, I annoyed the hell out of myself listing off all the reasons Kate and I wouldn't work and then playing the what-if game. What if we did work out? What if we got rid of Vincent? It went on for longer than I'd like to admit.

When I pulled into my driveway, Frank stood up from the front porch. He wore his deputy's uniform and an irritated expression. I couldn't help but notice his hat was missing and it made me chuckle. He'd do anything to get out of wearing that thing, and I couldn't blame him. They were hideous.

"What can I do for you, Deputy?" He hated when I called him that.

When I jumped out of my truck, my legs almost buckled. They felt like gelatin after the long drive. My back was sore, and I wanted to head inside and fall into my bed.

"Mayor." He smirked. "I'm sorry to wait out here like this, but I need to talk to you about an urgent matter." He walked toward me with an envelope in his hand.

"You texted me twenty minutes ago asking when I'd be home. Why didn't you just tell me then?"

"Because I needed to talk to you face to face."

I rolled my eyes. "Frank, can't this wait? I just got home from an exhausting weekend with my family, and I didn't get much sleep. Can we just talk tomorrow when I get back to the office? What's with the formalities, anyway?"

"I wish it could wait, but I want you to be aware of what's going on. The Lawrence brothers are back in town with another offer, and this time they're extending the properties they want to include in the proposal." He handed me the envelope. "You called me Deputy. You know I hate that shit."

I laughed and ripped open the envelope, pulling out a single piece of paper. It was another offer, all right. This time my name was at the top.

I looked up at Frank. "What the hell is this?"

"That's the urgency. They want your land for new development. They want to build condos that back up to the river. Along with a strip mall on the other two properties. They're coming first thing in the morning to meet with you about the new developments. They showed up today, but you weren't here. I think they're staying at a fancy hotel out of town. They said they expect answers. They want to break ground next Saturday," Frank replied.

"Frank, the answer is no. I said no the last time they came into town. The town took a vote and only agreed on the new town hall. This new project will destroy homes and force people to buy a condo or move away. I'm not leaving here. This is my home, my whole life. I won't be forced out by some money hungry boys in suits. That's my answer. Now help me unload my truck and come in for a beer," I said. I grabbed my duffel bag and turned for the door.

"Peter, you know they won't stop until they get what they want, right?"

"I know, and I'm still saying no. They can try all they want, but they can't build if the mayor doesn't approve, and I don't."

Frank walked inside behind me and stopped. "I can't have a beer. I'm on duty."

"When has that stopped you before? Let's go; I can't unload all this by myself. Thomas helped me load it up earlier. Some of it's going to the store. There are only a few items, so get your ass out there, and then you can have a beer with me. I'll even buy you a pizza for lunch or dinner, depending on how fast we get stuff done."

He huffed like a child and turned toward the truck. "Fine."

After unloading the dining room table and chairs into my living room, I headed through town to my store. Main Street was quiet, which was nice. I didn't want to stop and talk. Frank met me at the back entrance of my store where we unloaded everything else.

I gave Frank money to pick up the pizza I ordered and headed back home. I wanted to sit down and relax a little. I'd stocked my fridge with beer before I left for the weekend. Popping the top on one and leaning back against the kitchen counter, I let out a deep sigh.

The Lawrence brothers were once again a thorn in my side. It didn't matter what I said to them. I'd have to tell them, again, that we were not interested in building up the town. At least not how they wanted to do it. We were doing just fine without their help.

My stomach turned at the thought of having to pull the whole project. It would mean no town hall, and people were relying on that. I didn't want to think about having to deal with it. My trip home had been exhausting and thinking about work was making me sick.

Instead of shutting off, my mind wandered to Kate. I hoped she was doing well and wasn't in too much pain. I remembered my brother saying how he was going to show up and check on her and shook my head in disgust. He didn't deserve her, and he sure as hell needed to take a goddamn hint.

I walked into the living room and flopped down on my broken-in couch. The thought of losing my house and land made me feel sick to my stomach. My two-bedroom ranch wasn't much, and it looked like shit from the outside, but it was mine. I had done all the repairs and upgrades with my own two hands. I'd even added a screened-in porch out back.

But while the house was important to me, the land was sentimental. They could try to take away my home, but they would not get my land without a fight. I felt it was my job to protect the people of this town. Others like me whose land had been in their family for generations. The Lawrence brothers weren't only coming after my land, they were coming after my town.

My gut ached thinking about it. Frank showed up with pizza just in time, interrupting my thoughts. We sat in the living room and watched some sports game I didn't give a shit about. My trip to Pine Brook and dealing with my family and falling for a woman I could never have had taken a lot out of me.

I tipped my head back, finished my beer, and closed my eyes, letting the calm wash over me. The day was finally over.

Chapter 10

PETER

I STARTLED AWAKE, MY EYES snapped open and I groaned. I had a massive headache and a huge kink in my neck. Looking around, I realized I was still in my living room. Frank was passed out in my recliner. His mouth was open, and there was a drool spot on his chest. Frank spent so much time sleeping in that recliner it might as well have been his.

I looked at the clock that hung on the wall above the television. Nine. Shit, I was late getting into the office. I grabbed my cell phone from the coffee table. It was almost dead. Five missed calls from Elaine, and two missed calls from our friend, Sid. He happened to be Frank's partner, and I had a feeling I knew why he was calling me. I phoned Elaine while I kicked Frank awake.

"What the hell?" Frank snapped.

I kicked him again, and he sat up, ready to kill me. Wildly, I motioned to the clock on the wall.

"Shit," he said, jumping out of the chair.

Elaine picked up on the second ring, and I started talking before she could speak.

"Elaine, it's Peter. I know I'm late. I'll be there in thirty minutes."

"Peter, this is not a good day for you to be late. The Lawrence brothers called, and they'll be here in twenty minutes. Also, the sheriff called. Mrs. Anderson lost her cat up a tree again, and she asked for you. And they can't find Frank." Elaine sounded panicked.

"Stall the Lawrence brothers. Get them some coffee and donuts and set them down in the waiting room. I'll be there soon. Tell Mrs. Anderson to call the fire department this time. Frank is on his way to the station if they call again." I tried to balance my phone on my shoulder while I stripped my pants off. It was not an easy feat. I almost fell twice.

"Okay, Peter. See you soon."

Elaine hung up the phone, and I finished undressing. I made sure Frank left before I hopped in the shower.

Twenty minutes later, I left the house dressed in a gray pinstripe suit with a blue dress shirt underneath and wet hair. I needed to go straight to the office, but driving down Main Street meant there'd be at least one or two stops. I'd love to cruise right through to the office. The people of the town needed me, though, and it was my job to help.

I never imagined I'd be mayor. In fact, when someone approached me a few years ago about running, I laughed in their face. The job came with a lot of responsibility that I didn't want. I enjoyed blending in more than being the one people relied on.

Turned out I loved being mayor of this town. Trips, charity events, and even the dreaded town meetings. I loved helping people. The only downfall was all the attention that came with it. I was more of a behind-the-scenes kind of guy.

"Damn it," I mumbled as I rounded the bend toward Main Street.

Tom Tracy was standing in front of his store, Best Foot Forward, with Ken Marshall from the music store next door. Ken's arms were folded across his chest, and Tom gestured wildly toward the roof.

I tried to creep by without being stopped but had no such luck. Tom spotted my truck and ran toward me. I slowed and veered over to the curb.

"Peter! We need your help!" he shouted.

"I'm running late today, guys. Is there any way you could set up an appointment for us to meet later?" I asked through the passenger window.

"It won't take long. I was just pointing out to Ken that part of the rooftop of his building belongs to me." Tom pointed to the rooftop of On a Different Note.

I bent my head down and looked to where he was pointing.

"It is not yours. It's the top of *my* building; how could it possibly be yours?" Ken asked. "All the years we've worked next to each other, you've said nothing. Why now?"

"Because if you look at the way the building is, that part of the roof is over part of my store," Tom explained his logic to Ken. While they were both looking at the buildings, I seized my opportunity to escape.

"Call my office and set up an appointment. See you later," I yelled and pulled away from the curb.

I continued down Main Street. It was a quiet morning without a lot of foot traffic. Up ahead I noticed Beverly Anderson jumping, if you could even call it that. The poor older woman's feet weren't leaving the pavement.

It was obvious she still didn't have her cat. I pulled over to the curb again and got out. Rounding the back of the truck, I saw the black cat hanging on one of the lower branches, just out of Beverly's reach.

"Hello there, Mrs. Anderson. May I be of any help?" I asked.

"Oh, Peter, I'm so glad you're here. Duchess is stuck up in this tree. I've been trying all morning to get her down, but she won't budge. She's such a scared little thing." She shook a bag of cat treats. That wasn't working.

I assessed the situation. Sighing, I took off my suit jacket and handed it to Beverly to hold while I rolled up my shirtsleeves. The tree wasn't very high. I did this often, so I had a lot of experience. I put one foot in the center of the tree and pulled myself up.

I climbed a little higher so I could lean out onto the branch. It scared the cat, as usual, which made me nervous she'd move and then fall. I stretched out a little farther and, with one quick swoop, I scooped her into my arms.

Hugging Duchess to my chest, I climbed back down one-handed. The cat purred and snuggled into me. We had built up a good relationship over the years with all the trees I'd had to climb to rescue her.

"Here you go. Safe and sound." I handed Duchess back to Beverly.

"Thank you, Peter! I knew you would help me. I called your office, and Elaine said you weren't in yet. I told her you were the only one who could help me. Duchess trusts you. Elaine told me to call the fire department, but I knew that you would be the one to rescue Duchess for me. Thank you!" She threw her arms around my waist.

I gave her a quick squeeze and stepped back. "You're welcome. Now get Duchess home before she climbs another tree."

My tire rubbed the curb as I drove away. Maple Avenue, where I needed to turn to get to the small parking lot behind the stores on this side of Main Street, was just up ahead. I held my breath as I coasted around the turn and let it out when I pulled behind the store.

When I became mayor two years ago, I moved my furniture store from the front of my house to the small storefront off Main Street. The second floor was huge, and the previous owner had used it as storage. It was perfect for an office.

I figured being on Main Street would be a good idea. It'd make me more accessible to the people of the town. Sometimes that was a good thing; other times I regretted my decision. I stopped at least three times on the way to the office each day, and people could pop in whenever they felt like it. Elaine, to her credit, did a great job keeping foot traffic to a minimum.

I parked in my designated parking spot next to the door in front of the *Parking for the mayor of Oak Springs only* sign. When they first put the sign up, I laughed. I was the only one laughing, except for Frank. They were serious about it. I loved this town and all the people in it. Even with all its quirks.

When I walked into my store, it was business as usual. Hannah, the manager, was behind the register with a magazine in front of her. She stashed it below the desk when she heard me approach.

"Hello, Peter," she said with a smile.

"Hi, Hannah. How were things while I was away?"

I knew full well how things went. I had eyes and ears everywhere in this town. Also, I'd looked at what we sold over the weekend when I dropped off the furniture the night before.

"Business as usual. Oh, that large oak mirror you made last week sold on Saturday for twice the asking price. There was a bidding war between Frank and Sarah. Frank said he'd give up the mirror if Sarah agreed to go out on a date with him. Sarah got the mirror." Hannah laughed.

I smirked and shook my head. *Oh, Frank.* "Keep up the good work."

I walked to my office. When I reached the top of the stairs, it felt like someone had sucked the air out of the place. Elaine was pacing and had a panicked look on her face.

"There you are. The Lawrence brothers were angry that you weren't here. They said they'd be back in an hour."

"Did you offer them something to eat or drink like I asked?"

"Yes, but they said that this was unacceptable for a mayor, and they would keep a record of this. They were so unpleasant." She looked like she was going to cry.

"Elaine, they're two rich, stuck-up trust fund boys trying to take land away from people in our town. I'm not afraid of them, and you shouldn't be either," I said. I continued across the room toward my office with Elaine hot on my heels.

The whole floor was originally one giant open space. I'd put walls up to create a closed-in office. A break room, copier/storage room, and bathroom were off to the right.

"I know that," Elaine said. I didn't think she believed it though.

"You have some messages. One is from Mr. Lawrence himself." I turned toward her, and she handed me a few memos, then turned on her heels and hurried back to her desk.

I sat down, took my laptop out of my bag, and turned it on. I sorted through the mail piled on top of my desk then moved on to the memos that Elaine had handed me. One from Mr. Trent Lawrence, one from Tom Tracy, and one from Deputy Wilson. I called Frank first.

"Frank Wilson," he answered.

"Frank, it's Peter. I have a memo here that you called me. I also saw I had a few missed calls from Sid this morning, but I was running late."

"Forget about Sid. He was looking for me. Once I saw the time this morning, I knew I was screwed, but then I realized I was still wearing my uniform, so I grabbed coffee and donuts for Sid and rushed to the station," he laughed.

I shook my head. "Why'd you call then?"

"I wanted to apologize for yesterday, man. I feel bad about waiting outside your house and bombarding you like that. That's not what friends do. It's just that I knew you would want to know before your meeting today."

"Frank, it's fine. I understand you were under some pressure. I'll handle it. Poker tomorrow night?"

"You bet. Your house again?"

"Where else do we play?" I asked.

"I was just making sure. Geez."

I smirked. "See you tomorrow."

I hung up the phone, looked up, and saw Elaine coming down the hall with the Lawrence brothers. She paused and knocked on my open door.

"Come in," I said, closing out of my e-mail. The Lawrence brothers, Sam and Bill, walked in.

"Gentleman, have a seat." I gestured to the two chairs in front of my desk. "What brings you to our quiet little town?"

Sam was the older of the two. He spoke up first. "Mayor, let's just cut right to the chase. We're here again with another offer. This time it extends to some neighboring properties. We ran some numbers, and we can show you how Oak Springs will benefit from new development."

Bill continued, "We know that change can be very stressful, but we've done several of these expansions. We help with the whole transition process."

Expansions? Transition process? "Look, gentleman, I understand that you came a long way to go over some new numbers with me, and I received your generous offer for *my* property last night." I paused and leaned forward on my desk.

"However, we here in Oak Springs have not changed our decision. We do not want new development here. We like the small-town feel and we don't want to lose that. Your project would cost several people their jobs because the newer developments would put their small shops out of business. Also, you would be taking away homes."

"We understand all of your concerns, and you will not lose your small-town feel. You'll improve it. This project will create more jobs and add housing. Sure, folks will have to move, but we'll offer a condo to everyone we purchase property from. And we'll pay closing costs. Like I said, we help with the transitions, too. That's what sets us apart from other developers," Bill said. Sam nodded in agreement.

"We already have some new development happening on Grand Street behind us." I gestured to the street just outside my window.

"There are a lot of shops for sale or for lease. As you can see, we aren't having trouble expanding. It's just not the way you want to do it. As mayor of this town, I have to think about what's in the people's best interest. We take votes, and we let folks here share their opinions. Our next town meeting is in a week, and this will be the top order of business. Until then, please hold off on any more offers or talking to any of the people in this town," I finished and sat back in my chair.

"Mayor, I understand what you're saying, and we appreciate what you do here, but this can't wait that long. There is a lot at stake here, and we have a team waiting to break ground. The last time we spoke, everyone was all for the new town hall. Then we came back and talked about some strip malls, and we thought you were interested in that," Bill stated.

"I know it seems harsh asking to buy property out from under people, but I assure you we are doing no such thing. We just need people to temporarily relocate," Sam assured me. He took a sip of water from a bottle he was holding.

"Temporarily relocate? One property you're asking for is *mine*!" I shouted. I stood up and slammed my hand down on my desk.

"You will not force me or anyone else in this town out of our homes. Yes, we were all for the new town hall. You made a great pitch, and everyone went for it. There was a split vote on the strip mall, so it was unresolved. Taking someone's land out from under them and destroying their home? That is something that no one in this town will be okay with, and something I will not let happen.

"I'm sorry you drove all this way for something that could have been handled over the phone. The more you've pushed and tried to expand this project, the less interested we've become in the whole thing. There is a town meeting next Monday, and I'll request a vote. Until then, I would like you to stop calling, e-mailing, and bothering me and the people of this town. Elaine will see you out." I reached over and hit the button on my phone that buzzed the front.

"Yes?"

"Elaine, would you be so kind to show our guests out?" I asked.

She hurried into my office and ushered the brothers to the door. Once the door closed behind them, I sank into my chair, letting my head drop into my hands. On the outside, I may have appeared calm and collected, but I was a volcano waiting to erupt inside. This would not be the last time I'd have a run-in with Lawrence Development Company. I felt a storm coming.

Chapter 11

KATE

ROLLING OVER IN BED, I winced and grabbed my head. It was still pretty sore, and I'd been battling a nasty headache since the accident. I was scheduled to see my doctor at eight, and the clock alerted me I had forty five minutes before my appointment.

Groaning, I sat up and went through my stretches before heading to the bathroom. It took a lot of convincing for Mindy to go home last night after we'd spent the day curled up on my couch watching movies.

Just as he said he would, Vincent had stopped by with food. Mindy refused to leave, so he didn't stay long. Just long enough to pitch a fit about the for sale sign. He begged me to reconsider, about us and about selling the house. Vincent assured me we'd be happy this time around, and our dreams of having a family in this house would come true.

Before I could respond to any of it, Mindy kicked him out. That was another reason she was so adamant about staying with me through the night. She was afraid he'd come back and force his way in or beg to take care of me.

With Mindy around, he didn't say much. They hated one another, and instead of fighting Mindy, Vincent always walked away. It was like she repelled him, which I was grateful for. Sometimes I thought about stitching her to my side as a shield against him.

The hot water from the shower felt amazing. I was careful not to get any water in my stitches. I hadn't washed my hair in a while, and I didn't want to risk it. Even though I was hoping to go back to work after my doctor's visit.

Mr. Lawrence had called quite a few times asking when I'd be returning. I faxed the doctor's note from Thomas over and told him I'd return mid-week, but I hadn't given a specific day. I should have known that wouldn't be enough for him. The last phone call pissed me off, though. He said Vincent had told him how I was doing and that I needed rest and space so I should wait and come in next week.

Of course, when Vincent said something to my boss, he listened. When I tried to explain I just needed a few days, he tried to pressure me. It was sexist and annoying. Mostly because Vincent and I were no longer together. He didn't need to keep fighting my battles as if we were a couple, and my boss needed to respect confidentiality with employees and stop discussing my business with a *non-employee*.

I rushed out the door in my black dress slacks and a cream blouse in hopes of getting a cup of coffee and a muffin at one of the chain shops on the way to the doctor's office. There wasn't enough time to make a whole pot of coffee at home, and most of it would have gone to waste.

The lobby at my doctor's office was nearly empty when I arrived, coffee in hand. The wait time was minimal, and I was quickly seated on one of the exam tables waiting for the doctor. My butt slid on the paper. The room was cold and smelled stale.

Two magazines later, my doctor finally walked in. He was a tall man with a mustache and glasses. Mid-forties and kind. I'd been seeing him for the last five years since I moved to Bellport.

"Hello, Kate," he said as he squirted some hand sanitizer from the corner dispenser. He rubbed it in as he looked over my chart on the counter. Taking a seat on the rolling stool, he turned toward me and smiled. "Car accident? How are you feeling?"

"Better. Sore, and a headache that won't seem to go away, but it could be worse, I suppose."

He smiled again and nodded. "Yes, it could have been. You were seen by a doctor in… where was it? Pine Brook?" He flipped through my file.

"Yes. It was Vincent's brother, Thomas Bradbury."

My doctor knew Vincent well. That was another thing I needed to add to my list to sever ties with Vincent. Find a new doctor.

"Yes, I know Thomas. Very good doctor. I'm glad he was there so you didn't have to go to the hospital. I have his note here in your chart. Let's check the head wound, and then I'll want to send you to get a CT scan. Make sure we aren't missing something with those headaches." He stood up and stopped in front of me.

"Oh, that won't be necessary."

"It is necessary, Kate. With head wounds we like to make sure there isn't swelling or something going on internally that we've missed."

He must have seen my reluctance because he sat back in his stool and wheeled it over to me, looking me in the eyes. "I won't allow you to return to work until you've had the scan. Headaches are a good indication that something might be going on we can't see. But it can also be from the trauma. It's better to be safe than sorry."

I sighed. "Okay."

"Great," he said, standing up and looking at my head. "I'll see if we can get you in for a scan today so I can get the results tomorrow. The wound is healing nicely. Thomas did a nice job with the stitches. We'll schedule you to come back to get the stitches out Friday, and you should be able to return to work by Monday. Do you need another doctor's note?"

"Yes," I said quietly.

He nodded and hummed a tune I didn't recognize while he made some notes on the computer. "Let's do a quick check to make sure there isn't any significant bruising anywhere else, and then you'll be free to go. I'll have your return to work note at the front desk waiting for you."

The scan of my body took less than five minutes since most of the cuts on my arms and legs from the glass had already begun to heal. The bruising and the burns from the airbag were already healing as well.

"You were very lucky, Kate; this could have been a lot worse. Most of the cuts are surface and will heal quickly. You shouldn't see any lasting marks from the burns. They weren't bad. Overall, I'd say in another week you'll be back to normal."

"That's great news. Can I exercise?"

"What do you do?"

"Mostly run, occasional cardio."

"Wait for the results of the scan, and if it's normal, then you can start with a light jog and increase the pace at your own discretion."

"Thank you, Dr. Parks."

"You're very welcome. Tell Vincent to give me a call sometime. I'd love to hit the golf course again."

I nodded, unable to form words. It was becoming clear that I was not going to be able to continue to live here. The connections to Vincent were far too deep.

After getting the script for my scan, I headed to the hospital. On the way, I called my office and then Mindy. She insisted on staying with me for another few days to make sure Vincent didn't weasel his way into taking care of me. I was grateful for that because I didn't know how many more times I could have the "we're done" and "leave me alone" talk. When would he take a hint?

MONDAY FINALLY ROLLED AROUND, and I was ready to return to work. The scan had come back normal, the doctor refilled the pain medication Thomas had given me, and my stitches were removed. I was feeling back to normal and ready to tackle the mountain of work I knew I'd have from being gone.

I was going stir crazy at home by myself. My mind drifted to Peter often. I could not stop thinking about his beautiful mossy green eyes and strong jaw. The kind smile and caring expressions. He was everything I wanted in a man and not anything I could ever have. It was frustrating.

It didn't stop my body from wanting him and my mind from dreaming about him. Most of the dreams involved the forest. Lumberjack Peter, scruffy Peter in a cabin, Peter hunting and finding me stranded in the woods, making love to me on a bed of leaves. That last one was last night, and I woke up aching and wishing he was there.

As I was drinking my coffee before work, my mind had wandered back to the dream, and I accidently poured the coffee on my shirt. I needed to change and was almost late leaving for work. I had to get Peter off my mind. We'd never see each other again, and if he wanted something more, he'd have left his number. It would never work out between us anyway because of Vincent.

My fingers tapped a beat on my desk as I waited for my computer to boot up. I'd worked from home a little last week but wasn't able to do much. My e-mail was probably full, and I had a report I needed to finish up.

Bonnie popped her head into my office. "Kate, Mr. Lawrence would like to see you." By the time my eyes lifted to the doorway, it was empty.

It wasn't how I wanted to start my day. I had a routine I liked to follow to get the day started off right. With a long sigh, I stood and headed for the door. My second cup of coffee would have to wait, along with my e-mails.

Mr. Lawrence's office was across the hall from mine. He had a larger corner office that overlooked a small pond. There was a small waiting area in front of his office. I was about to take a seat in one of the armchairs when his door opened. He ushered me in with a jerk of his hand.

"Kate, good morning. How are you feeling?" he asked as he walked back to his desk. He wasn't the most personable or approachable boss.

"Better, thank you. All healed up." I took a seat in one of the black leather chairs in front of his desk.

I smoothed down my pencil skirt, and then folded my hands in my lap. I took a few calming breaths to prepare for whatever he would say. He sat down at his desk and leaned forward. He pressed his fingertips together, and a long sigh fell from his lips.

My heart rate picked up. Was I going to get fired? I'd missed the last week, but I had tons of vacation time saved up. Four years' worth to be exact. This was the first time I'd taken a day off. It was for a good reason, or so I thought.

"Kate, you're my best, and I need you now more than ever," he said. I relaxed just a little. "Sam and Bill were in a little town called Oak Springs, about three hours west of here. There's an offer on the table for new development, and it's big, one of my biggest yet."

Excitement zipped through me. I could tell there was a lot riding on this. Tweedledee and Tweedledumbass messed up a lot, and I loved going in after them to clean up their messes. It made the close sweeter. Things moved quicker because of how badly they screwed stuff up. Clients were happy when I smoothed things out and showed them the positives.

Mr. Lawrence continued, "The mayor of the town is being difficult. He agreed to a new town hall, but nothing more. We offered to build up the surrounding area with strip malls, create new jobs and such. They have these town meetings, and they vote on things like this. I had my boys take an offer with them last week. It was for more money and to buy some of the surrounding properties. To build condos and a strip mall. You know, to build up the community and bring more people and business to an otherwise dying town. It's what we do." He sat back and took a sip of his coffee.

I nodded in agreement. We helped small towns by making them more appealing and creating more jobs. People were drawn to bigger, more well-known areas. We put the small towns on the map, so to speak. They appreciated all we did for them, and they flourished. We always gave back by giving something they needed. In this instance, a new town hall.

"So, you want me to close this?" I wanted to be sure I was understanding what he was asking of me.

"I want you to make them see that without the development, the town will die. A town like that cannot stay small forever. They need more money, more people, and more jobs. We want to help create that for them. Sure, people will have to sell their homes and property, but you know very well that what sets me apart from other big developers is that I stay to help set things up. We will find temporary housing for those folks, and then when the condos are up, we'll pay all the closing costs for a new condo. It's a win-win for everyone," he said with a smile.

"Sir, I think there are a few things that we need to talk about. In case there are negotiations. I need to know what I'm allowed to take off the table and what I'm allowed to add. Also, I'll need some time. So if you can give me two weeks, I'm sure I can come up with a solid plan and will be able to close it." Mr. Lawrence was already shaking his head before I finished talking.

"That won't work. We need this closed, and fast. Time is money. You leave tonight, and you have until Saturday to close it. This is an enormous deal, Kate." He leaned forward on his desk. "Close this, or else."

"But sir, that's less than a week, and you said yourself they have a town meeting on Monday where they vote on big projects. That's tonight, so I'll be behind. I need a little more time. At least give me until next week," I pleaded.

"You have one week."

I swallowed hard. "Mr. Lawrence, you promoted me to work alongside you because I get things done. I plan to get this done, too, but I need time to persuade them. I need to experience the town a little so I can get a feel for how it's doing, and that way, when I speak to the mayor, I'll have more information to provide. This is how I do things, and I haven't let you down yet."

"I promoted you because you are the best, and I only work with the best. You can do this, Kate; I believe in you. Take a company car and credit card. We've arranged for you to meet with the mayor first thing in the morning. In the meantime, you'll stay at a little bed and breakfast right off Main Street in the heart of the town, called The B&B." He snorted.

"See? They need our help to come up with some better names for things. Names that will attract people to the town. Transfer the Mullins case to Quincy and go home to pack. If you hurry you can get down there by five and attend the town meeting. Bonnie has all of your travel information at her desk." He turned his chair away from me and faced his computer.

This conversation was over. He had dismissed me. There was no way I'd get out of this or be able to buy more time. I'd just have to stall once I was down there. Instead of replying, I stood and turned to go.

"Oh, and Kate." He turned his chair toward me a little. "Make sure you close this deal, or don't bother coming back here."

My stomach plummeted to my feet. I felt weak and grabbed the doorjamb to stay upright. He'd never threatened my job before. I wanted to cry. Instead, I walked back to my office with my head held high. No matter the cost, I'd get this done.

I met with Quincy and transferred all the information I had on the Mullins case. Quincy was new, and I wasn't sure about him, but as Mr. Lawrence said, he only worked with the best. So I had to let go and trust everything would be okay.

"Do. Not. Blow. This," I said. "I've been working extra hard on this. You just need to go down there and deliver everything that I just told you."

He looked like a small animal caught in the middle of the road with a car barreling down on it.

"Quincy?"

He nodded and took the envelope from me. As I watched him scurry down the hall, I felt more uneasy about the situation. I shook my head and returned to my office.

A pad of paper sat on top of my desk; there were pages of notes. I flipped to a blank page, tore it out, and started making a list of all the things I needed to take. Organization and list-making helped keep me calm. It was a good feeling to know I was prepared, even if it was over the top at times.

The weather app on my phone said Oak Springs would be warm. It was crazy how the weather had changed from this past weekend. We were in a heat wave now, but I'd still need some sweaters and long pants for the evenings. The nights would still cool down since it was only spring. Once I finished my list, I went to talk to Bonnie.

"Here's the information you need for picking up the car. You need to go to this lot." She tapped the paper with her pen.

"Here's the address and your reservation for your stay. Check in time is after three today, and I've booked you to stay through to next Wednesday," she said with a wink. I smiled. "If you need to extend your stay for any reason or leave early, talk to Betty. She's a very sweet lady."

She handed me another piece of paper. "This is the information on your meeting with the mayor. I've already spoken with Elaine, his secretary. She knows you're coming and will schedule the meeting for tomorrow morning at ten. She also said he's a real looker, so wear something sexy." Bonnie waggled her eyebrows and handed me a few more sheets of information on the town.

This was a big packet of information, and I needed to keep it all together. I dug around my desk until I found a spare folder. If I had more time, I'd go home and organize it all into a binder with color coding and dividers. This would have to work for now.

I called Mindy for a ride. While I waited for her, I looked over my list once more and changed one pair of dress pants to a tight pencil skirt. The outfit appeared in my mind and I knew it would be perfect. Might as well play into my strengths.

There was a knock on my door. "Come in."

The door slowly opened, and Vincent poked his head in. I rolled my eyes and suppressed a groan.

"Vincent. I don't have time right now."

"I was wondering if you wanted to grab some lunch," he said, taking a seat in front of my desk.

"I can't. I'm going on a business trip."

"Now? This is your first day back. How are you feeling?"

"I'm fine. Stitches came out, head scan was clear." I had no idea why I was telling him all of that information. He was always able to pull it out of me.

He nodded and looked off to the side in thought. "Let me come with you."

My eyes widened. "Excuse me?"

I saw the look of steely determination in his eyes and braced myself for what he was about to say. "I'm coming with you. Trent won't mind. In fact, he'd probably encourage it."

I shook my head frantically. "No way. Absolutely not. This is my job! A job that I'm damn good at, I might add. Vincent, this has to stop. We are through. You cannot keep dropping by here and showing up at *my* house uninvited. I can't keep doing this with you."

"Katherine, we were good together, and we can be good again. I see the error in my ways. Just let me come with you and we can use the trip to rekindle our relationship."

My mouth dropped open and then snapped shut. "No. There is nothing to rekindle. Now kindly leave. Do not follow me, and do not show up. I have a job to do, and I need to focus. I'm sure if Mr. Lawrence found out that you were there to rekindle a romance, he'd be really angry."

He frowned and looked to the ground. When his eyes met mine they were dark and cold. Almost like a storm was brewing behind them.

"This is not over, Katherine. We belong together."

"No, Vincent. We don't."

He laughed, and it sounded crazed like the night of the memorial service. A chill ran down my spine. He stood and buttoned up his suit jacket.

"Have a good trip. I'll see you when you return."

Before I could respond, he walked out. My cell phone buzzed with an incoming text. Mindy was downstairs waiting. I put my laptop into my bag and closed the door, locking it on my way out.

"Kate, I'm trusting you to close this. Don't let me down."

I jumped at Mr. Lawrence's voice. He was standing next to Bonnie's desk. I nodded and scurried to the elevators with my heart beating out of my chest and my stomach in knots. This was a hell of a way to start a business trip. Especially after a traumatic accident. Fingers crossed everything else worked out.

THE DRIVE TO OAK SPRINGS wasn't bad at all. I had expected to hit traffic around rush hour, especially since it took me forever to pack, pick up a company car, and ditch Mindy. My GPS led me down country roads, and I seemed to miss all of the traffic. I had never been to this part of the state before. It was almost like a whole different world.

About an hour before I was set to arrive in town, the road opened up wide; there were farms and never-ending countryside to my left. A wooded area appeared on my right, and the GPS told me to turn right on a dirt road called Old Cedar Road. I almost missed it.

The road was long and winding; I drove about another two miles before it dumped me right onto Main Street. I slowed down to a crawl. The street seemed empty.

It was eight o'clock, and most of the stores appeared to be closed. I read some store names as I crept by. Grateful Cup, Best Foot Forward, and Pizza Pan. I didn't know what Mr. Lawrence was talking about; the stores had very original names. They were catchy and drew attention.

I drove a little farther down Main Street. Instead of storefronts, houses now lined the street. The GPS said I had arrived. I stopped in front of a two-story house and peered through the window. A wooden sign out front read *The B&B*. Okay, the bed and breakfast could use a little help with its name.

I turned into the driveway and parked. My legs were cramped from the long drive, and stretching felt good. I lifted my arms above my head, breathing in the sweet country air. I tipped to the side to get a deeper stretch.

Maybe I could use this time to relax, too. I thought I'd spotted a massage parlor on Main Street. A run sounded great, and the park I passed on the way in looked like the perfect spot.

I grabbed my suitcase from the back seat and walked up the pebble stone walkway. Beautiful flower beds lined either side of the walkway by the large front porch. Two white wooden rockers sat at one end of the porch, and a porch swing hung on the opposite end. I was already in love. I snapped a picture for Mindy.

I opened the screen and read the sign that hung on the solid green door. *Welcome. Rest your heads upon our beds and feast upon our breakfast spreads.* That little sign was a lot more eye-catching than the name of the place.

I wasn't sure if I should knock or just walk in. I'd never stayed at a bed and breakfast before. The door opened before I could decide what to do.

"Don't just stand out there, darling; come in. We've been expecting you," a large woman wearing a white apron said.

She had salt and pepper hair pulled up into a tight bun, and she wore a long dress to her ankles and black boots. Had I just stepped back in time? The woman took my suitcase and ushered me inside.

There was a couch and chair in front of a fireplace to the left. A large tall oak desk that looked similar to the pieces of furniture in Violet's house was to my right. I wondered if the store Violet got her furniture from was here in town.

"Katherine Miller?" The woman asked from behind the desk.

"Yes, that's me," I replied.

Behind the woman's head were more wooden signs. One read *The B&B.* Another read *If you want breakfast in bed, sleep in the kitchen.*

I laughed out loud, and the woman looked at me funny.

"What's so funny?" she asked with her hands on her hips.

"I was just reading your sign." I pointed to the last one I read.

"Oh yeah, got those all over the house. Laney Walters is the best sign maker there is. She uses wood found around Oak Springs. She has a store down there on Main Street called Limbitless Expressions," she explained.

"I'll have to check it out while I'm here." I collected things from every town I visited, and a sign with a cute saying on it was just what I needed.

My eyes roamed the room. There were little knickknacks all over the place. Wooden signs hung in the living room. An older gentleman I hadn't noticed before was asleep on the couch.

"My name is Betty, and this here is my bed and breakfast, The B&B, as the folks around here call it. I do all the cooking and cleaning myself. There are a few guests who will be in and out during your stay. They shouldn't give you any trouble. Come on; I'll show you to your room," she said. She grabbed a key from one of the hooks behind the desk.

Next to the desk were the stairs. They creaked as I followed Betty's wide frame up. Photos covered the walls on either side of the stairway. There was a large picture window with a bench seat at the top of the stairs. I wanted to sit down and read.

At the top of the stairs, a hallway branched out to the left and right, with three rooms on either side. The place was a lot bigger than I thought. We turned to the right, and Betty unlocked the second door.

"This is your room. The bathroom is attached, and I left clean towels on the sink. Kitchen is closed for the night, but if you're hungry, I'm sure I could find you something." Betty set my suitcase down on the chest in front of the bed. The décor in the house reminded me of my grandma's house.

"I'll be okay tonight, thank you. I'm just going to get to bed early so I can get an early start tomorrow," I said as I looked around the room.

"Well, good night then, and see you in the morning. Breakfast is at eight," Betty said.

I stopped her before she closed the door. "Betty?"

"Yes?"

"Is the town meeting happening right now?"

She nodded. "Oak Springs residents only. No outsiders."

"Thanks," I said with a shy smile.

She nodded again and left.

That seemed like a silly rule, but I guess it made sense. I thought about sneaking into the meeting, then I remembered I didn't know where it was being held and decided against it. I took out my phone and snapped more pictures to send to Mindy. It was her kind of place with the trinkets and wooden signs with the witty sayings.

The room was a bit outdated, but the homey feeling of it had me letting out a deep sigh and the tension rolling off my shoulders. I could feel myself really relaxing. Sheer gold curtains hung in front of a set of French doors. Two heavy panel curtains in cream hung on either side of the doors. I stepped outside and smiled. The balcony overlooked Main Street.

Leaning forward with my hands on the railing, I looked up and down the street. To the right looked like a residential street. All the shops were to the left. Everything was so quiet I could hear crickets. Was it always like that here?

Walking back inside, I went into the bathroom to brush my teeth and get ready for bed. I wanted to look over the proposal again to make sure I didn't miss anything. The quicker I closed this, the quicker I could go back home.

Chapter 12

PETER

"ALL IN FAVOR OF the new town hall," Tom Tracy called out.

"Unanimous," I called out. Laney nodded.

"All in favor of the strip-mall."

Split vote. Damn.

"All in favor of the new condo complex," Tom called.

"Ten," I said. There were forty of us in attendance this evening.

"All opposed."

I raised my hand and counted. "Thirty."

Laney smiled before recording the numbers. That concluded the meeting. Surprisingly, it went by quickly, and I was happy to be on my way back home. The week had been long and tiring. After the Lawrence brothers left town, people were in and out of my office with worry over what was happening to the town. Tom and Ken returned, still arguing about their stores' roof situation.

We had to retrieve the building specs to find out who actually owned the roof. The true reason came out, and it made total sense. Apparently, there was a leak in Tom's store, and when he looked at where it was coming from, he discovered the roof issue. Tom was a cheapskate, so he was trying to get Ken to pay for the repairs. Now it involved me. Tom almost took it to a vote tonight, but I stopped him. That was not official town business.

Frank, Sid, Tom, and Ken had all come over last night for an impromptu poker night. Our normal night was Tuesday. It ended with Frank passed out on my couch and Tom and Ken arguing over a hand and then their roof situation. Sid and I gave up, and we called it a night.

After the town meeting, I drove straight home and threw some leftover pizza into the microwave before heading to my room to change. I heard the microwave beep and shuffled out to grab my pizza and a beer before heading back to the living room. The couch was calling my name. I flopped down and turned on the television. Just as the pizza was up to my mouth, someone knocked on my front door. I had a pretty good idea who it was.

I sighed and threw my pizza back down onto the plate, setting it beside my beer on the coffee table. My bare feet shuffled on the carpet as I made my way to the door. Frank was standing on my porch tugging on the back of his neck. He was anxious. That was his tell.

"What are you doing here?" I asked, a little annoyed.

"I was coming by to see how you're handling everything. I thought maybe you could use a friend, and I could use a beer."

He was still in his uniform, so I know he hadn't gone home yet and likely wouldn't tonight. He was avoiding his responsibilities there. Frank walked past me toward the kitchen and came back out with a beer and a slice of cold pizza.

I rolled my eyes and closed the door. Frank plopped down in the recliner, kicked off his shoes, and put his sock-clad feet on the coffee table. I picked up my beer and pizza and sat back on the couch with a sigh.

We sat in silence and watched a football game. There was something going on with Frank, but it appeared he didn't want to talk about it, so I didn't press him. It was kind of nice to have some company. I'd never let him know that though. That would be like issuing an open invitation for him to come over any time, which I guess he did anyway. I just didn't want to keep encouraging it.

I must have dozed off during the game because I woke up with a start. I sat up and looked around the now dark living room. Frank was passed out on the recliner with his mouth hanging open. His shirt was open, revealing his white undershirt.

I pulled myself off the couch and walked down the hall to my room. Peeling my clothes off, I climbed into bed. The second my head hit the pillow, I was out.

MY ALARM WENT OFF at six fifteen for my morning run. I liked to get up early and run through Main Street and the park before stores opened and people recognized me. The town was nice and quiet. I threw on a pair of sweats and a hoodie and headed out the door, leaving a snoring Frank behind.

I went through a set of stretches on my porch. My house sat off Old Cedar Road, about two miles from Main Street. I jogged down the road and cut through the trees just before Main Street. The park was just on the other side. I picked up my pace to a run.

When I was rounding the path at the far end of the park, I thought I saw a woman heading toward Main Street. Normally the park was empty. Sid was one of the few other people who ran in the mornings. I wondered who was out, so I ran hard to the entrance of the park and up the side street that cut back to Main.

When I got to the street, no one was there. I stopped at a bench and stretched, allowing my heart rate to come back down. Then I turned and headed back to the park to run the loop once more before heading home.

I checked my schedule on my phone when I got back to the house. Frank had gone, so I cleaned up the living room before heading for the shower. A 10 a.m. meeting with Lawrence Development Company popped up in my calendar.

I didn't remember setting up a meeting. In fact, I'd told the Lawrence brothers to back off until after our town meeting. I wanted to buy some time to think about my next move. They didn't waste any time. Day after our vote and they were back.

I jumped in the shower, got ready, and then headed into town to stop at Grateful Cup where I got my coffee and fresh banana nut muffin every morning. It was a gorgeous morning. The sun was shining, and it was already getting warm. The weather had shifted, and now it was an unusually warm spring.

"Good morning, Mayor Bradbury. Can I get you the usual?" Elouise asked from behind the counter.

I smiled at her. "Yes, thank you."

Elouise owned Grateful Cup and was one of the best women I knew. She'd been in this town since the beginning. Her parents moved here when the town was first established; she was just a little girl. She opened Grateful Cup when she was in her early twenties.

I spotted Frank sitting by the window with Sid. So I walked over to the table and pulled up a chair.

"Hey," Frank mumbled. He lifted his cup in the air. "Elouise, I'll take a refill when you have a minute."

"Looking a little rough there, Frank. What time did you leave this morning?" I asked with a laugh.

Sid shook his head. "You slept there again?"

Frank punched Sid in the arm. "Yes, and it's none of your damn business. I'm fine. I just need more coffee to wake up."

Sid punched him back. Then Frank turned to me and punched my arm.

"What was that for?" I asked as I punched him back.

"None of that in my store, boys. I'll throw you out, even if you are the mayor and the police," Elouise barked. She placed my muffin and coffee in front of me and refilled Frank's coffee before heading back behind the counter.

"I've got to get to work." I pushed my chair back to stand.

"Us too," Sid said, joining me.

"I just got my refill," Frank whined.

"Get it to go," Sid replied, a little annoyed.

I laughed. The two of them were hilarious together. Frank always acted like a kid, and Sid was a little too uptight and reserved. How they became friends long ago, I'd never know.

"See you guys later," I called as I headed out. "Bye, Elouise." I smiled and waved at her. She winked and waved back.

Hannah was behind the counter counting the cash drawer when I arrived. The store was opening in fifteen minutes.

"Good morning, Hannah," I said as I headed up the stairs.

"Peter," she called after me. "I have a question for you."

I turned and walked back down the stairs toward her.

She poked her head around the wall. "I was wondering if you'd join me Thursday night at that new place on Grand Street, Simply Cook It. The class is at eight. They're cooking rack of lamb."

She made a disgusted face, and I held back a laugh. She'd asked me twice before, and I'd turned her down. I felt bad and gave her a chance. It would entertain me, at least, to see her eat lamb.

I smiled down at her. "I'd love to."

A big smile spread across her face. "Great." She ducked back around the wall.

I walked up the rest of the stairs wondering what I had just done. I wasn't interested in dating anyone right now and I couldn't stop thinking about my brother's ex-girlfriend, Kate. I regretted not leaving my number with her. I wanted to check in on her. If it had been someone here in town, I would have checked on them. I felt terrible that I hadn't done that.

When I reached the top of the stairs, Elaine was sitting behind her desk, looking at her computer screen and banging away on her keyboard.

"Good morning, Elaine. What's this meeting at ten with someone from Lawrence Development Company, and why wasn't I informed of it yesterday?" I asked her.

"It was a last-minute addition. I received a call yesterday, but I didn't want to add to your stress, so I added it in for today at ten." She handed me a few messages.

Elaine arrived at the office every morning at eight and answered voice mails and office e-mails for me. She helped weed out the serious calls and e-mails from the ones that didn't need the mayor's attention.

I walked into my office and closed the door behind me. Sitting down at my desk, I thumbed through my messages and then returned a few phone calls. I thought about giving Bill or Sam Lawrence a call to inquire about this meeting, but then decided I'd just let it play out. I wanted to see what they would throw at me next.

Chapter 13

KATE

THE TOWN WAS REALLY CUTE and very quiet. I always loved the quiet of country living. The first rays of sun were just beginning to appear in the sky. I stood on the porch and stretched my legs, inhaling deeply and getting ready for a run. Betty had said breakfast was at eight, so I figured I had plenty of time. I wanted to check out the stores on Main Street before they opened for the day.

I walked up the left side of the street; there wasn't a car or person in sight. A peaceful feeling settled over me. On the corner was Lavish Locks, a hair salon. Next door was Tips and Toes Nail Salon.

The names of the stores were clever and catchy. Mr. Lawrence was wrong about them. Had he even visited the town? He normally made at least one visit during the whole process. I wondered who scouted this town. I usually had all of that information, but when I was combing through the file last night, I noticed that was missing. Along with all of the person's data collection.

Whenever we went in to scout a location for new development, we followed an extensive format that was set up by Mr. Lawrence, myself, and a team of scouts. Brenda, Max, and Sylvia were the scouts, and they'd been with the company for years. They were always thorough and documented everything.

I made a mental note to call Bonnie and see if she could send me a copy. Maybe they were missing by mistake. This whole thing seemed a little messy, and I was in the dark more than I liked.

The next store was Knead to Relax Day Spa. I was so excited I couldn't contain it. After the car accident, a massage was what I needed. I couldn't wait to book an appointment later. The store window said they opened at nine, which meant I'd have enough time to call before my appointment with the mayor.

I continued down the street, my smile so wide it almost hurt my face. This town was so charming. Black trash cans and streetlights lined the street on either side, with matching black benches every few stores. I spotted Limbitless Expressions—the store Betty had told me about that sold those cute wooden signs—across the street.

I made my way over to the store and peered in through the large front window. Wooden signs of all shapes and sizes covered the walls. Coffee mugs, key chains, and smaller wooden signs sat on rotating display cases in the middle of the store.

It opened at eight. I'd have to visit after my meeting. The play on words in the store's name was a nice touch and gave the store originality. Again, I rolled my eyes at Mr. Lawrence for thinking the stores were boring. This store was quaint just like the rest of the town, and I was falling in love with every step I took.

A small side street off to the left of the store led to a park. *Parkway.* Even the streets had clever names. I stretched once more and sped up to a brisk walk. Just to warm up a little. The path went in a big circle and didn't seem like it would take that long to get around.

Black benches that matched the ones on Main Street sat at the edge of the path around the park. I increased my speed to a jog. As I came to the first curve in the path at the back of the park, a river appeared, separating the park from the woods. The woods that Mr. Lawrence wanted to tear down so he could build one of two sets of condos.

I slowed down to a walk and paced back and forth, staring out into the woods. Such a peaceful backdrop for the park. A bench sat at the edge of the water, and I made my way over to it. The water lapped at the edge at my feet.

To my right I saw the back patio of the pub. It overlooked the pond and the woods. No doubt a selling point for whoever bought the pub. The condos would be a huge eyesore, and the pub would lose some of its appeal.

I jogged the rest of the circle back toward Main Street. Stopping at one of the streetlamps, I went through my leg stretches. I checked my fitness watch; it was six forty-five. I needed to head back.

There was just enough time for me to shower and get ready before breakfast. But not before stopping in for a quick coffee from Grateful Cup. Luckily, the coffee shop was located next to the park.

The bell chimed above the door, and a portly woman behind the counter with gray hair and kind eyes smiled at me. The smell of roasted beans and baked goods filled my nose, and my stomach growled.

"Welcome to Grateful Cup," the woman said. Two older gentlemen looked up at me from a table beside the door. I smiled and made my way to the counter.

"Thank you. I'll take a medium brewed coffee and a…" I paused and peered into the glass display case. "Glazed donut."

"Sure thing. Here's your cup; coffee is at the end of the counter," the woman said. She handed me my donut and cup. "That'll be $4.12."

I dug out a five from my pocket and handed it over. After I got my change, I moved down the counter to the coffee. I felt eyes on my back, but I kept my head down and filled my cup. I didn't want to linger and risk being the center of attention, so I left and made my way back to The B&B.

THE GPS SAID THE MAYOR'S office was one minute away. I looked out over the balcony, then back at the map on my phone. The office had to be across the street. The sign on the building said Double Oak Furnishings.

I walked to the store and stared at the sign for far too long. I was sure I looked lost and confused. "You have arrived," my GPS announced in an Australian accent. This was, in fact, my destination. *Strange.*

Shoving my phone back in my purse, I opened the door and stepped inside. The blonde woman behind the desk didn't lift her head, even though the bell had announced my arrival. I gazed around the store in awe of all the hand-crafted furniture.

A small round table with the same markings as the one in Violet's house sat next to a larger square one. I ran my fingers over all the fine details. This had to be the store where Violet purchased all her beautiful furniture. A smile spread across my face. I couldn't wait to place an order.

"Can I help you?" The blonde asked as she flipped through a magazine. Her eyes were glued to the pages, which were turning too quickly for her to actually read them.

"Yes, I'm here to meet with the mayor. Am I in the right place?" I asked, walking toward the desk.

"Upstairs." She pointed to the wall behind her. Her eyes never left the magazine.

I walked toward the back door. A set of stairs appeared to the right. The upstairs was brighter and more modern than the store below. Light gray hardwood throughout the space looked nice with the stark white walls.

A small sitting area with black furniture was to the left of the entrance. Just beyond that was a water cooler. The walls were bare, and my mind was instantly teeming with ideas to fill the space. It was a blank canvas.

The space was huge and bright, but somehow it still felt cold, almost stale. I'd liven this place up with warm colors, more furniture, and some photos for the walls. A big area rug would bring in some extra color and make the waiting area more inviting.

An older woman sat behind a large oak desk that had to be from the store below. Her eyes were on her computer screen, and she didn't seem to notice that I had come in. Behind her was a half wall made of tinted glass. I walked up to the desk, my heels clicking on the floor and echoing through the large space.

"Hi, I'm Katherine Miller from Lawrence Development Company. I'm here to see the mayor. I have a ten o'clock," I announced.

The woman looked up at me in surprise, then quickly smiled before looking back at her screen, "Have a seat, dear. The mayor will be right with you." She pointed to the black leather sofa against the wall.

The couch wasn't as comfortable as I had imagined. My bare legs squeaked against it as I tried to get comfortable. A nervous zip of energy ran through me. That always happened before meeting with a client.

After about ten minutes, the woman stood up from her chair and walked around her desk. "The mayor will see you now."

She led me around the partitioned wall toward a smaller room. A hallway went off to the right and led to another room that I assumed was a break room of sorts. At the end of the hall was the bathroom.

The room seemed out of place, like it wasn't part of the original floor plan. I looked around and realized this was just one large open space. The mayor must have had it renovated. Why this place? Why not an office in town hall or somewhere more important?

We stopped in front of a frosted glass door with the word *MAYOR* on it. The woman knocked on the door.

A deep muffled voice came from the other side of the door, "Come in."

Even though my secretary, Bonnie, had mentioned the mayor was attractive, I still pictured an older gentleman. Salt and pepper hair and glasses. Sitting behind a desk and stuffed into a small space. Papers surrounding him and perhaps a frown on his weathered face.

Elaine opened the door and stepped to the side so I could squeeze past her. All the air left my lungs, and I froze. Not at all what I just pictured. The room was void of clutter. The desk was clear except for a phone and laptop. And Peter sat behind it with an expression that I'm sure mirrored my own.

"Elaine, we need two cups of coffee. Black for me and two creams, two sugars for Kate here."

My eyes opened wide. He remembered. I'd had a cup of coffee the morning after the accident in Pine Brook. He must have watched me pour cream and sugar into it and committed it to memory. It would have impressed me if I wasn't so shocked.

Elaine gave him a funny look before she walked out of the room, closing the door behind her.

"Have a seat." He gestured to one of the black armchairs in front of his desk.

My legs felt shaky, and my heart rate increased. *Not now.* There had to be some mistake. Peter was the mayor of Oak Springs? I was here to pitch an idea to Peter? My lungs felt tight. I sat down and rubbed my hands together. My palms were sweating.

Peter looked as good as the day I met him, if not better. He was wearing an expensive-looking black suit that stretched tight across his broad frame. His bright green dress shirt brought out the color of his eyes. He looked comfortable without a tie and the top button undone. The man could wear the hell out of a suit.

His hair was neatly styled today, and damn, did it look good. Tight on the sides with one of those sharp lines cut into it and longer on top. It was swept to the side and held in place with some gel instead of tousled like when we first met.

He had a shadow of facial hair on his jaw again, and I wondered what it would feel like on my skin. If I wasn't mid-panic attack, I might have drooled. How did he not have a line of women out his door every day?

I couldn't bear to make direct eye contact with him, so instead I looked down at my lap. Why had I listened to Bonnie? I ran my hands over my tight black pencil skirt to wipe some sweat off my palms. The skirt was one of my favorites and showed off my subtle, almost nonexistent, curves.

I'd thought the skirt and short-sleeved, sheer blouse I wore over a lacy white tank top would entice him and persuade him to listen to me. But now I was worried I looked cheap, like I went around seducing men into signing contracts with our company.

My shoes weren't any better. Black peep toe with a thin ankle strap and a three-inch heel. My favorite pair that I wore when Mindy and I went out for a night on the town.

Oh, who was I kidding? I'd dressed sexier than usual because Bonnie had mentioned that the mayor was hot. She was right. I'd had fantasies starring *this* man for days. I dropped my head into my hands and wished to disappear.

I never did things like this. The man I was trying to convince to sign the contract was the same man I had been lusting after for the past four days. My stomach started to hurt, signaling the beginning of an attack. I tried and failed to ward off the panic. This was bad—terrible in fact.

The silence between us seemed to drag on forever. Elaine came back in with two cups of coffee. She set them down on the desk and then left the room again. Peter stood up, reached across his desk, and handed my coffee to me.

"It's good to see you, Kate," he said with a smile. "How are you feeling?"

My stomach dipped. I couldn't answer. My heart was beating out of my chest. The panic attack was taking over. I hadn't had a full-blown attack in years. I did a lot of deep breathing exercises to keep them away. None of the exercises were working, and the anxiety grew stronger each minute.

"Could I get some water?" I asked. It came out as a whisper.

I rubbed my hands together, and then ran them up and down my arms as if I could physically ward off the attack. My mouth felt like I'd swallowed a giant cotton ball. My head started to pound. It was a full body attack. One that I wasn't going to win.

Peter stood up and walked over to his door. He yelled to the front, "Elaine, could I get a glass of water, please?"

He walked back over and sat on the edge of his desk in front of me. I couldn't take my eyes off the floor. In my head, I was counting backward from ten. Peter grabbed my hands and held onto them. I'm sure they were a sweaty mess, and I started breathing heavier. My pulse increased, and I was losing my battle against the attack.

"Kate, take a deep breath. It will be okay," he said in a calm voice. "Look at me."

I couldn't look up. The attack drew all my focus. My breathing became shallow. It felt like there was no air in the room, and I couldn't breathe, which then caused me to panic more. My eyes slammed shut, and I counted back from ten again. *Why wasn't it working?*

"Kate, look at me," he repeated in a commanding tone.

I opened my eyes just as he knelt in front of me. His green eyes were staring up at me, causing a flutter in my stomach. I focused on the depths of green and the small yellow flecks in his irises. They were gorgeous and mesmerizing.

"Take nice deep breaths. Can you breathe with me, Kate?"

I nodded, still focused on the subtle color variations in his eyes.

"Oh my, is she going to be okay?" Elaine asked. "I think Gerald is out of town for the day, but I could call his assistant."

"Everything will be just fine," Peter said. He handed me a cup of water. "Take a drink, Kate."

"Do you two know each other?" Elaine asked.

"Elaine, not now," Peter snapped. "We don't need to call Gerald either. Or his assistant. Kate will be fine in just a few minutes."

His eyes never left mine. I stared into the depths of them again. They matched the spring greens outside, and I focused all my attention on that. I'd never seen anyone with such beautiful eyes before. It was like they weren't real.

I followed his breathing. *In and out. In and out.* I took another sip of water and felt my heart rate almost return to normal.

"Thank you. I'm sorry about that," I croaked out.

Peter sat down in the chair beside me and turned it so we faced each other, all while keeping hold of my hand. It felt amazing and reminded me of how close we were last weekend. My head resting on his chest and his arm wrapped around me. I wanted more of that. I wanted to climb into his lap and have him tell me this wasn't real.

"What are you sorry about?" He drew small circles on the back of my hand with his thumb.

"Having a panic attack. I'm so embarrassed," I said as I tried to pull my hand away.

He wouldn't let it go. It wasn't the same way Vincent had held onto my hand over the weekend; this was more of a gentle way of letting me know that I wasn't alone.

"You have nothing to be embarrassed about. This is not an ideal situation."

"No, not at all," I agreed. "This is your town. I'm here to prompt you to accept the proposal for the Lawrence brothers' project."

I turned my head away and took another sip of water. Peter released my hand, and I missed his touch. He sat back and reached for his cup.

"Pitch it to me." He propped his right ankle on his left knee and took a sip of his coffee.

"What?"

"Give me your pitch. I want to hear what you have to say and how it's different from what Sam and Bill have already said. Why are you here? When I asked for time, why did Mr. Lawrence send you?" He took another sip, never taking his eyes off me.

No wonder they appointed him mayor. He had a way of being intimidating while remaining calm. I'd met many men in my line of work who acted the same way, and I broke them all. Normally I was strong and confident, but this situation threw me off guard. I was struggling, and that wasn't like me.

I hated that in both of my encounters with Peter I had appeared weak, like some little girl who needed saving. That was the way Vincent had always treated me. When he left me, I poured my heart into my work.

I focused on becoming a stronger person. I practiced on Vincent a thousand times a day when I had to continually reject him.

Yet, in a matter of minutes, this situation took me right back to where I started. I took a deep breath, sat up straight, and faced him head-on. After counting to five, I was ready. He was like any other client.

"I've been crunching numbers and going over property lines. There are a few properties that have housing on them. We're prepared to offer the affected families housing in the new condos. Mr. Lawrence always stays to see his projects through. Once the buildings are up and running, he comes in to make sure the transitions are flawless. The amount of money he will offer is over double what the land is even worth. And he will still build your new town hall."

Peter said nothing. He didn't even move, so I continued, "There's some vacant land over there on Old Cedar Road that backs up to the river across from the pub. That's where he'd like to put one set of condos. A second set would go on one property where the river runs through. I've driven over there to see what we're working with. I think there are only two properties we'd need to make offers on. The second would be where part of the strip mall would go."

Pausing, I took a sip of water. Peter's jaw ticked, but still, he said nothing.

"He's made very generous offers to the owners of the properties and offered to pay closing costs on a new condo for them to move into, on top of the money for the property. He wanted two strip malls, but I talked him down to one. The strip mall would generate new jobs and open up the town for more revenue. It would be a great benefit to the town. The condos would create more housing and attract more families to the town. It's a win all the way around," I finished.

I picked up my coffee and took a sip. It was perfect, and I curled my lips in to hide my smile. I studied Peter's gorgeous face for any signs he would bend. He was skeptical, but I thought maybe I could persuade him over to my side.

"I have numbers and charts and building plans if you want to see any of them. I've also brought along growth models from previous small towns that have accepted similar developments and are now thriving."

Peter took a large gulp of his coffee and studied me. Finally, he said, "You're good. This must be why they sent you. You create the perfect pitch. How could anyone say no to you?"

I smiled. "No one has. My record is perfect."

"Well, I'm sorry to do this, but I'm going to be the first one. The answer is still no," he stated. He seemed cold and closed off now as he buttoned his suit jacket and walked back around his desk.

My mouth started to drop open, and I snapped it closed. I thought he would understand where I was coming from. See things from my perspective and want to do what was in the best interest of the town. This was it.

"No? You aren't even going to consider what I've just told you? This could benefit your town. You could bring in more revenue, which means you could do more things for the town. There is no way that this little town makes enough money to make repairs to buildings or fix roads and such. Small towns die," I nearly shouted, my eyes locked with his.

I couldn't read his expression. Panic started in the pit of my stomach again, and I pushed it down. I would not back down, not now that I'd found my backbone again.

He smiled at me, and it confused me. "This little town has more to offer than you know, and I'm going to show it to you. Are you hungry?"

I hesitated, unsure of what game he was playing. I needed the upper hand. "I think we need to stay here and talk this through."

"I understand, but I'd rather show you the town. How long are you here for?"

"A week, unless we finalize everything earlier."

I bent down to pick up my briefcase, and a warm sensation ran up my spine. I turned around and caught his eyes below my waist. His gaze snapped back up to my face, and heat flooded my cheeks. Great, I was blushing. Was there any way that I would not embarrass myself in front of him?

"Then I have a week to convince you to change your mind," he said as he walked past me to the door.

"I doubt that will happen, but you sure can try," I said as I followed him.

I felt sick to my stomach. No matter what happened, someone would get hurt. One of us would get burned. It was just a matter of which one.

Chapter 14

PETER

KATE WAS HERE, IN MY TOWN, and working for the pain in my ass. Not only was she working for him; she was the one sent in to force my hand on the development. The one that would take away my home. There was no chance in hell we'd ever be together now.

The business side of me needed to tell her no, pull the plug on the whole thing, and find a different way for the town to get the new town hall. The other side of me—the one thinking with the other head—couldn't walk away just yet.

Hell, I couldn't stop thinking about her, and she showed up. I wanted to spend as much time as possible with her. To get to know her. There was no way we'd ever have a future together, but there was something between us. I couldn't let her go without exploring it further.

"I'm going out for the rest of the day, Elaine. Only call me if it's an emergency," I said as I passed by her desk on the way to the stairs.

Pausing at the bottom of the stairs, I let Kate pass me, then placed my hand on the small of her back to guide her through my store. She flinched and then relaxed back into my hand. I straightened up a little taller, a smile crossing my face.

I felt a sense of pride leading her through my store. I knew she admired my work. As if she couldn't help herself, she ran a finger over one of the pieces as we passed by. I committed it to memory so I could gift it to her later. When I could show her everything in more detail.

I leaned forward and whispered in her ear. "By the time this is over, you will fall in love with this town." *And hopefully me, too.*

Her short intake of breath told me the effect I had on her, and I smiled again. It was the same effect she had on me. At least I wasn't in this alone.

"I think someone is a little suspicious of me," she mumbled.

She pointed back toward the store where Hannah was watching us from the window. I shuddered.

"Yeah, about that, I sort of agreed to a date with her Thursday night. She'd asked me a few times before, and I always turned her down. I felt bad this time, so I agreed."

"Peter, you don't owe me an explanation," she said, glancing up at me.

Her blue eyes sparkled in the sun. I thought I saw a flash of disappointment for a second, but it quickly disappeared. She lifted her hand to block out the sun as she looked around Main Street.

"Ok, let's pick somewhere to eat. Pizza Pan is cool. They use all organic, home-grown ingredients and cook their pizzas in a stone oven." I pointed down the street.

Then I pointed across the street to one of my favorite places, "If you want a healthier option, there's Lettuce Eat. They have salads and lettuce wraps. Their salads are great and made from organic, home-grown ingredients. Tommy Davis from Davis Farms supplies most of the ingredients and produce to the town. He's also the owner of Lettuce Eat. I like to stop there after a long run.

I led her over to a nearby bench so she could sit down while we talked. I didn't know if she was still sore from her accident or not. It had only been a week.

"How are you feeling?" I asked.

"Better. Almost back to normal. Had my stitches out the other day," she said with a smile.

"If you need a follow up with a doctor, Gerald Stevens is who you'll want to see. He owns a small practice a few miles from here. He's visiting the next town over, Ridge Point, today making some house calls. He should be back in tomorrow. I'll give you his number."

She placed her hand on top of mine. My skin tingled under her touch. The same type of lightning feeling under my skin that I got each time we touched. My eyes lifted from our hands to her face. Her smile was beautiful and aimed at me. "Peter, I'm fine. Thank you, though."

I smiled back at her, and a pink hue appeared in her cheeks. She looked back over the street, crossing her legs. Her skirt rode up, revealing more of her gorgeous tanned legs. I wanted to run one hand up her bare leg while the other explored under her thin, almost see-through shirt. The sheer white top was doing nothing to hide the cleavage spilling out of her tiny tank top.

I didn't normally act like a caveman around women, but there was something about Kate that had me wanting to cover her up and throw her over my shoulder. Was this how she always dressed for meetings? I nearly growled. The thought of other men looking at her like that only fueled my inner caveman more.

Flaunting herself to get what she wanted was cheap, and that's not who she was, or so I thought. Really, I knew nothing about her. I could have her pegged all wrong.

"You run?" she asked, drawing me out of my thoughts. I tore my gaze away from her legs.

"Yup. Every morning." I looked out over Main Street.

The wind blew her long hair around her face, and she pushed it aside. It was a gorgeous chestnut color with blonde tones that shone through in the sunlight. My fingers itched to get tangled in her long locks. I wanted to touch her, needed to touch her. I clenched my hands into fists to keep from doing it.

"I run every morning, too," she said.

"Great, then we can run together tomorrow," I declared. I wasn't asking. Now that she was here in my town, she was stuck with me.

She looked over at me and smiled. "Okay, Mr. Mayor. Sounds like a date." Then her eyes opened wide. Pink ran up her neck and settled in her cheeks. "I didn't mean a date. It was just an expression."

I kept my eyes locked on hers. "It's a date."

She smiled again, and then looked away. She was so damn beautiful. I was an idiot if I thought I could spend time with her without developing feelings. I was already captivated, ever since I had her wrapped up in my arms. She'd occupied my mind every damn day and night since. Now she was right here in front of me, and I still couldn't have her.

I changed the subject. "Let's get back to picking somewhere to eat. Sandy's Country Diner is the only real sit-down restaurant in town. There's no chain restaurant here or anywhere close by. Local restaurants run by the people of the town are better, anyway. They all use ingredients from Davis Farms or from the farmer's market we have very Saturday and Sunday from spring to fall."

Kate chewed on her lip as she thought. I tried not to watch as her teeth moved back and forth over her plump bottom lip. Okay, maybe I was watching a little.

She turned and looked at me. "That's a lot to choose from. I think, since you're showing me the town, Mr. Mayor, you pick."

I took a minute to think about where I wanted to take her. I had a week to show her the town, and I needed to make a good first impression. Sandy's would be the perfect spot for that.

Sandy had been in the town as long as Elouise, and she would be helpful in convincing Kate that this town didn't need all the extras her company was proposing. I needed all the help I could get.

"Okay, I know the perfect place. Come on."

I stood up and held out my hand for her. She looked down at it, and then slid her hand in mine. It was small and delicate, and my hand fit perfectly around hers. I helped her stand, and then dropped her hand. I wanted nothing more than to continue to hold on to it, but now wasn't the right time for that. There wasn't going to be a right time for us. The thought had me rubbing at my chest.

It had been easy to walk away from her the first time, but fate, if that's what you called it, brought her back to me. It was like a second chance. Except now we were on opposing sides. The odds were stacked against us. The thought made me sweat even more than I already had been.

It was hot out and felt even hotter with my damn suit on. I took off my jacket and draped it over my arm. My fingers itched to grab Kate's hand again as we walked, but I knew that was only asking for trouble. I shoved my hand in my pocket to keep from reaching for her. There was no way that we could ever be more than what we were right now. Even if it killed me.

WE WALKED DOWN MAIN STREET, and I showed her all the mom-and-pop shops that lined the street. I told her stories about all the people who owned the stores. She asked a lot of questions, and I was glad I had the answers.

"Why is your office located where it is?" she asked.

"I wanted to be right on the main strip where it would be easy for everyone to find me. I didn't want to seem like I was better than everyone else. That's not how I wanted to run things. I started here just the same as they did, and I wanted to be someone they could feel comfortable coming and talking to. Someone they trusted," I explained.

The sun was beating down on us, and even though I had taken off my suit jacket, I was still dripping sweat. I stopped in front of a store and told her how it got started while I rolled up the sleeves of my dress shirt.

My eyes focused on Kate in the store's reflection. Her eyes moved over my body, and she bit down on her bottom lip. She watched intently as I finished rolling up my sleeve, revealing the tattoo on my forearm.

I turned around slowly; her eyes locked with mine. Her cheeks turned pink as she stared at me. I couldn't look away. There was something about Kate that sent all rational thought flying from my brain. She was attractive, yes—gorgeous actually—but it was more than that. I waited to see if she'd give me a sign that she was feeling it, too.

She took a small step toward me; I wasn't even sure if she was aware she had moved, and that was the sign I needed. My long legs ate up the space between us until we were standing inches apart. I wanted to pull her close, to feel her body pressed against mine again.

My fists were at my sides, and my jaw was clenched. The intensity between us was something I hadn't felt before with another woman. It was as if we were surrounded by an invisible force. I just wanted one kiss from her. To see if this thing between us was real or just my imagination.

Aware of my surroundings, I stayed put with my arms pinned at my sides. I didn't need to be seen making out with the enemy. Even though Kate was anything but. She was stuck in this situation the same way I was. It wasn't her fault this was happening.

Her big blue eyes dilated as she stared into mine, and when she pulled her bottom lip into her mouth, I nearly lost it. I couldn't hold back anymore. I leaned forward, her lips mere inches from mine. If they touched, would it blow open a force field, destroying whatever was in close range? It was possible I had been watching too many superhero movies with Frank recently.

Her lips parted, ready to accept mine, and my head was lowering slowly toward hers when sudden shouting had my head snapping up. Laney ran toward us, waving her arms and shouting something I couldn't make out.

I took a giant step away from Kate and adjusted myself in my pants before turning toward Laney. She looked panicked, and I knew it wasn't good. Laney was rarely frazzled.

"Peter! I'm so glad I found you. It's Mrs. Anderson. She's up a tree!"

What the hell? "Where?"

Laney turned toward the park, and I took off in a sprint. I ran around the corner and up Parkway. Kate was keeping up well considering she was wearing heels. I could hear them clicking on the pavement behind me. I tossed my suit jacket to her, and then took off at a full run.

A crowd had gathered around the bottom of a tree, alerting me to where Mrs. Anderson was. I looked up and saw her on one of the lowest branches. Still high enough to be dangerous. Duchess was sitting a few branches above her. I let out a curse and assessed the situation. Mrs. Anderson was yelling to Duchess and shaking the damn cat treats again.

"Beverly, what are you doing? You could get hurt," I gritted out.

"Oh, Peter, there you are. It's Duchess; she got out again, and I followed her to the park. I tried your office, but they said you were out for the day. I thought maybe I could climb the tree myself like you did yesterday and get her down." She held onto the branch for dear life.

"You are seventy-eight and should never climb a tree. I told you to call the fire department next time," I yelled up at her.

"Where the hell are the fire department and the deputies? Why hasn't anyone called them?" I asked all the people standing around the tree. Tom shrugged.

"I called. Frank and Sid are on their way. I don't know what's taking so long. Tom and I are the volunteer firefighters for the day, and I'll be honest; I'm not gonna climb the tree," Ken explained.

I couldn't wait for Frank and Sid; besides, what were they going to do? I needed the damn fire department. Why did no one ever call them for things like this?

As if reading my mind, Laney shouted, "I called the fire department. They should be on their way."

We lost half our fire department in a freak accident on Harry's farm a few months ago. Our Chief lived in Ridge Point but oversaw both firehouses. He had a few of his men from Ridge Point come help us out. Because of the accident, there weren't always firefighters available. Volunteers from town filled in the gaps. Men and women willing to step up when needed. Except for now, when my volunteers were Tom and Ken.

"I told her that she shouldn't have climbed that tree," Ethel said.

"She's stubborn like you," Rose remarked.

"She's in love with her cat," Mary Ann added.

I ignored the three gossiping ladies and put my foot in the tree's crook, hoisting myself up with ease. I wasn't going to wait around to see how long it would take for the fire department to arrive.

"I'm going to put my arms around you, and I want you to let go of the branch, okay?" I said to Beverly as I grabbed her around the waist.

She let go of the branch, and with the help of the two officers who finally showed up, we guided her down to the ground. I climbed a little higher into the tree and grabbed the cat. I held her close—even though at this point I wanted to strangle her—and climbed back down.

Once my feet were on the ground, I handed the cat to Mrs. Anderson. She hugged Duchess and rocked her from side to side. And that was why I couldn't kill the cat, no matter how badly I wanted to.

A fire truck pulled up, and Chief Hanson jumped out, followed by Lieutenant Smith and Captain Ward. They made their way over to the tree while the crowd that had gathered began clapping. I hated praise and attention. I wasn't doing this for the applause. I was doing it for Mrs. Anderson, who was like a grandmother to me.

"Beverly, please, never do that again. The next time Duchess goes exploring, please call the fire department or Frank here," I said, slapping him a little bit too hard on the back, "They can better assist you. I can't keep climbing trees in these suits." I patted her on the back and looked around the crowd for a certain brunette.

"Peter," Chief Hanson barked out. He was an older man with gray hair and a handsome handlebar mustache that had won several awards.

"Chief. Thanks for coming," I said, shaking his hand.

"You seem to have everything under control here," he stated.

"Looks that way. Although this isn't a job for the mayor."

He chuckled. "No, but by the time we get here, you've already got the damn cat out of the tree. Beverly needs to keep that thing locked up."

"No kidding," I said. My eyes scanned the crowd.

Kate was standing off to the side talking with Laney. Both women had dreamy looks on their faces and I didn't like it. The two men standing next to the Chief were young and attractive. I felt the need to stake my claim.

"Excuse me, Chief." I clapped him on the back.

"We'll take over. Although there isn't much for us to do."

I made my way over to the women, arriving at just the right time.

"He's something, isn't he?" Laney whispered to Kate. Loud enough for me to hear.

Kate's eyes met mine, and I winked. She looked away and turned a bright shade of pink. I smiled. I hated all the attention that came with things like this, but I'd climb ten more trees just to see Kate look at me that way. I shifted my weight to hide my growing erection. Adrenaline mixed with the sexy woman in front of me was not helping me around all these people.

"I'm Laney. I own Limbitless Expressions," Laney said, breaking our connection. She shoved her hand in Kate's direction.

It took a minute for Kate to register what Laney was saying. Her eyes darkened as they roamed my chest and arms, and her teeth slowly sunk into her plump bottom lip. I wanted it between my teeth. Laney's hand brushed against her and she looked down, shaking her head like she was coming out of a fog. I smirked.

Laney laughed and repeated herself.

"It's so nice to meet you," Kate said. She turned to face Laney. "Betty has told me so much about you and your store. I want to make sure I stop in before I have to return home."

"I'd love to show you the store," Laney said with a smile.

She was so proud of her store, and I was proud of her too. It had taken a lot to get it up and running. Plus, she was talented, and I loved everything she did there. Laney walked away, leaving the two of us alone.

"Sorry about that. Mrs. Anderson doesn't like to call anyone but me. I've been getting her cat out of trees for six years now. Come on, I'd like you to meet some other people from town," I said, grabbing her hand. Kate followed me, and I tried like hell to ignore the shock of electricity coursing through me.

"This here is Tom Tracy. He owns the shoe store, Best Foot Forward, on the corner."

Tom was short and skinny with gray hair on just the sides of his head, and he wore an outfit that looked like it was straight out of the sixties. He dressed that way all the time. We were always ribbing him on poker nights about his outfits.

"Pleasure to meet you, dear," Tom said. If I hadn't been holding Kate's hand, I was sure he would have kissed the back of it. I resisted the urge to squeeze tighter.

"This is Ken Marshall. He owns the music store, On a Different Note, right next door to the shoe store," I said, pointing at Ken.

Ken was Tom's opposite, tall and skinny with long gray hair down to his shoulders. It was a wonder the two of them became friends. They were always bickering like an old married couple.

"These two goons who should have been here sooner and climbed the tree so I didn't have to are Deputies Frank Wilson and Sidney Lewis." I punched Frank in the arm.

"Ouch. Sorry man, we were on another call," Frank said as he rubbed his arm. He turned to Kate, "Well hello, beautiful. What brings you to our town, and how do you know Peter here?"

"I work for Lawrence Development Company. I'm here to meet with the mayor about signing the proposal for new development," Kate announced. I winced.

Everyone seemed very displeased with her answer. Ken shook his head and walked away. Tom stood there waiting for more of an explanation. Frank's eyes widened, and he smiled and nodded. He looked at her like she was crazy. I needed to smooth this over, and fast.

"Nothing is set in stone, folks. We're just discussing things. So I will remind you to keep your opinions to yourselves and to treat Kate with respect. She will be observing our town while she's here. Let's give her the best treatment and show her what Oak Springs is all about."

Chapter 15

KATE

I STOOD BACK AND WATCHED the way Peter interacted with the people of the town. They had all cheered, and clapped, and patted him on the back when he climbed down out of the tree. Some had even given him hugs.

He quietly accepted their praise, which was something I admired about him. That, coupled with the way he climbed that tree, made him that much more attractive.

He was obviously proud of his town and all the people who owned the stores and restaurants. The way they worked together to help and provide for one another was not something you saw much in the world anymore. Even just waving to someone else in passing was rare. They'd all been waving to me since I arrived here, and I was a stranger.

In Bellport, everyone was so bottled up and closed off. They didn't help one another out. In fact, in all the years I'd lived there, I only knew three of my neighbors, and we didn't do anything together.

I watched as all the people talked amongst themselves, taking the opportunity to chat and catch up. I was so lost in the way everyone interacted and how cute this town was, I had almost forgotten why I was here.

The two younger firefighters who had come to help Mrs. Anderson were attractive, but I only had eyes for Peter. There was something about him I just couldn't get over. It could have been the way he cared for me after the accident, or the way he looked at me. Whatever it was, it was something I knew I needed to stay away from. Question was, could I?

Peter winked at me as he led me into the group to introduce me to some of the townspeople. A shiver ran through me that was quickly replaced by guilt when I looked around at all the happy faces. Eager to meet me.

Irritation and doubt swirled around in my stomach. Who had scouted this town for development? I needed to look into it further. Something didn't feel right.

As Peter addressed the town, a panic attack started to make its way to the surface. The townspeople were not happy to hear where I was from and what I was doing in their town. More people gathered around, and I started to worry that I was going to become the center of an angry mob.

The urge to run was so strong that my feet almost started moving on their own. What was it about this town that made me panic so much? I needed to get away from here. My palms started to sweat, and my breathing was shallow. I was minutes away from another full-blown attack.

This one came on much quicker than the one from earlier. It was like a runaway train, and I was unable to stop it. I stepped back, my heel caught in the grass, and I almost fell.

A hand grabbed my arm to steady me.

"Whoa there," Sidney said.

I needed to escape. Turning to the left, I saw a row of bushes and trees. If I took my shoes off, I could sprint behind them. Sidney still had me by the arm, though.

"Are you all right?" he asked.

I felt like a fish out of water as I gasped for air while I searched for somewhere to go. The panic attack was taking over, and I needed to get away from the crowd. Ignoring Sidney, I looked to my right. Parkway was much closer and the best option.

"I'm sorry. Please excuse me," I gasped out.

I waved my cell phone in the air and then pretended to take a call. Sidney released my arm, and I hurried over to the street. Once I was a good distance away, I sprinted as fast as my heels would allow around a building onto Main Street. I leaned back against the wall and gave in to the panic attack.

My breaths were coming short and quick, and my vision started to swirl. Blackness was creeping in, and I knew I was a few minutes away from passing out. I hadn't passed out since I was a little girl; I fell off the jungle gym at the park and landed flat on my back. I couldn't get up, and I freaked out.

Leaning forward and placing my hands on my knees, I shoved my head down between my legs. My hair draped over my face like a curtain. Strong, calloused hands gripped my arms, and then I was moving.

I looked up at the strong figure standing in front of me. Peter. His brows were knitted together in worry. I couldn't speak. My breathing was too heavy, and the darkness was closing in. I fell into his arms as my legs started to buckle.

Peter scooped me up into his arms and walked toward the back of the building. He sat me down on the ground and propped my back against the building. His hands ran up and down my arms as he knelt in front of me.

"Kate, look at me. Deep breaths, remember? In and out."

He demonstrated what he wanted me to do. I mimicked his breathing and started to count backward from ten. I felt my pulse slow, and my breathing started to even out. He had the ability to calm me down fast.

Embarrassment swept over me. This was the third time since we met that he had seen me in a weakened state. I wanted to forget this whole thing and run back home. Far, far away from Peter. This was a nightmare that I so wanted to wake up from.

I pinched my arm and winced. Nope, this was a living nightmare. No escape was possible. Tears welled up in my eyes before I could stop them. Damn it, now I was crying in front of him. He would never see me as anything but weak. A damsel in distress in need of rescuing.

Peter pulled me into his chest and held me close. His hand rubbed up and down my back in comfort. I shoved him away from me.

"Stop it! I don't want your pity. I'm fine," I snapped. I pushed up to a standing position.

Peter stood up and looked at me, a shocked expression on his face. "Pity? Kate, this has nothing to do with pity. I like you, and I want to help."

"You like me because I appear weak and in need of rescue like that damn cat in the tree," I yelled. Peter took a step away from me. I was aware I sounded like a crazy person, but I needed to put distance between us as fast as possible.

"Kate, you're anything but weak. I've never met anyone like you. Please, let's just go get something to eat and forget about what happened here." He reached out for my arm.

Taking a step back, I turned away from him. "I'm not hungry anymore. I'd like to meet you tomorrow in your office to discuss numbers and property lines."

His brows pulled together, and a scowl slowly formed on his face.

"Fine. You can call my office and set something up with my secretary," he snapped. He turned to walk away and stopped. I saw him take a deep breath before he turned back to face me. "Just know that the answer is still no."

I stood there in the back alley alone, and a chill ran up my spine. I shook it off, and then stomped my way back to Main Street. Peter may have seen me in a moment of weakness, or several, but that would not happen again. I was here to do a job, a job I was damn good at. As soon as I regrouped and made sure everything was airtight, I'd get Peter to sign the papers, and then I'd go home.

My cell phone rang and I looked to see who was calling. I punched answer and cried into the phone, "Mindy, I'm so glad you called. I have so much to tell you."

Before Mindy could respond, I launched into everything that had happened. About finding out Peter was the mayor, and about my two panic attacks. I cried, and I couldn't stop, which only pissed me off more. I missed Mindy a lot. I was all alone here and an outcast in the town.

To make matters worse, this was Peter's town. The people here were his friends, and they looked up to him. He had the final say in this, and I had a terrible feeling that he wouldn't budge. He needed to do what was best for everyone and the pressure sat on his shoulders.

I knew it wasn't easy for him, but it was worse for me. I was at risk of losing everything. I had built my life around this job and my success. I'd worked to prove myself for years, and I was still proving my worth. Especially with Vincent always lurking around every corner of my life.

I couldn't believe that after all my success, I could still lose everything over one failure. It wasn't even my fault. They sent me here to close something that wasn't even possible. They had their answer, repeatedly according to Peter, and yet Mr. Lawrence still sent me.

"Kate, do you want me to come there?" Mindy asked.

"No, don't do that. I already look weak to him. Having my friend come and save me would make things worse."

I sighed and sat down on the front porch swing. "Mindy, I don't know what to do. If he doesn't agree and sign the papers, then I'll lose my job and everything I've worked so hard for."

"I don't know what to say," Mindy whispered.

I laughed. "Well, that's a first."

"Hey now! Let me think," she said.

I waited quietly. She always gave the best advice, and at this point I was at a loss.

"Okay, I think you need to find him and apologize for pushing him away. Then I think you need to take a few days to relax and get to know the town. You need to go with your heart. You know what's best. If it seems wrong, then you can't do it. And if that means you lose your job; well, then you can come work for me."

I sighed again while I thought about what she said. She was right. Taking some time to relax would be a good thing. I could enjoy the town and the solace it offered. I needed to get to know the town and the people in it better so I could make the best choice.

I always followed my heart, and most of the time I agreed with Mr. Lawrence's choices for development. This was the first time he'd ever tried to build in a small town that was already thriving and expanding. I wasn't one hundred percent sure about this, and that's what scared me the most.

"You're right, Min. I need to shake off what happened today and do my job. Thanks for the advice."

"Anytime, and next time you feel you're starting to panic, call me first. We talked about that, remember?" Mindy asked.

We had talked about it. Many years ago, but until recently I could always calm myself down. Now everything in my life felt out of control. I felt so mixed up.

"I will, thanks," I replied as I headed inside.

After I ended the call with Mindy, I stopped at the front desk, rang the bell, and waited for Betty. She greeted me with a big smile. I asked her a few questions about the town, and what her favorite place was to eat, and then I headed to my room to make notes.

I LEFT KNEAD TO RELAX, the massage parlor on Main Street, feeling refreshed. My sixty-minute massage with just-the-right-pressure Sarah had me melting into the table. She didn't go too deep since I was still recovering. The peppermint oil mixed with the soothing music calmed me in a way I hadn't felt in a long time.

Sarah was a bit too chatty for a massage therapist, though. She talked about people in the town as if I knew them. She was a sweet girl, and I'm sure we could have been friends under different circumstances.

Today was not that day. I needed her to quit talking so I could fully relax. I didn't respond or engage in the conversation. Sarah finally took the hint about halfway through, and the rest of the massage was quiet, with only the sound of the calming spa music filling the room.

I was looking across the street toward Peter's office when I turned out of the store and ran right into Sidney Lewis. He wasn't in his uniform, which is why I didn't recognize him at first. He was an attractive man, just not my type. In fact, few men were my type since meeting Peter. He set the bar high.

Sidney's chin-length thick wavy hair was blowing in the breeze, and I could smell his spring-fresh shampoo. A fitted black t-shirt stretched across his muscled arms, and his jeans fit him well. They looked designer, with a few rips on the front, and I wondered where he got them around here.

"Whoa there," he said, stopping me from falling again. "We have to stop meeting like this."

We were standing so close that I could see the variation of color in his warm brown eyes. He smiled, and that drew my eyes to his well-manicured beard. Sidney was shorter than Peter but still had a few inches on me.

I smoothed my hands down my yoga pants. "Yes, you're right."

"You ran away from the park pretty fast earlier; is everything all right?"

"Everything's fine. I had an important call. Thanks for asking, Sidney." I tried to scoot around him. Not because he made me uncomfortable; I just didn't want to explain myself to him.

"No problem. And you can just call me Sid. Can I walk you to wherever it is you're going?"

I wanted to say no, but I didn't want to be rude. I could take this opportunity to get to know him better and see how he viewed the town. "Sure."

"I'm glad I ran into you. A few friends of mine are going to this new place that just opened in town called Simply Cook It. It's become a big hit and has even drawn some out-of-town guests. The next class is Thursday. Would you be interested in going with me?" he asked as we walked.

I wondered how that would work out. Peter would be on a date with that blonde from his store, and I didn't think I could stand to watch him with her. It wouldn't be fair to Sid, either. I wouldn't be able to give him my full attention and treat him like a date because I'd be too busy watching Peter.

"I think that would be a little too much for me. Is there somewhere else we could go? You know, just the two of us?" I asked, trying to persuade him to change his mind.

"It'll be fine," he said with a smile. "I think it would be a great time for you to see some of the popular stores in action. Plus, you can get to know some of the people here."

We slowed down and stopped in front of The B&B. "You know what? I think you're right." I turned to face him. "I could use some fun, and I've been taking some cooking classes back home."

It was time to be strong and face things head on. I needed to quit thinking about Peter and start thinking about my job. Nothing could ever happen between Peter and me, so I needed to move on from that crazy fantasy and get back to work. Maybe watching him on a date with someone else would help.

"Great!" It looked like Sid was about to jump up and down, and I couldn't help but smile. It had to be hard dating in a small town like this. The pool was only so big.

"I'll pick you up here at seven. We can walk there; it's over on Grand Street. Does that sound okay?" he asked.

"That would be great," I said. I turned on my heels and headed inside. Time to put my game face on.

Chapter 16

PETER

SITTING IN MY OFFICE, I thought back over my day. Kate was here, and all she was doing was panicking. I didn't blame her; anyone would panic in this situation. Hell, I wanted to panic. As mayor of the town, I had to be strong and keep it together at all times.

I let out a sigh. Stressed didn't even begin to describe how I was feeling. It all started when Lawrence Development Company first brought their development proposal to the town over a month ago. They kept returning and asking for more property, and now it was out of hand.

To add to the stress, my visit home had been horrible. Aside from meeting Kate, that is. I couldn't believe she had dated my brother for so long. She's not the girl I'd pictured him with, and he didn't deserve her. I wasn't sure I did either.

I picked up the phone and called Frank.

"What's up?" he answered.

"Hey, poker tonight? I could use a distraction," I said as I shut down my computer.

"Why are you even asking? Isn't this Tuesday?" Frank asked.

I nodded. "Yeah. I was just making sure. I'll get the pizza and beer."

"I'll bring the liquor," Frank said.

"Let's just stick to beer. We all have to work tomorrow."

"I don't. I'm off for the day," he scoffed.

"Aren't you on call even when you have a day off?"

"Technically, yes. It'll be fine, man. Stop worrying about me," he gritted out.

I put my laptop in my bag and slung it over my shoulder. "You know I can't. We're family."

"Yeah, yeah. See you tonight."

He hung up. I'd have to figure out another way to get him to talk to me. Another thing added to my plate. Everyone was always relying on me for one thing or another.

I thought about going over and talking to Kate after what happened today, but I decided to give her space. It was better if we kept our distance from one another. Maybe it was time to look at this for what it was, strictly business. She was here to do a job, and I had to do mine.

Speaking of my job, I almost forgot something important I needed to do today. Kate filled my mind all afternoon. Picking up the phone, I sat back down behind my desk. My stomach was in my throat while it rang. I was calling in a favor, and I hoped it wouldn't cost me.

"Peter," the voice on the other line answered.

"Yeah, Kel, it's me," I whispered, even though no one could hear me.

I still felt like I needed to keep this quiet. Kelly Stevens was an old buddy of mine from high school, and he was great at digging up information and people. Which is why he worked as a private investigator.

"Shit, I haven't talked to you in a long time. Ever since you needed me to find that information on the Davis brothers."

I rubbed the back of my neck. "Yeah. Thank you for that. I still have it in my back pocket just in case."

"No problem. What can I do for you now?" he asked.

"I need another favor."

I explained the situation and how fast I needed the information. The development couldn't move forward if I didn't approve it, but Lawrence Development Company wouldn't stop pushing. They could try for years to get the development, and if someone else became the mayor down the road, it could go through. This was my last shot to find something to stop them for good. It was my Hail Mary.

"I'll see what I can dig up and be in touch," he said.

"Thanks. Maybe we could get together soon. I was just in Pine Brook this past weekend, but it was for a family gathering. I'd like to visit on different terms."

"Yeah, no shit. Your family is something else, man. Let me know when you're free. Listen, I've got to go, but I'll make sure I move your request to the top of my pile."

"Thanks. I appreciate it." I felt a little lighter knowing someone was in my corner. Even if it was a long shot.

I hung up the phone and locked my office door behind me. Then made my way to the stairs. My feet froze mid-step. Hannah was standing at the bottom looking up at me like I was a snack.

"I heard that you're the town hero today," she purred.

"Hero? Hardly. How did you hear about that so fast, anyway?" I asked.

She smiled and leaned against the wall, tilting forward just enough for me to see down her shirt. I cleared my throat and shifted away from her. I didn't want to encourage this any further. I kept my eyes fixed on a crack in the wall. I'd need to patch that before it spread.

"Tom called and told me you were saving Mrs. Anderson and her cat. I didn't want to abandon the store, and I figured by the time I got down there it'd be over. So I stayed here, but he gave me an awesome play-by-play. Great job!"

I glanced at her and she leaned forward more. I looked away again. I was still standing on the damn stairs, and I felt trapped.

"Thanks. What kind of person would I be if I just let some elderly woman fall out of a tree in the park?"

"I know you would never let that happen. You have too big a heart."

She stepped up to the next step, and I took a step up and back. I wanted to run up the stairs and lock myself in my office, but I knew that running from Hannah would only make things worse. She'd enjoy the chase too much. She'd been chasing me for months already.

I'd hired her five months ago after she blew into town like a storm. Tom approached me and asked me to please hire his niece to get her back on track. I did because I can't say no to people in the town when they need help, and I needed someone to help me run my store. Dating her was never part of the plan, though, and I regretted saying yes.

"Are you looking forward to our date? I know I am."

She slinked up the stairs toward me like a lioness stalking its prey. I felt like a damn water buffalo, unable to move and afraid of what was coming. Sweat covered my brow. I needed to get out of there, but she was blocking my only exit.

The only other way I could go was up and there was no way to leave from there. There was a flimsy fire escape on the side of the building that led from my office window. It'd be a miracle if I made it down alive from there, though. The fire escape needed repairs, and I had put it off.

"It sounds like fun," I said, tugging on my collar.

"Oh, there will be fun, but not from cooking."

She stopped on the step just below me and placed her hands on my abs. She leaned in and whispered, "I won't be wearing any underwear."

"Very good. I have to go. I'll see you later."

Reaching out, I eased her to the side and darted down the stairs as fast as I could without face planting on the ground. Although, I'd take that over being trapped with her anytime.

"LOOKS LIKE I'M JOINING you guys tomorrow night at Simply Cook It," Sid announced as he grabbed a beer from my fridge.

I grabbed the paper plates from the cabinet above the stove. Frank had just arrived with four pies from Pizza Pan. Tom and Ken were already in the living room setting up the poker table. Tom always insisted he bring a real table and chips. If it made him feel better when we took his money, then it was fine with me.

"Who did you get to go with you? Mrs. Anderson?" Frank mocked. I laughed.

"Ha ha, hilarious wise guy. It's the new girl, Kate," Sid said.

My hands fumbled the plates, and I set them down next to the pizza. I ran a hand through my hair. "She said yes?"

"She did and seems excited," Sid replied. He had a big smile on his face, and I felt like crap for being upset about it.

"You realize I'll be there with Hannah, right?"

"Yes, and Frank with Sarah; what's your point?" Sid asked, taking a sip of his beer.

"Yeah, what is your point?" Frank questioned.

He grabbed two beers from the fridge and handed one to me. He popped the top of his beer and leaned back against the counter, waiting for me to explain.

"Remember Monday night when you came over and I told you about a girl I met over the weekend and couldn't get off my mind?"

"Yeah, what's that got to do with this?" I waited a beat and his eyes widened. "Oh shit. Kate is the girl."

I nodded and took a sip of my beer.

"Well, I'm still taking her out. You're taking another girl. Plus, she and I have something in common being the two newbies in town," Sid said. Sid transferred to Oak Springs six months ago, but he and Frank had been friends for years.

"Why don't you take Hannah, and I'll go with Kate?" I suggested.

"No way! I've already been down that road, remember? I took Hannah out when she first arrived here. She's way too high maintenance for me, and she spent the evening complaining about everything. Where we went, what we ate, what I was wearing. I can't go down that road again," Sid said as he grabbed some pizza slices. "But it might work out for you, man."

What a huge mess. Maybe I could fake sick and get out of the date altogether. If Kate wanted to date Sid, that was her choice. We needed to remain professional with one another, anyway. That was the lie I was telling myself and I was sticking to it. I grabbed my beer and then another, along with a box of pizza. At least I'd have poker to distract me.

THE SOUND OF A CAR HORN startled me awake. When the hell did I change my alarm to that? *Frank.* After silencing my alarm, I debated going back to sleep, but then I remembered I told Kate we'd run together. The room did a nasty spin when I sat up. I'd had too much to drink and lost too much damn money. When was the last time I had let loose like that?

The night before was a blur. Hearing that Kate had agreed to go on a date with Sid had sent me into a tailspin of jealousy. That upset me, but I was angrier with the mess I was in. Torn between wanting to pursue Kate and wanting to keep her at arm's length. I could lose everything important to me if we gave things a try, and there were a thousand reasons why it would never work out. I was so messed up over it all that I drank my feelings away.

The nausea and pain in my head reminded me of the shots I took with the guys and the bottle I finished with Frank. I groaned and got out of bed to make my way to the kitchen. Every step I took felt like an explosion was going off in my head. My mouth was dry, and my stomach threatened to expel its contents from the night before.

My eyes scanned the living room as I passed by. Frank was snoring on the couch. If I felt this bad, Frank felt worse. He drank more than I did.

I walked into the kitchen and grabbed a large power drink I had stashed in the fridge, some pain medication from the cabinet, and an energy bar. Then I walked to my bedroom and threw on my sweats, a t-shirt, and my running shoes. Running a hand through my hair, I tried to fix all the wild strands that were sticking up everywhere. Then I grabbed my cell phone and checked the time: six-thirty. Shit, I was already late.

I ran down Old Cedar Road, stopping a few times to throw up. Thank God it was so early because this was not a good look for the mayor. I was a fucking mess. Instead of going to Betty's, I ran toward the park to get a hold of myself before I met up with Kate.

My foot slid in the mud on my usual path through the woods that cut to the park. I tripped twice over branches. By the time I entered the park, I was nearly crawling to the bench.

The pizza I ate the night before was trying to make a reappearance. I fell onto the bench and put my head into my hands. After a few seconds I lay down and closed my eyes. I needed to get my shit together.

Chapter 17

KATE

I WOKE UP AT SIX and waited half an hour to see if Peter would show up. Not wanting to waste a beautiful morning and perfect running weather, I headed out toward the park. Feeling pretty good, I started at a run on Parkway.

My feet pounded the pavement, and my music blasted through my earbuds. Inhaling deeply, I felt myself completely relax. I took in the beautiful scenery as I jogged. I could only imagine what the park would look like in late fall. Orange and red colors on the trees and ground. Leaves crunching under my feet. A chill in the air to replace the intense heat of the summer.

It was one of my favorite times of the year, and I wished I would be here then. I imagined they had some kind of festival as most towns did. Fall was probably much more enjoyable here than back home.

As I rounded the bend toward the back of the park, I saw someone lying on a park bench. I got closer and realized it was Peter. His long legs hung over the side. One arm was draped over his face.

"Peter, are you all right?" I asked as I approached with caution.

"Yeah, never better." He opened his eyes and attempted to sit up. His face looked a little pale. Shaking his head, he laid back down. "Nope, not yet."

"What's wrong? Are you hurt?"

"No. Just hungover and embarrassed." He threw his arm over his face again.

I stifled a laugh. "Stay there. I'll be right back."

I ran back to Main Street and then back down to my car. A few minutes later, I pulled up and parked on Old Cedar Road near the wooded area. I remembered seeing a small clearing in the trees when I was checking out the surrounding properties.

"Can you walk?" I asked when I reached Peter again.

"Yes, I can walk. I ran here," he bit out. My eyes widened at his tone.

He sighed, and then said in a more normal voice, "Sorry. Yes, I can walk."

After he stood up, he bent forward and put his hands on his knees. I stood by and waited for him to follow me to the SUV. I tried not to laugh at him. It wasn't easy.

"Tell me where I'm going," I said as I slid into the driver's seat.

Peter pointed straight ahead. He put his seat back and rolled the window down, throwing his arm over his face again. I was worried he was going to get sick in my rental.

I enjoyed having the roles reversed. To not be the one in need for a change. I glanced over at him and bit my lip to hold in my laughter. He looked horrible and smelled like a brewery. Why did he even get out of bed?

"Peter, I'm not sure where I'm going," I said, looking around. I followed the winding road for about a mile. Peter lifted his arm off his head and leaned up a little.

"First house there on the left."

I pulled into his driveway and froze. This was his house? Now I was the one who wanted to throw up. This was one of the properties we were trying to buy. The house seemed so run down from the outside I had figured the owner would happily sell.

The front porch ran the whole length of the house. Two white rocking chairs, old and in need of new paint, sat on it. The paint on the porch was peeling, and the railing was broken and falling off. One shutter on the front window was hanging askew, and the other one was missing. Based on the state of disrepair, I would have assumed someone older lived here.

"This is where you live?" I said in disbelief.

One eye looked up at me from under his arm. "Sure is. Look familiar?"

I didn't appreciate his tone. I had more at stake here than he did. If he turned down the development, his life stayed the same. I could lose my job if this didn't pan out.

I turned toward him. "I didn't know this was your house."

He sat back up and looked at me. His brows pinched together, and he looked mad. "Would it have made a difference whose house it was?"

He opened the door and got out, not waiting for my response. My blood boiled. What the hell? He wasn't even going to give me a chance to explain?

I opened my door and hurried to catch up to him. "Honestly, no, but this makes it more complicated."

He walked up the front porch steps and I hesitated at the bottom. They looked unsafe.

"Peter, can we talk about this?" I asked.

"What is there to talk about? You want my property, and I won't give it to you. You want to tear down my house, and I won't let you." He unlocked the front door.

I stood at the bottom of his front porch, stunned to silence. He was hurt and angry, and I could understand, yet I still wanted to smooth it over with him. I didn't want things to go this way. He really wasn't being fair. It was hard on both of us.

He looked back over his shoulder, "Well, are you going to at least come in and see the place?"

Hurrying in behind him, I stopped just inside the door. The front door opened right into the living room. Frank was asleep on the couch. My eyes widened at the state of the room. Empty beer bottles and pizza boxes littered the room. They had shoved the coffee table up against the stone fireplace, and someone's clothes were on top.

I snorted when I saw a piece of pizza lying on Frank's stomach. His arm hung down off the couch, a beer bottle dangling loosely from his fingers. Taking my phone out, I snapped a picture. It was too good to pass up.

Peter had disappeared, so I looked around a little. A small hallway went off to the left. From the look of it, the house had one bedroom and one bathroom. The living room was large, but part of it was set up as a dining room.

The large oak table with four matching chairs caught my eye. I recognized the huge table as the one from his grandmother's house. It was a lot smaller without the leaves in it. Some of the chairs were missing too.

The table sat in front of two French doors that led to a large screened-in porch. The porch looked new or at least updated. I walked over to the doorway that opened to a tiny kitchen. Peter was standing in front of the coffee pot.

"Coffee?" he asked.

"Yes, please. Your house is much smaller than I thought it would be."

He laughed. "This is temporary. I'm in the early stages of building a home."

"Then why are you turning down the offer for your property?" I demanded.

I was a little more than upset at this point. The man could take the money and use it for the house he was building and move the location. It didn't have to be complicated.

"Because the property is what I love. It's secluded, yet close enough to town for me to take care of business the way I need to. I don't want to move. This small house was nothing but a shack nine years ago. I threw a tent out back and began renovating. I did everything on my own."

I watched as he poured two cups of coffee and added two cream and two sugars to mine. He handed me a cup and walked out of the kitchen. I followed him out onto the screened-in porch.

"You did all of this? Wait, why didn't you fix the front of the house?"

"There's no point in fixing the front when I'm going to build something new, but the inside of this place was unlivable for a while. I plan to build my new house. That's why it has taken so long. I want to make sure everything is just right. Let me show you something," he said, taking me by the hand.

He led me off the porch and through the backyard. We walked for a while, through a forest of trees, hand in hand. I loved the feeling of my hand in his. It fit perfectly and felt right. We stopped at the bank of a river, and he dropped my hand.

"This is why I don't want to sell my property. When I need a break from being the mayor and some peace and quiet, I come down here and fish. This property has everything I ever wanted." He gestured in front of him.

I closed my eyes. I could hear birds chirping and the river lapping in front of me. It was so peaceful. I wished I had this back home. I opened my eyes and took a sip of coffee; it was perfect. I wanted to capture this moment and bottle it. That way, whenever I was feeling stressed or anxious, I could relive it.

"This is still your property?" I asked. "What about beyond the river?"

He turned to face me and frowned, "Don't you know that? You said you had looked at the properties. Lawrence wants to take this whole thing and bulldoze it. He said the river would be a great selling point for the condos." He looked back at the river. "I own half an acre beyond the river, too. Mr. Lawrence said he'd let me live there. Like that was a kind gesture on his part. I'd have the damn condos as my backdrop."

My gut ached like I'd just been punched. I didn't know that's what Mr. Lawrence was doing. I realized that I really didn't have a good idea about anything when it came to this development. He had sent me in blind.

Part of it was my fault, too, though. When I drove by and saw a poor-looking house, I decided it wasn't worth looking into further. I thought the owner could benefit from the money. I pictured an elderly man with a large beard and a shotgun living here.

It was time I dug deeper and did some research. My gut was telling me this was a bad proposal. Mr. Lawrence had said this was his biggest yet, which meant he'd put a lot into it. I had a feeling he was hiding something, though. Why was he pushing so hard to develop here?

"I'm sorry. It looks like I need to do more research before meeting with you again."

Peter remained quiet as he led us back up toward the house. He walked ahead of me, and I missed the connection of his hand in mine. We entered the screened-in porch and stopped. Frank was seated in one of the patio chairs. He looked awful. His head was in his hands, and his short brown hair stuck up like he'd been struck by lightning.

"Hey man," Peter said.

"Don't 'hey man' me! Why the hell did you let me drink that much last night? I have ten missed calls from the station. I finally answered, and Sid chewed my ass off before handing it over to the sheriff. What time did Sid end up leaving last night?"

Frank's eyes looked sunken in, and he had more than a five o'clock shadow going on. It looked like he was working on a beard. I was worried about him. He needed food and water. At least some coffee.

"Relax, I drank just as much as you did. I feel horrible, too. Sid left about three, I think, and he didn't drink as much as we did. You and I sat on the sofa and polished off that whiskey after everyone else left. How about some coffee?" Peter walked past Frank and into the house. "You remember Kate, right?"

"Hi Frank," I said, taking a seat at the table.

"When did you get here? Wait, am I interrupting the morning after breakfast? I should go." He got up.

"The morning after… what?" I asked, confused.

My face burned as I realized what he was talking about. "Oh no. I just got here a little while ago. I found Peter on a park bench and brought him back here."

Frank barked out a laugh. "He was passed out in the park?" He grabbed his head and then his stomach and fell back into his chair. "Oh, not a good idea to laugh so hard. What was he doing there?"

"I think he was trying to go for a run." I hid my smile behind my cup of coffee.

Peter walked back outside at that moment. He shoved Frank's coffee cup into his chest. "Don't laugh too hard, asshole."

Frank laughed again and then winced. "I can't believe you went for a run feeling like this. You are a dedicated S.O.B." He took a sip of his coffee. "Unless you were trying to impress a girl."

Frank wiggled his eyebrows at me. I felt my cheeks flush again. How was this town so full of attractive single men? Mindy needed to come visit. If not for the town itself, then for all the man candy they had.

Peter slapped Frank on the back. "Frank and I met when we were kids. We didn't become best friends until years later when he tried to ticket me for trespassing on my own property. He thought I was a homeless man camping somewhere I shouldn't be." Peter laughed. "Even though he was irritating as hell, and still is, he's my brother."

Frank looked down at his lap for a second and then back up. "Well, doesn't that just seem weird? A house that looks like the wind could blow it over, and then this burly looking dude camping out behind it. Seemed like something fishy to me. Back then, he had a huge bushy beard and shaggy hair. I didn't recognize him."

"I was going through a transition!" Peter shouted. He took a seat next to me.

"Well, you sure came out looking like a butterfly, didn't you Mr. Mayor?"

"I'm still the same guy inside. I'm just more polished now," Peter said, smoothing a hand over his stomach like he was wearing a fine suit.

I laughed and studied the two of them. They were about the same height. Frank was fit, but not as muscular as Peter. His hair was also shorter and lighter. Frank had dazzling blue eyes and could pull off the boy-next-door look if it wasn't for his mischievous smile.

Peter pushed up his sweatshirt sleeve, revealing his forearm tattoo I didn't get a chance to look at before. Frank ran a hand through his hair at the same time, and I noticed one on his forearm too.

"Wait. Do you guys have matching tattoos?"

They both laughed and looked down at their arms.

"Yeah. Funny story, actually. Peter was afraid to get his, so I told him I'd get one, too. We had a little to drink and decided we would each get something that represented ourselves but keep them similar enough to match." Frank held his arm out for me to see.

His was a cowboy riding off into the sunset done in color. Peter sighed and held his arm out. I looked his design over; a black and gray tattoo of a lone wolf howling into the night with a wall of trees behind it. It seemed very fitting.

I leaned back in my chair and asked Frank, "Do you ride horses?"

He ran a hand through his hair and seemed uncomfortable. "Yeah, but not as often as I used to. That's how I met Sid and his brothers... well, I think I'm going to take off and get some food so I can get to work."

"I'm going to go walk him out." Peter followed Frank into the house.

I stood up and walked to the window to look out over the vast backyard. Shadows from the trees danced across it. How would I get him to sell this place when I wanted to move here myself?

Warmth trailed up my spine, and I turned around slowly. Peter was standing inches away from me. Intense green eyes bore into me, making me shiver. Warmth pooled between my thighs. I had wanted Peter the moment I saw him at his grandmother's house. The connection between us was electric. It was stronger than anything I'd experienced before, even with Vincent.

He stepped closer and ran a hand slowly up my arm. His rough fingers brushed against my skin, setting it on fire. One hand stopped at the nape of my neck, the other rested on my lower back, pulling me flush against him. I inhaled sharply as our bodies melded together. His hard muscle pressed against me felt so right.

"I've wanted this from the moment we locked eyes in that dining room," he whispered. "Not being able to touch you after having you in my arms and feeling your body pressed against mine has been torture."

He lowered his face, and my lips parted on a sigh. His lips crashed down onto mine, and the kiss pulled me under like a wave. It was deep and passionate, full of promise. I melted into him and pressed my hands against his broad chest. His chest was a solid wall of muscle.

This was perfection. This was everything. My heart pounded in my chest, matching the beat I felt against my palm. Not being able to touch him was torture for me, too. I wasn't one to believe in instant connections or love. Maybe I'd been wrong.

I felt safe with him. As if we'd known one another for so long. His tongue wrapped around mine and it was pure bliss. My tongue twisted around his, drawing out a moan. There wasn't a fight for control, just passion and desire. He poured himself into the kiss, and my chest tightened. This was more than just a physical attraction.

The way his tongue moved in my mouth had me writhing against him. My hands fisted the fabric of his shirt while my leg wrapped around his. His hand moved to my ass, holding me in place as he ground his hips into mine. I dropped my head back and moaned, rolling my hips into him. His warm breath on my neck sent shivers through my body.

Peter's lips were soft and hot, searing my skin as they trailed down my neck. His teeth sunk into my shoulder, sending a jolt of pain straight to my core. His lips closed over the spot as he lightly sucked the sting away. My leg tightened around his, pulling him tighter against me. He ran his tongue slowly over the swell of my breasts which were threatening to break free from my tank top. My nipples so hard they felt like they were poking holes in my sports bra.

Pleasure swirled through me as the pressure built. I was wet and throbbing. I needed him inside me. I had seen the bulge in his pants when he woke up next to me last weekend, but it was nothing compared to feeling it rubbing against my center.

A low growl came from the back of his throat and vibrated through his chest. My hips were grinding against him shamelessly. I needed the friction to ease some of the ache. I reached for the hem of his shirt, but his hand grabbed hold of my wrist, stopping me.

Suddenly I was aware of where we were and the fact that I was dry humping him on his damn porch.

"We have to stop," I panted against his mouth.

He groaned. His chest rose and fell in time with mine. There was disappointment in his eyes mixed with the hunger I'd seen earlier. I didn't want to stop. I wanted more with him, but that wasn't possible. There were a million reasons why we wouldn't work. The biggest one was Vincent.

If Peter and I got together, it would only be a fling, and there were already too many feelings involved for that to work.

"Baby, you have no idea how hard it is for me to stop," he said as he rested his forehead against mine.

I rocked my hips forward. "I think I have a pretty good idea."

He groaned. "Spend the evening with me."

"I can't. I need to work."

"Tomorrow then."

I looked away and bit my lip. "Fine. Only for ice cream."

He smirked. "Not a chance. I want the whole damn night."

"Peter, you know that can't happen. I'm here to do a job. Sleeping together will only make it more complicated."

He sighed. "There's no one else I want to be with, Kate."

That was the sweetest thing anyone had ever said to me. Whatever this was between us was strong, and it had the potential to be something beautiful. If only things were different.

"I can't be with you for one night," I whispered. It needed to be said. This was more than just a one-time thing.

He smiled. "I'm glad you said that, because once will never be enough. I want you to be mine."

I closed my eyes. I wanted that too. More than anything. It just wasn't possible, and it was tearing me in two. I put my foot back on the ground and stood up straight. His arms tightened around me, and he pulled me close, pressing his lips down on mine once more. Before I could fully sink into the kiss, he pulled away, leaving me breathless and wanting.

"Okay, get out of here before I take you to my bed."

He turned around and walked to the other side of the porch, facing away from me. I was rooted to the spot. I wanted him to take me to his bed. I wanted it more than the air I was breathing.

"Go now, Kate."

His hands gripped the railing, and it looked as though his restraint was slipping. Despite my desire to stay, I ran. My legs felt like putty, and they weighed me down, but I got them moving.

I didn't want to run away. I wanted to run to his bedroom with him. But we needed to sort through things first before any of that could happen. I ran out the front door and down the driveway to my car.

With my chest heaving and my heart racing, I sat behind the wheel and stared at his house. I looked into the rearview mirror and saw my face was flushed. This was such a mess. If I was going to change things and possibly have a chance with Peter, I had a lot of work to do. I put the car in reverse and got out of there as quickly as I could before I changed my mind.

AFTER MY STEAMY RUN-IN with Peter, I threw myself into work. I called Sam Lawrence to double check a few items on the proposal, and then checked the properties we wanted to purchase in more detail. There were a few properties for sale that I checked out. Maybe we could build on one of those instead of forcing someone out of their home and taking their land away from them.

I was grasping at straws, but I had to try. Everything was falling apart right before my eyes, which never happened. I never ran into this much trouble. By the time I got to a town, everything was ready to go. I just had to give the client a little nudge in the right direction—our direction.

This project was a mess, though, and I had a sneaking suspicion it was because Mr. Lawrence was giving his sons a chance to prove themselves. A chance to show him they could take over the family business one day. It was a dumb idea since they were idiots.

This proved that, and instead of them getting in trouble or fired, I would lose my job. There was a protocol for how we scouted new areas, and this project didn't feel like it followed the protocol. They had dealt me a crap hand and now I had to play it and win.

Frustrated and hungry, I took a break. I had skipped breakfast since I spent that time lip locked with the sexy mayor. Thoughts of the morning flooded my mind, and my body heated. I could practically feel his hands on me again, the roughness of his fingers against my bare skin.

I shook my head, trying to refocus on the task in front of me. My body was on fire, and I was standing on Main Street. I was reaching for the door handle to Lettuce Eat when someone called my name. It was Sid, dressed in his uniform.

"Hey, Kate, how are you?" he asked, stopping in front of me.

"Hi, Sid. I'm good; how are you?"

"Great. Lettuce Eat, nice choice," he said with a nod toward the building. "Their Caesar salad wrap is amazing."

Maybe Sid could tell me more about the town over lunch. "Would you like to join me?"

A smile spread across his face. "I'd love to."

The minute we walked inside, I fell in love. A chalkboard menu hung from the wall above the counter with the items listed in a beautiful curly font. The walls were decorated with artwork. A few round tables sat in front of the large window overlooking Main Street.

More tables ran along the wall from the front door to the back of the store, which was darker and had a more relaxed feel to it with a large area rug and comfy armchairs. The whole place had a very artsy vibe, and I knew Mindy would love it, too.

"Welcome to Lettuce Eat. What can I make fresh for you today?" a young girl wearing a green apron with the store's logo on it asked us from behind the counter.

"We need a minute, Faith, it's Kate's first time here," Sid said.

He explained the menu to me and the different ways to customize my order. I settled on a Caesar salad with chicken and Sid got the wrap he'd told me about. He paid for our meals and carried them to a table by the front window.

"So, how are you really doing?" he asked as he took a bite of his wrap. His eyes closed in pleasure as he chewed.

"I'm okay; it's just complicated. Even though everyone is being nice to me, I know they have their guards up considering what I'm here for." I took a bite of my salad. My taste buds sang. It was the best Caesar salad I'd ever eaten. "Wow, this is amazing."

Sid nodded. "Secret homemade Caesar dressing recipe. They make all the meals fresh every day. All the ingredients come from their family farm. The dairy comes from there, too. Big Red is the dairy farmer."

I covered my mouth and laughed. "Big Red?"

"Yeah. He's Faith's dad and the only dairy farmer for the town. He's also a huge guy. Faith's grandpa started Davis Family Farms, and Big Red and his brothers have kept it going. Tommy Davis is the one who owns the store. All the brothers live on the farm together. It's the largest one in the county. They have three houses on it," he explained. "We should go there sometime. They love to give tours."

That sounded like a good idea. A great way to understand the inner workings of the town a little better. And how could one farm supply everything the town needed? Peter had mentioned the farmers' market. Were there other people who contributed as well?

"That sounds like fun," I said. As long as we could go as friends.

"Are you excited for our date?"

I wasn't, really. Instead of excited, I'd been stressing about it. The whole thing just sounded awkward. I felt bad letting Sid know that, though. He seemed excited.

I forced out a smile. "Of course."

After we finished eating, Sid asked if I wanted to go for a walk down Main Street to see some stores. He also offered to introduce me to more people. It sounded like a fantastic idea. Sid told me a lot of the same things Peter had, but some of the information was new, and I tucked it away. It wasn't helping me with my work. It was only causing me to fall more in love with Oak Springs.

Sid and I stopped at The Frozen Spoon ice cream parlor and got two cones. I found a new favorite flavor called Dipsy Swirl. It was cake batter and their chocolate lava flavor swirled together and dipped in a raspberry coating. I inhaled it.

"Have you been inside?" he asked as we stopped in front of Limbitless Expressions.

"No. Not yet."

"Let's go."

The store looked so much better in person than through the front window. Laney smiled and rushed over to greet us. Her short brunette hair bounced as she weaved through the shelves. She wore jeans, a flowing t-shirt and a pair of Birkenstocks; she reminded me so much of Mindy. I could see them being instant friends, sharing their love for sandals and crocs.

"Hey, guys, what brings you in?" Laney asked.

"Kate's never been in here, and I thought maybe you could show her around," Sid said. He checked his phone and frowned. "I'm sorry to do this, but I have to go. I'll see you later tonight."

I smiled and waved at him. Laney grinned at me and I shook my head. "It's complicated."

She held up her hands, "Say no more. I know all about complicated. Come on, I'll show you around."

I spent too much time in Laney's store and bought too many signs. I also ordered a few custom signs to take home. It was my kind of store, and I couldn't resist. Before heading back to The B&B, I checked out a few other stores.

Back in my room, I dumped all my treasures onto my bed. I would need another suitcase to get all my new goodies back home. I'd let my shoe obsession get the best of me in Best Foot Forward.

My phone rang just as I sat down on the bed and picked up my laptop to work.

"Katherine Miller," I answered without looking at the caller ID.

"Kate, what the hell is going on down there? Why are you taking so long? You're giving this guy time to wiggle out of this," Mr. Lawrence shouted as a greeting.

I rolled my eyes. Such little faith in me all of a sudden. "Mr. Lawrence, hello. How are you today?"

"You know what you are there to do, so why aren't you doing it?" he shouted, ignoring my greeting.

"I just need a little time to make things happen. I don't know what your sons did, but this deal was a mess. The mayor was closed off and saying no to everything from the start. I need to do some research and find my in. I will make this happen," I assured him. Even if I was unsure of how I would do that.

"Mr. Lawrence, while I have you on the phone, were there any other properties you were looking at, preferably ones with the river behind them?"

"If there were, I would have bought those, too. The river will be a huge selling point for the condos. Why are you asking? We are not moving locations. We're way past all that, Kate. Just close the damn deal."

"I understand, Sir. I was asking because—I'm not sure if your sons told you or not—but one property belongs to the mayor, and he is not willing to sell. I thought if I could find another property similar to his, then maybe he'd be willing to sell and we could write it into the proposal." I bit my lip and waited for his response.

"I don't care whose property it is. I will not run around trying to find land to offer these people. They can do that themselves with the very generous amounts I will pay them for their land. Now, I want that property, and I am going to get it with or without you. Do you understand?"

"Yes, sir."

"Good. Then get this done by Monday or don't come back here at all!" he screamed and hung up on me.

I sighed. I had to do this, or I would lose my job, which meant I needed to stop thinking about Peter romantically and start doing what I was sent here to do. This was business, and I needed to get my head back in the game.

Mr. Lawrence was taking property that already belonged to people and uprooting their lives. He wanted their properties and would stop at nothing to get them. So I could either join him or lose my job.

This wasn't how we did business. Normally we sent our scout in first. They'd stay for a week and get to know the town to see how things were doing and determine whether it was worth it for us to get involved. The scouts would feel out whether the mayor or the council were open to what we could offer them.

Then we'd send in someone from our sales team with the proposal, and the town would either agree or decline the offer. If they declined our first offer, then we'd move on to negotiations. If the town needed the help, it was over and done with quickly.

However, if they were stubborn and couldn't see that what we were offering was a good thing, then Mr. Lawrence sent me in. It never took this long. The mayor or council were usually already on the fence and just needed a little nudge in our direction. It was the first time a town had locked me out from the start, and it was throwing me off my game.

Chapter 18

KATE

MY ALARM WENT OFF earlier than usual this morning. Partly so I could get my run in early and get back to work, but mostly to avoid running with Peter. After working for the rest of the day yesterday, I had dinner alone at Pizza Pan and then took an evening walk through the park. A few people stopped to say hello, but most of them looked at me like I was the devil, here to burn down their town and use it as a hub for Hell.

After showering and drying my hair in soft waves, I headed downstairs for breakfast, which was probably my favorite part of being here. My mouth watered when I entered the kitchen. Betty had made biscuits and gravy. When the first bite hit my tongue, my eyes rolled back in my head, and a soft moan slipped from my lips.

It was so good. My taste buds were ruined. I'd never be able to cook as well as Betty. My mouth and stomach were going to be disappointed when we returned home. Maybe she would teach me a couple simple meals I could try on my own.

It was becoming harder and harder to do my job each day that I spent here. I loved this town, and the people in it were quickly growing on me. Implanting themselves into my soul one tiny seed at a time. It was going to hurt like hell to leave.

Speaking of leaving, I needed to meet with Peter again to go over the proposal and negotiate terms. There wasn't a way for me to give him what he wanted. Mr. Lawrence wanted his land, and he was pretty set on getting it. I could, however, make things easier for Peter and the town. Maybe give them something else they wanted that would also benefit our company. It was the best I could do.

First, I wanted to walk around and see more of the town. Find out what made Oak Springs so special.

"Betty, where is the best place to really get the full experience of the town?"

She laughed. "Honey, just go sit on Main Street. The full experience will come to you."

"I don't understand."

"Sit down on one of those benches out there and relax. Someone will come sit down next to you and talk your ear off."

I smiled. "While that's good and all, I was hoping for sightseeing or something."

"Do you hike?"

I shook my head.

"I figured as much. Well, if you have a friend, you could go tube down the lazy river."

I perked up. "There's a lazy river?"

She nodded and stirred something on the stove. "Not too far from here. I wouldn't go it alone, though. It's more of a buddy system thing."

I sat back in my chair. I didn't bring a buddy, and everyone else around town was working. Plus, I didn't know anyone well enough to ask them to do something like that with me.

"I think I'll head down to Grateful Cup with a book and figure it out from there," I said, pushing away from the table.

I headed out of the kitchen just as the front door opened. Peter stood in the doorway dressed in his usual suit, this one black with a light blue button up. His hair was perfectly styled, and he had his usual stubble on his chin. I resisted the urge to leap into his arms and kiss his full lips.

He smiled, and I sighed. My core tingled, and I pressed my legs together.

"Hi."

"Hi," I said breathlessly.

"I was looking for you this morning. Did you skip your run?"

"No. I just went a little earlier than usual. I forgot you mentioned running together."

He took a step closer. "Forgot? Or are you avoiding me?"

"Why would I be avoiding you?"

He took another step, and my breath hitched. He reached out and trailed his fingers up my arm. "You are avoiding what's between us. You can't run from it, Kate."

I lifted my chin. "I'm not running from anything."

He tugged my arm and pulled me into him. "Good. Then let's spend the day together."

"We both have to work."

"I can work from anywhere."

"You're wearing a suit," I pointed out.

He smiled. "I can change."

"Do you have an answer for everything?"

He grinned. "I have an answer for all your excuses. Come on, let's go. You can pick what we do first after we grab coffee and donuts."

I placed my hands on my hips, "I want to sit down and negotiate terms so you can sign the proposal and we can move on."

The grin dropped off his face, and his jaw ticked as he stared at me. "Later."

"Peter," I started.

"Later, Kate," he gritted out.

"Okay."

I raced up the stairs and closed the door to my room. This was a terrible idea, yet there wasn't anything I wanted more than to spend time with Peter. My heart raced like I was back in high school, and the boy I liked was picking me up for a movie.

That had only happened once, and my dad had scared the boy away. I wasn't very social, and I didn't go out all the time like my older sister did. I was the one with my nose buried in my books. But I still remembered the way I felt the night Bobby came to my door. It was the same feeling I had right now. A mix of nerves and anticipation.

After grabbing my phone and some cash, I headed back downstairs only to stop in my tracks. A small woman with long, bright red curls was standing in front of Peter. She was looking up at him because she was so tiny and gesturing wildly with her hands. He looked up and smiled at me over her head.

"Mindy," I squealed and leapt down the last few steps.

She turned around just in time for me to lift her into my arms and spin her around. Her feet dangled in the air as we spun since she was only five feet tall.

"What are you doing here?"

"You said I had to see the town for myself, so here I am. I need to get checked in, and then I'll get out of your way."

I tilted my head at her, and she thumbed behind her toward Peter. He was sitting on the sofa talking with Pa. They seemed comfortable, which was weird. Pa didn't seem comfortable with anyone, and he sort of blended in with the sofa most of the time.

"Come with us. Peter was just going to show me around town," I said.

Mindy couldn't have come at a more perfect time. I needed her as a buffer. Peter and I were supposed to be spending the day together and I knew he wanted it to be something more.

I slid my arm through hers and pulled her toward the desk. "I need you to come with us."

She laughed. "Okay. If you insist."

MINDY SETTLED INTO HER room while I talked her ear off, filling her in on everything that happened in the last few days. After she changed, we met Peter in the lobby, still in the same spot where we had left him, and headed down toward Grateful Cup. Mindy's face was like a kid on Christmas morning as she took in the town.

"I want to live here," she said on a sigh.

"You could," Peter said. "There are houses for sale."

I shook my head. "No she couldn't. She can't leave me."

"Then you both should move," he said with a smile. I knew he was kidding, but it didn't stop the flutter in my stomach at the thought of moving here and being with him.

"Ooh, ice cream. We'll have to get some later," Mindy said with a wink in my direction.

Peter wrapped his arm around my waist and pulled me into his side. "Kate and I were going to go there on our date." He smiled down at me and I melted into his side. He was irresistible.

"Don't worry about me, I'll have plenty to do," Mindy said, crossing the street and heading for the coffee shop.

"She'll have no problem fitting in here," I said dryly.

"You wouldn't either," Peter said, placing a kiss on the side of my head.

The smell of coffee hit me the minute Peter opened the door. He held it open for me, and I floated in nose first. I loved coffee shops. Everything about them helped me to relax. Mindy and I left our orders with Peter and found seats by the big window that overlooked Main Street.

"I really love it here," she whispered.

"You haven't been here for more than an hour."

She sat back and smiled. "I know. It's a feeling though. Like when you put on a broken-in pair of jeans and they fit just right. They feel good, and you like how you feel in them. The minute I stepped foot here, that's the feeling I got."

"Really?"

She nodded.

Peter set down our coffee and donuts on the table in front of us and took the empty seat beside me. He put his arm over the back of my chair as he sipped his coffee.

"What are you ladies talking about?" he asked.

"Mindy was just telling me how in love she is with your town," I said.

He smiled at her. "It really is a great place."

"I can see that," she said with a seductive smile. I knew she wasn't just talking about the town anymore. Something inside me stirred, and I had the urge to crawl into Peter's lap and claim him as mine. The door chimed, and loud voices carried over to us.

"Hey, there you are," one of them said. I turned my head and saw Frank making his way over to our table. He stopped beside it with a grin on his face. "We were looking for you."

"Well you found me," Peter said looking up at him. Sid stood behind Frank.

Frank's eyes drifted over the table and stopped on Mindy. They widened, and he pulled a chair from the table next to ours and flipped it around backward before sitting down.

"Hello, gorgeous. What's your name?"

Mindy crossed her arms over her chest and looked him up and down. "Not interested."

He barked out a laugh. "You're feisty."

"And you're cocky. I know your type."

He reared back, "My type? Sweetheart, don't put me in the category with others. I'm in one all of my own."

Peter snorted into his coffee. Sid rolled his eyes and headed for the counter.

Mindy leaned forward and licked her bottom lip. "I bet you are."

Frank leaned in, "You want to find out?"

She bit her bottom lip and smiled, "When hell freezes over." She leaned back in her chair and picked up her coffee, taking a big sip.

Peter laughed and smacked Frank on the back.

Frank stood up. "This isn't over. Not by a long shot."

"Whatever you say, Slick."

"Slick?" Frank asked with a smirk. "We've already advanced to nicknames?" Before she could answer, he walked toward the counter and got in line. But his eyes were still on Mindy.

"Is that the company you keep?" she asked Peter.

"Yeah. He's got layers."

Mindy laughed. "Like an onion?"

Peter nodded.

"Does he turn into an ogre at night?"

Peter chuckled. "Nah, Prince Charming."

Mindy snorted. "I doubt that man could ever be someone's Prince Charming."

Frank lifted his cup of coffee toward our table as he and Sid headed out the door.

"Definitely not Prince Charming," Mindy muttered.

AFTER COFFEE, MINDY WENT back to The B&B to take a nap, and Peter and I headed to the park.

"We need to talk about the elephant following us around," I said.

Peter gestured toward a park bench. I took a seat and waited for him to talk. Instead, he stretched his arm on the bench behind me and pulled me to his side. "This is nice."

I agreed.

"I know that you're here to do a job, Kate. That's one of the many barriers between us. But I can't help but feel like I'd be wasting an opportunity if I didn't get to know you on a personal level. To explore this. Just enjoy the day with me, and we can meet first thing in the morning. We have a date tonight, with other people, and it's going to be awkward. I just want a few hours to enjoy your company. Will you give me that?"

I nodded.

"Good."

My phone buzzed in my pocket at the same time Peter's rang. He dug into his suit coat and pulled it out.

"I've got to take this. Excuse me," he said stepping away from the bench to take the call.

I checked my phone and laughed at the name—Mindy must have changed it—before cringing because of who it was.

King asswipe: *Kate, what's going on? I thought you would have closed the deal and been home by now.*

Me: *There's been a setback. I'll be home soon. Quit stalking me.*

King asswipe: *I'm not stalking; I'm concerned. Trent told me you're stalling. Do you need help? I am a lawyer. I could force their hand.*

I rolled my eyes.

Me: *No! I do not need your help. Quit trying to save me. Leave me alone, Vincent. I'm fine.*

Three dots jumped and then disappeared. I waited a few minutes before slipping my phone back in my pocket. Peter walked back over, shaking his head.

"I've got to get back to the office. I guess I'll see you tonight."

"Yeah, guess so."

He looked around, and then pulled me up from the bench into his arms. They wrapped tightly around me, cocooning me in his warmth. The fresh scent of his body wash and spicy cologne filled my nose. My eyes drifted closed, and I rested my head on his chest, inhaling deeply. He smelled amazing, and being in his arms felt like home.

I startled. That was a weird feeling. I pushed back from him and took a step away to put some space between us.

"I've got to get going, too. I have a few phone calls to make," I lied.

His eyes were a dark shade of green as he stared at me. I shifted on my feet and looked away.

"Right. Well, I'll see you later, Kate."

"Yes. Later."

Without waiting for him to say anything else, I bolted. The awkwardness of the conversation mixed with my confusing feelings made me feel panicky and jumpy. I jogged back to Betty's and headed for Mindy's room.

"I DON'T SEE ANYTHING WRONG with enjoying yourself. Work be damned," Mindy said as we headed to Lettuce Eat. It was noon, and I was starving. Plus, I really wanted Mindy to experience the restaurant. I knew she'd fall in love.

"You'd willingly throw your job away for a man?" I questioned. I knew damn well she wouldn't.

"No, but I'd put it on the line for some hot, spicy sex."

A woman I didn't know passed us just as Mindy said that. She scowled at us. I was about to apologize when Mindy pulled the door open to Lettuce Eat.

"This place is amazing!" Mindy said from the doorway. Her eyes scanned the room, taking it all in like a kid in a candy shop. "You know what they need?"

"What?"

"An art store!"

I laughed. "Yeah, they don't have anything like that here."

"Yet," she said with a devious smile. That smile scared me. It meant she was thinking, and usually there was a big change that came with that. Especially here, where she was already in love and looked like she wanted to buy some land and build a house.

We ordered lunch and settled in the back in the armchairs. Mindy studied the art on the walls. I loved seeing her light up whenever she looked at art. She was so passionate about it. Back home, she owned an art gallery where she sold some of her own pieces.

"Eat your meal, we've got some clothes shopping to do. Is there a place around here, or do we need to take a road trip?" Mindy asked. She had insisted on coming along to Simply Cook It tonight for our date.

She wanted to make things less awkward. She would be the only single in the group, but Mindy didn't care about things like that the way I did. I envied her take-no-shit attitude and wished I had an ounce of her confidence. She didn't care what others thought of her and always spoke her mind. Something I was working on. Slowly

.

Chapter 19

KATE

DATE WITH WAS CANCELED. The group before us at Simply Cook It started a fire in one of the kitchens, and they closed it down for the evening. Peter invited Mindy and me to Frosty Mug Tavern. I had been wanting to check out the pub anyway, so it worked out perfectly.

"Do you think they'll have pretzels with that beer cheese?" I asked as we walked up Grand Street toward the pub.

"It's a pub, Kate. I'm sure they'll have something similar."

"You'll have to order for me like you do at Lucky's."

"Yeah. Okay."

"Do you think I look okay? I'm so nervous. I put on extra deodorant already," I said as we got closer. Mindy didn't answer. I looked behind me and saw her standing in front of an empty storefront that was for sale. Her face was pressed to the glass.

"Whatcha doing?" I asked, stopping beside her. I already knew she was envisioning a store of her own here. I could tell by her broad smile.

She jumped and spun toward me. "Nothing."

I laughed and tugged her along. "Come on. You can call about it tomorrow."

"I have no idea what you're talking about."

"Mm-hmm."

Frank and Peter were standing out in front of the pub, waiting for us. Mindy stiffened beside me when her eyes connected with Frank's. A smirk crossed his face, but he didn't move. Both men looked deliciously handsome. Peter's hair was styled the same as earlier. Instead of the suit, he was wearing dark gray shorts and a burgundy shirt that made his arms look a little tanner.

Peter wrapped me up in his arms when I got close enough and pulled me against him. He breathed in deeply, and I relaxed into his embrace. It felt so good to be in his arms. My body burned with desire. All I could think about was Peter's mouth on me and the way his hands had cupped my ass earlier.

He stepped back, still holding my hand, and said, "You look gorgeous." My skin burned as his eyes raked over me, taking in my tiny white shorts, flowing yellow tank, and black blazer. It was classy, yet sexy, and I loved it. Along with my new heels. I was a sucker for a good heel.

"Mindy and I went to The Oak Wardrobe earlier. Vivian helped us out."

He smiled. "She's an amazing woman. She and her husband have owned that store for years. It's been great to watch it grow with the town."

I smiled and looked away. Would a store like that be able to compete with a large strip mall? Usually, small shops went out of business as the bigger, more well-known stores moved in.

"No Hannah tonight?" I asked, looking around to make sure I didn't miss her. That would have been awkward.

Peter scrunched up his nose in disgust. "No. I told her I'd like to remain friends and that I couldn't go on a date with her when I had feelings for someone else."

"Oh," I said quietly.

His tongue ran along his bottom lip, and his eyes dropped to my mouth. It might have been my imagination, but it seemed Peter had leaned in closer to me. I swallowed hard.

Frank coughed, and Peter stepped back. "Shall we go in?" he asked.

I nodded as Frank sidled up next to Mindy. "Hello again," he said with a grin.

Mindy rolled her eyes. "You again."

Frank laughed and stuck out his arm for her to slip hers through.

She crossed her arms instead.

"Come on, let me walk you in," he said.

"I'm not a helpless female," she replied.

"No, you certainly aren't. Just humor me."

She lifted an eyebrow at him. "No."

"Do you know how to be nice? We've just met and I'm trying to be a gentleman."

She laughed. "That seems like a stretch for you."

"What is your problem? You don't even know me."

"I don't need to. I know your type."

He huffed.

"What's the matter? Mad that I'm not fawning all over you?"

He frowned and looked at the ground. "If you must know, yes. It's not something I'm used to."

Mindy patted his chest. "Come on, Slick. I'll let you buy me a drink." She walked past him and around us, throwing open the door to the pub. I followed quickly behind her.

It was amazing inside, unlike any of the pubs or bars I had been to back home. City bars were different from the ones in small towns or more rural areas. I loved how each one had a different feel. I'd been to some that were hole-in-the-wall bars and others, like Frosty Mug Tavern, were modern, yet still rustic.

The ceilings of the pub were high and open with wooden beams running across them. A long mahogany bar ran the whole length of the wall to my left. There were booths along the walls and round high-top tables and chairs in the center of the room.

The lights were dim, and lanterns hung on the walls. The wood floor looked scuffed, but that only added to the appeal. I walked in a little farther and took in all the pictures on the walls. Some were of people I recognized from around town. Everyone was so close here.

My mind whirled with possibilities for holding events in the space. I had always wanted to be an event planner; I just never pursued it.

The pub was much larger than it appeared outside, just like a lot of the stores and buildings here. There was a small half partition wall, and I craned my neck to see what was behind it.

"That's just more seating," Peter whispered in my ear, sending goosebumps down my arms. I hadn't realized how close he was standing to me.

A hostess, Mariah according to her name tag, was flirting pretty heavily with Frank. She wore a short black skirt that flared out slightly at her hips and a tight black tank top that stopped above the skirt, exposing a little skin. Her breasts were spilling out of the top; the whole outfit seemed extremely unprofessional.

Mariah led us back to the patio. There were more tables and booths around the small wall, just like Peter had said. The space was slightly more open.

"Sometimes they have karaoke, and on the weekends it's a dance floor," Peter said, pointing to an open area.

We sat down at one of the lower tables near a black gate. It overlooked the river, and the sun was setting. It was beautiful, like something out of a painting. I took out my phone to capture the moment and sighed.

"It's really beautiful," I breathed.

"Yeah, it is," Peter whispered.

I looked up and realized he was staring at me. My stomach fluttered, and heat crawled up my spine. I couldn't look away. His green eyes burned with desire, but also something more. Something deeper.

"Yuck," Frank cringed.

I turned to find his gaze bounding between Peter and me. I quickly looked away to hide my embarrassment. Mindy punched Frank in the arm.

"Ouch. What the hell was that for?" he asked rubbing at his arm.

Mindy glared at him, and my face burned hotter.

Thankfully, our waitress, a busty blonde, appeared. She took our orders while she flirted shamelessly with Frank and Peter, ignoring Mindy and me altogether.

"What is it with these women?" Mindy asked. "Have you slept with them all?"

Frank smirked. "Not *all* of them."

"You're disgusting."

"Hey, it's a small town. There's not much to do here, and I've come to the pub a lot since it opened," he defended.

"Why? Hitting the sauce a lot?" Mindy asked. She leaned forward on the table like she was interested in a juicy story.

Frank scowled at her. "I'll have you know that I don't drink that much."

"Sure you don't," Mindy said goading him.

"I don't," he shouted.

"Mm hmm."

"Whatever. Let's just let loose and have a good time tonight. Plus, no one has to work tomorrow."

Before anyone could argue with him, Frank ordered a round of shots and a plate of nachos. Peter ordered pretzels with beer cheese for me, and I fell for him a little more.

THE NEXT MORNING, I WAS slightly hungover for my jog through the park. Peter dodged me again for our meeting. This time claiming he was out of town all day for a meeting. I was starting to get the impression that he was giving me the runaround.

Especially since he promised he'd be back in time for our date tonight. The date that he tricked me into when I was drunk. It wasn't hard, though. Everything in me had shouted *yes* when he brought it up. He was so hard to resist.

A black lab ran toward me from the side. I slowed my pace almost to a stop and yanked my earbuds out. The lab sat down in front of me and wagged her tail. I bent down and ran my hand over her head and then scratched behind her ears.

"Hey you, where did you come from?" I cooed.

"Shiloh," a male voice yelled from behind me.

I looked over my shoulder and saw Sid jogging toward us with a leash in his hand. His hair was held back with a band, and he was wearing black gym shorts, a gray t-shirt and tennis shoes.

"Is she yours?" I asked.

"Yeah. Sorry about that. Normally when we're out running, she doesn't stop. She must have sensed you were someone new."

I smiled at him while I petted Shiloh behind the ears. "She's really friendly and beautiful."

"Thanks," he said, running a hand through his hair.

I could sense he was a little nervous. Last night when he called about our canceled date, he asked me to go to the pub, but Peter had already called. Sid showed up at the bar and saw us on the patio. He turned around and left. My heart sank; I should have been more honest with him.

"Want to walk with me?" I asked.

He held out his hand, gesturing for me to go ahead.

"I'm sorry about last night," I blurted out. "I should have told you the truth."

"I understand. You and Peter have a connection. I can tell. Hell, everyone can tell."

"Well, I'm really sorry. You deserved an explanation."

He shook his head. "Really, it's okay."

I looked away and focused on the path ahead of us. We walked lazily through the park toward the river. It was nice. The sun was out, and the trees provided some shade that helped with the growing heat. The breeze felt good, and the smell of spring swirled around us.

"Were the river and the forest behind it a huge selling point for the pub?" I asked, changing the subject.

Sid nodded as he hooked Shiloh to her leash. "Yeah. The owner was trying to decide between here and another location in the city. He chose this one because of the backdrop for the patio. There wasn't a building there. He hired builders, and now we have Frosty Mug Tavern."

I felt like crap. How would the owner feel when Lawrence Development Company ripped out the trees and built a huge building there? It would destroy the view from the patio.

I had experienced that view firsthand. The sun setting behind the trees was beautiful, and I couldn't get enough pictures. The river caught some light as the sun dipped low in the sky. It was an awesome picture that I planned to blow up and frame for my wall back home.

"I'm sure he'll be pretty upset when the backdrop becomes a large building," I muttered as I stared off into the trees. The words just slipped out.

Sid stopped and turned toward me, "You're kidding. They want to build there? That would ruin the view from the park too. We really don't need any help, you know."

I could sense his annoyance, and I really didn't blame him. The condos would be a huge eyesore. The park and the pub were the center of the town.

"I know," I whispered.

"Do you? Ridge Point is twenty minutes south of here, and they're doing just fine, too. They have fewer businesses than we do. This idea that the town won't survive if you don't build here is ridiculous. Why can't you just build the new town hall like you originally proposed and leave the rest alone?"

I chewed on my lip.

His eyes widened. "They're not going to build it, are they?"

I turned to face him. "He rewrote the proposal; it's all or nothing. If you say no to one thing, then he'll pull the whole project. No town hall."

"Dammit," he shouted. "No playground for the kids then, either." He gripped at his hair.

I shook my head. "I'm really sorry. I'm trying to find ways around it, but there really aren't any. He wants to build here, and he'll stop at nothing to do it. I think he figured he could force Peter's hand by pulling the town hall if he said no."

Sid scowled. "This is bullshit."

I was about to say sorry again but held it back. What good was my apology when I was here to mess things up? It was useless. Even I could see this wasn't a good idea. I didn't blame any of them for being upset or voting against it.

"Come on, Shiloh, let's go. I don't really feel like finishing my walk." He yanked on Shiloh's leash to get her to move. I wanted to say more, but I knew nothing I said would change the way he or anyone else here felt about me or the project.

"Hey, is everything all right?" Mindy asked, appearing on the trail ahead of me. Laney was walking behind her.

I pursed my lips and exhaled as I turned to face them fully. "Yeah, I'm fine."

"I heard Sid yelling," Laney said. "What was that about? He never gets angry."

Great, I'd managed to piss off the only person in town who never lost his temper. "He's upset about the condos that my company wants to build." I pointed to the pub. "Right over there."

"Are you serious?" Laney asked.

I nodded. "One of the two sets. The strip mall will be down off Old Cedar Road."

Laney folded her arms across her chest. "The whole thing is ridiculous. This park is the center for everything. The pub, too. People go there to relax after a long day at work. It's where out-of-town guests come to visit. It's where we meet with friends and family and share a meal and drinks. Putting condos behind that will ruin it all."

"I know, and I see that now. There's not much I can do, though. If we don't build the condos and strip mall, then he won't build the town hall. It's all or nothing now. He wants it all."

Laney frowned. "I can't believe this."

"I know." I sat down on a park bench, defeated.

"There are a lot of people who have grown up here. Not just older folks, either. People like me and Frank. My dad met my mom in high school and that was the same school Frank and I went to. It was where I met my high school sweetheart, before he moved away, but that's a story for another time. The point I'm trying to make is that this is home, and it will always be home. Building it up and putting a lot of awful gaudy buildings here will ruin the feel of the small town. It's more than just a location; it's community and family and friends. It's the support we give one another when we need something. It's coming together and forming committees to run all the events we hold. Peter became mayor here because he loves this town and he believes in everything we stand for. If you build here, it will change things. I'm sorry; I like you, but I have to say no to this, too."

Laney walked off, and I slid down on the park bench feeling like someone had gut-punched me. There was no point in staying until Monday. The longer I stayed here, the worse it got. These buildings weren't a good idea, and deep down I knew that. Mr. Lawrence had been wrong.

"Come on. Let's go get some coffee," Mindy said, pulling me up.

"I feel like a piece of shit," I mumbled, resting my head on her shoulder.

"I know. I'm sorry, but I agree with everyone. This town is great, and so are the people in it. If I were you, I wouldn't be able to stand behind something like that."

I looked at her and frowned. "Thanks a lot. That's not helpful at all."

She shrugged. "Sorry, just speaking my mind."

"When do you not?"

She laughed. "True. That's why you love me, though. I will always tell you the truth."

Even if the truth hurt like a knife to the gut. I had a choice to make. I could either stick it out and meet with Peter and the town council on Monday or go home with my tail tucked between my legs and try to convince Mr. Lawrence that this was all wrong and we should scout another location.

Chapter 20

PETER

THE DOOR TO MY OFFICE flew open, scaring the shit out of me. My heart pounded out of my chest. I'd been trying to avoid meeting with Kate and was just packing up my things to head to Ridge Point, the next town over, to hide out.

Tom Tracy sat down in front of my desk.

"Tom, what can I do for you? I'm on my way out."

"You can tell me why Hannah is home packing her stuff and crying about you breaking her heart."

I rolled my eyes and took a seat in my chair. I knew this was coming. Last night, I stopped by the store after walking Kate home. I went into my office to catch up on things I'd let slip by in the store and that's when I found all the errors. Things were not adding up, and the more I searched the worse it got.

"Don't roll your eyes. This is serious. What happened?" he asked, leaning forward.

"I fired her, Tom."

"Fired her? What the hell for?"

"For stealing."

His eyes widened as he mulled over my words. Then they narrowed on me and he sat forward in his chair. "What proof do you have?"

"The books, the cash drawer, and her confession."

"Confession?"

"She broke down and cried. Told me that she needed the money and promised to return it all. It was too late, though. She's stolen over three hundred dollars since she started."

He shook his head. "I don't believe you."

"Then ask her, but what's done is done."

"Listen, my sister doesn't know what to do with her anymore. This was her last shot at getting her life right. Can you just hire her back? I'll keep an eye on her."

I shook my head. "No. It's not my responsibility. I gave her job because we're friends, Tom, and she stole from me. That's the end of it."

He huffed. "Fine."

I stood up and shouldered my laptop bag.

"What are we going to do about the development?" he asked. He was in no hurry to go.

I looked to the door and the time on the wall before sitting back down in my chair.

"Tom, I've really got somewhere to be."

"I have a right to know."

"I'm working on something."

He scoffed. "You sure are. A relationship with the enemy."

"That's uncalled for," I shouted.

"Is it? Because everyone has seen you with her and you look mighty cozy."

"What I do outside of this office is no one's business. She's not the enemy. She's caught up in this just as much as we are. Now, I'm working on something that will help all of us, and it's not here in Oak Springs."

"Fine, but people talk, Peter."

I leaned forward on my desk and narrowed my eyes at him. "If you and Laney print one goddamn word about either of us, you're going to see a side of me you wish you hadn't. I will strip you of all your town privileges."

He put his hands up in the air, "Okay. You won't hear a word from me."

"Is there anything else?"

He shook his head and stood.

"Then have a nice day, Tom."

The door shut, and I breathed a sigh.

AFTER A LONG DAY OF HIDING out in Ridge Point, I was more than ready for my date with Kate. The one that I secured the night before when I walked her home from the pub. She may have been slightly intoxicated, but she seemed really excited.

I texted her during the day to see if she was still interested, and she said she couldn't wait. The feeling was mutual. I was dying to spend time with her. Mindy helped me plan everything so we would get some privacy later and I could surprise her.

Every Friday night from spring until fall, weather permitting, the town showed a movie on a giant screen in the park. I wanted to do something special for Kate, but I also wanted her to experience this. It was something important to our town, and it brought everyone together. We even had a popcorn vender, Tom Tracy. He'd raised money to buy a machine after the first two showings. It had gotten a lot of use, and everyone loved it.

We had monthly theme night where we showed a movie, and the town planning committee brought food that corresponded to the theme. Once a month in the summer, we also had a pub night, where Arthur Hughes, the owner of Frosty Mug Tavern, set up a beer tent.

Every other weekend on Sunday nights, we showed a kid's movie. We'd started out only doing it once a month, but the event was really popular. The parents really enjoyed it, and sometimes we set up sitters so parents could leave their kids in the park and have some time to themselves. Sid and Frank usually took turns staying to keep an eye on things at the park.

My stomach was a jumbled mix of excitement and nerves as I walked from my store, where we would have dessert, to The B&B. My walk turned into a jog when I saw Kate sitting on the front porch swing waiting for me. She was so beautiful. The light hit her just right, making her look angelic.

"Hey," I said casually when I stopped in front of her.

She smiled and stood up. Tonight, she was dressed in tight jeans that looked painted on her long legs and a tight red top with a plunging neckline. I temporarily blacked out staring at her cleavage. I wanted to bury my face in it.

"Hi," she whispered. I peeled my eyes away from her breasts and up to her face. One eyebrow was cocked, and her hands were on her hips. Busted.

I pushed up the sleeves of my gray henley and ran a hand through my hair, which I had left a little messy. Kate tracked my movements. I smirked at her, and she dipped her head to the side, looking coyly at me. It was like we were high schoolers. I smiled and grabbed her hand, pulling her down the steps to the street.

"So, you're in for a treat. This is something we do every weekend if the weather is nice," I explained. I was buzzing, not only from the date, but also because this was such a cool thing about our town, and I was dying to show it to her.

"Hey son, you almost forgot something," Betty called from the porch.

I spun on my heels and jogged back up to her. She held out a wicker basket.

"Thanks, Aunt Betty."

"Have a lovely evening," Betty said, kissing me on the forehead.

"Aunt Betty?" Kate asked.

"Yeah, that's my grandma's youngest sister on my mom's side. Uncle George, or Pa as he's known in town, is her husband. I visited here a lot growing up, and I got very close to this side of my family. Nine years ago, my grandpa Jack got really sick. I moved in with him to help take care of him." I grabbed her hand as we walked down Main Street.

"Tell me more. Does your mom visit?" Kate asked.

"No, my mom hasn't been back here in over twenty years. My dad was passing through on business and stayed at The B&B. One day, my mom came to visit Aunt Betty and saw my dad. She fell in love with him and followed him out of here." We crossed the street toward the park.

"She's too good for this place now that she has money, even though the money isn't really hers. She never worked a day in her life. Her relationship with my grandfather was very strained because of it. When we were born, she would write to my grandma and send photos, but she never came to visit. She sent me here when I was older because I was 'troubled.' It ended up being the best thing that could have happened to me. I learned so much from my grandma and grandpa. Aunt Betty and Uncle George, too."

"Did your brothers ever come to visit?"

"Vincent visited once when I was too little to come. He hated it so much he never came back. He didn't like being away from mom. Thomas came when he was younger, but once he got to high school he stopped. He went through an 'I'm too rich for that place' phase. Unfortunately, it stuck with him." I slowed our pace. She seemed to enjoy getting to know me and the parts about my family she didn't already know from Vincent.

"Tell me more about when you moved here," she requested.

"My grandma, Eleanor, passed away fourteen years ago. My grandpa lived alone and fell apart. He let himself and his house go. He didn't want anyone to visit him anymore. He was lost without grandma. At first, I respected his wishes. I stayed away for a few years. When he got sick nine years ago, Aunt Betty called me. She said he wouldn't let anyone in, and his house and yard were a mess. The former mayor was threatening to fine him if he didn't start taking care of his property. I came right down and moved in with him. He was pissed, but I didn't give him a choice. The conditions were pretty much unlivable. I moved him to Aunt Betty's. He died about two years later."

"Your mom never fixed things with him before he died?"

I shook my head. "No. She started drinking a year before he passed. She changed a lot. She's bitter and selfish now."

"I'm sorry, Peter. That's so sad," she said, and then quickly changed the subject. "So, what are we doing here?"

"We're meeting up with friends," I said, purposely keeping things vague.

I spotted Mindy waving at us and headed that way. Mindy had helped me get a group together. Small-town people talk, and word spreads quickly. I didn't want rumors spread about Kate and me.

There were three blankets spread out on the ground. Frank was on one of them, and Sid was on another. Mindy grabbed Kate's hand and pulled her down onto her blanket. I sat next to Frank and nudged him a little. He grumbled as he moved over to make room for me.

I emptied contents from the picnic basket onto the blanket between Kate and me. Two mason jars full of sweet tea, Aunt Betty's famous pulled pork sandwiches—which Frank almost snagged—and some fruit. Overall, it was a nice spread.

"Where the hell is my food?" Frank asked.

"You should have eaten before you got here," I said through gritted teeth.

"I thought tonight we were having theme night, and it was Pizza Pan's turn to provide the food."

Sid nodded. "I heard that too. Where's the pizza? I didn't eat, either."

"Oh, for fuck's sake," I grumbled.

Kate laughed, and Mindy swatted Frank's hand away from our food.

"Woman, I swear to God, if you hit me tonight, you will be sorry," he warned.

She stuck her tongue out at him, and I thought for a second I saw him smirk. He was enjoying this.

Lowering my voice, I leaned into Kate and said, "Listen, if you want to go sit somewhere else, we can. I just thought being seen alone together wouldn't be the best idea since people would talk."

She nodded. "Yeah, it would make things weird."

"In that case, let's eat. These bozos can get their own food."

She smiled and unwrapped her sandwich.

"This is some bullshit," Frank scoffed as he plopped back down next to me. I hadn't even noticed he had left. "Laney said Pizza Pan isn't coming. Apparently, that's next weekend. I'm going to starve."

"You could always go home," Mindy suggested from behind her cup. She was smart and had brought snacks and drinks.

"What do you have over there?" Frank asked, sitting up tall to peer over Kate and me.

"Nothing you need to worry about, Slick."

He narrowed his eyes at her. Then stood up and walked behind us. She squealed as he tackled her to the ground to steal the bag of chips she was holding.

"You're holding out on us. You have a whole picnic basket of food for yourself."

"That's not true," she giggled. "I just have a bag of chips. The guy who's selling the popcorn has a friend who's sitting behind a table with other snacks and drinks. Go buy your own."

Frank ran to the table with Sid not far behind him. I let out a sigh. Maybe this wasn't such a good idea.

THE MOVIE ENDED, BUT KATE didn't make a move to leave. Instead, she leaned back on her hands and looked up at the stars. The view was really great here, unlike the city. She couldn't stop talking about how much she loved the whole movie under the stars experience. And I couldn't stop thinking about how I wanted more of these nights with her.

"Meet me behind Double Oak in ten minutes," I whispered to her.

My heart was pounding out of my chest the entire way to my shop. This part of the date was important. I needed to know where she stood with everything. The store was dark except for a few small lights in my workshop. Perfect mood lighting.

In the center of the room was my grandmother's coffee table that Kate had admired. I planned to give it to her as a gift, along with whatever else she wanted. I covered the table with a white sheet and set down two plates of chocolate cake, which Mindy had told me was Kate's favorite, two wineglasses, and a bottle of wine in a bucket of ice. Then I stepped back to look at everything.

The roses were missing. Mindy had stashed two red roses under the counter for me earlier. I placed them in the center of the table and resisted the urge to snap a picture. I was pretty impressed with myself. All that was missing now was Kate.

My stomach felt twisted in a knot. It was a huge risk pursuing her with everything going on, but I couldn't stop myself. It felt like there was a magnetic pull between us. She was gorgeous, sure, but it was more than just the physical attraction.

Every time we were together, it felt like pieces of my soul I hadn't even known were missing clicked back into place. I'd always been closed off to love and relationships, but with Kate it was natural, easy.

I wished we had met under different circumstances. Maybe I'd been holding onto the past too tightly. Was the land really that important? It had belonged to my grandfather, and he had passed it down to me. One day, I'd like to pass it down to my kids. But what good was building a new house if there was no one to share it with? I tossed back a glass of wine and then poured another one, straightening everything out again as I did.

The back door opened, and the clicking of Kate's heels echoed in the quiet store. My heart rate increased as I stood, waiting for her. I took a deep breath, trying to calm my nerves. The air left my lungs when she stopped in the doorway. She was so beautiful; it was like my brain had forgotten what she looked like already, and I was seeing her for the first time again.

She smiled at me, and her face lit up. I would do anything in the world to keep that smile aimed my way. Shit, I was in too deep already. I watched as she walked farther into the room and ran her hand over my workbench. Her fingers lightly touched my tools.

"This store is amazing. Who owns it?" she asked.

"I do."

She whirled around; eyes wide. "This is your store?"

I nodded.

"Do you make the furniture, too? The sign said handcrafted."

"I do."

"Peter, that's amazing. I can't believe you made all of this. It's so beautiful. I am so in love with that end table out there. It matched your grandmother's coffee table that I loved."

I pulled the corner of the sheet back from the table. "You mean this one?"

"Yes!" She ran her fingers over the carvings etched around the side. "It's my favorite."

"It's yours. You can have the matching end table, too."

"Really?"

I smiled and nodded. She flung herself into my arms, hugging me tight. Surprised, I stumbled, but quickly regained my footing. I wrapped my arms around her and pulled her tight against me. She smelled like vanilla, and I squeezed my arms tighter around her, remembering holding her while she slept.

I was so fucked. I was falling so hard for this girl, there was no way I could stop it. I wasn't even sure I wanted to.

She was gorgeous inside and out. Her smile made me feel like a king, her passion and drive made me want to work harder to be a better man, and her body drove me crazy, but her spirit and goodness really pushed me over the edge. I couldn't ever let her go. Consequences be damned.

I buried my nose in her hair and inhaled the fruity scent of her shampoo. She hummed and tilted her head to the side. I trailed kisses down the column of her neck while my hands slid down her sides. She moaned, and the sound went straight to my crotch. I bent at the knees and slid my hands to her legs, just under her ass, lifting her up so I could carry her to the chair beside the table.

It felt so natural to have her in my arms. She kissed a trail from the base of my ear down to my collarbone, and then back up again. I was a goner. My dick pressed so hard against my jeans it was painful. It didn't help when she straddled my lap and ground her hips against my length.

I groaned, loud and deep. God, it felt so good. I traced my fingers down the plunging neckline of her shirt and dipped them inside. Her head dropped back, and she pushed her chest forward in invitation. The small moan she let out was so sexy.

I bent forward and kissed down her neck, following the neckline of her shirt to the swell of her breast. Finally, I'd get a peek at the body that had been driving me crazy. The one I'd spent nights dreaming about. I pulled one cup of her black lace bra to the side and sucked her perfect breast into my mouth. She moaned, and her fingers wound into my short hair, keeping my head in place.

Her hips rocked into me again, and I moaned around her breast. I wanted her so badly I couldn't think straight. I told myself to take things slow, but all my good intentions went out the window once she was in my arms. With the way she was grinding against me, I'd say she felt the same.

I sucked on her breast with long slow pulls, and then teased her nipple with my teeth. Her hands moved to my belt and started undoing it. I wanted to keep going, but I needed to slow this down. It wasn't the right time. There was still a lot hanging between us that we needed to sort through.

For one, this damn development project. Two, my brother. If there was any chance she still had feelings for him, I needed to know. It would tear me apart, but I wouldn't be the other man.

I stopped her busy hands and looked into her eyes. She looked confused. I really didn't want to stop this, but I had to before things got out of control. We needed to talk.

"Not yet. I want you; believe me, I do." I pushed my hips up so she could feel just how badly. "But I want you when there is nothing standing between us. For now, let's take it slow. We don't have to go any further than this tonight."

I ran my thumb over her pebbled nipple. She flinched against my touch and then pushed back. My hand slid off her chest.

"Take it slow? This is how you take things slow? This could never work out, one of us will end up hurt. Then there will be nothing between us but pain and heartbreak."

She stood up and adjusted her shirt. I missed her warmth and touch. The connection between us had been severed and replaced with tension and hurt. The reminder of why we were both here and in this situation to begin with cast a pall over the evening. This was not at all how I wanted things to go.

"In case you didn't notice, I've already developed feelings for you. There is no way this will end well for me," she said.

"Kate, I have feelings for you too," I said grabbing her hand.

Her eyes searched mine. "You do?"

"Yes, I do. There has to be some way that we can work this out so it benefits us both."

She yanked her hand away. "I've been trying to find another property for either you or Mr. Lawrence to build on. That way, it's a win for both of us."

I took a step toward her, and she took a step back. "Is that all that you want, Kate? To win?"

"Of course not, but if you don't sign the papers, I'll lose my job." A tear escaped the corner of her eye and ran down her cheek. She wiped it away and turned her back to me.

"Kate, I'm sorry you've been put in this position, but I can't sell my property."

"Why the hell not?" she asked, whirling around to face me.

Her eyes were red, and tears dotted her cheeks. It gutted me to see her like this. I wanted to comfort her, but I wasn't sure how. Things between us were so new. This was basically our first date. I was trying everything I could think of to help her calm down, but maybe that wasn't what she needed at all. We hardly knew each other.

I was used to being in control, and this situation was getting away from me. I was pretty upset by all of this, too. It was my land they were going after.

I pulled at the ends of my hair, frustrated. "Because it's my grandfather's land!" I shouted.

Her eyes widened, and she took another step back. I didn't mean to raise my voice, but I was losing my patience with this whole thing. I was ready to shut it all down and move the hell on with my life.

She said nothing, just stared at me with wide tear-soaked eyes.

"He gave it to me when he passed away. I pitched a tent out back like Frank said and got to work renovating it so I could live there. It's more than just a piece of land, a shitty house, or even a place to build a new house; it's my whole life. It's the only thing that ever meant something to me. The place that changed my life. It's where I learned what true family was and how to laugh and love. The place I learned to fish, build furniture, and cook. It's a giant part of me and made me everything I am today," I explained.

I stepped toward her and reached for her hands. She stepped back and shook her head. Tears spilled down her cheeks. I felt like someone was sitting on my chest. It hurt to see her so upset. My heart was breaking.

"I have to go," she cried. She turned and ran from the room.

I heard the back door shut, and it echoed through my chest. I didn't bother to go after her. What was the point? There would always be something standing in the way of us. A job, a family member, hundreds of miles. I tossed back both glasses of wine and cleaned up the back room before heading home

Chapter 21

KATE

RUNNING IN HEELS WAS NOT EASY. I wasn't even sure why I'd worn heels to the park to begin with. I wore heels a lot. For work, to go out, to feel sexy. Tonight, I had been feeling very sexy, and things were going really well with Peter. For a minute, I almost forgot what brought me here. I let go and just let myself feel something I never had before.

Now I was running back to The B&B angry, hurt, and confused. I couldn't stand behind this project, no matter how badly I needed to. There was no way this would work, and I didn't know what else to do. This proposal would take things away from people here that really mattered to them. People like Peter, with farms and properties that had been in their families for a long time and passed down through generations.

No one was interested in anything new, either. I'd asked around. I was shocked our company was even trying to develop here. Oak Springs wasn't hurting for money or closing down shops. Just the opposite, actually. People weren't moving away. In fact, the population had increased recently. And lots of people visited from neighboring areas, bringing money into the town.

Mr. Lawrence had told me this was a dying town, but that wasn't true. I'd seen dying towns, and Oak Springs was far from it. They were creating more jobs without the help of big-time developers. Peter was just doing what I would in this situation, protecting the town from people like me.

When I got back to The B&B, I went in search of Mindy. I knocked on her door, but there was no answer. I went to my room to change and tried her phone. I needed her help to sort this out, even though I already knew what I needed to do.

She picked up on the first ring. "Kate, are you okay?"

"No, I'm not okay. I don't know what to do. I need help!"

"Okay, give me ten minutes, and I'll be back," she promised.

I hung up with her and changed into my sleep shorts and tank top. My hair was a mess from Peter's hands, and that made me cry again, so I piled it on top of my head. The small pieces sticking out everywhere made me feel a little more relaxed. I had makeup smeared under my eyes. I washed it off and climbed into bed.

Taking out my laptop, I opened a blank document and made two columns. At the top, I typed *Pros* and *Cons*. I was an organized person, and if I could organize the good and bad things about this project, maybe I could figure this out. If I could prove to myself that this development was a pro for the town, then maybe I'd be able to persuade others.

Problem was, there weren't many pros, and the cons list was long. Most of all, my heart was on the cons side. I couldn't get behind this project, and that meant I couldn't go through with it. Which meant I had to decide what I was going to do now. I slammed my laptop closed and set it aside, resting my head in my hands.

Mindy strolled into my room fifteen minutes later with a big paper bag. I laughed when she dumped the contents onto my bed. Ice cream, wine, and face masks. She handed me a spoon, and then bounced a few times on my bed, getting situated. She poured wine into two red plastic cups before sitting back against the headboard.

"So, tell me what's going on," she said around a huge bite of ice cream.

She was just as obsessed with The Frozen Spoon as I was. The Dipsy Swirl was our favorite, but their Layered Caramel Bourbon Delight was quickly becoming a close second. Mindy had somehow managed to snag a big tub of it.

I told her everything, including my internal conflict and pros and cons list.

"I can't go through with the project," I finished.

She nodded slowly and took another bite while she mulled that over.

How could I just walk away from my job? I'd put so much of myself and my time into it. After Vincent and I broke up, it took a lot of hard work to convince Mr. Lawrence to keep me. I had to show him I wasn't just some frail woman who needed a man to get a job.

I worked hard to prove myself and show that I was an asset to his company. After months of doing shitty jobs to prove myself, I finally worked on a project where I could shine. He was so impressed with my work that he gave me my first project the next week, and I nailed it.

I proved over and over again I could do what he asked and that I wouldn't be pushed around by clients. I'd built such a name for myself that clients knew who I was before I even showed up.

This was the first project I had failed to close, and it would be my downfall. What does that say about things? I burst into tears over my ice cream. Mindy wrapped me up in her arms and let me cry it all out. I didn't even feel this kind of pain when Vincent left me.

Okay, maybe the first time, when I left him and ran to Mindy's. I cried over my ice cream then, too. But when he left me the second time for good, I was so mad at him I couldn't feel anything else. I was just pissed that I had believed him the first time and gone back. I'd wasted so much time on that relationship, and I blamed myself. I'd sacrificed so many pieces of myself and changed to please him. And it was all for nothing.

This was different. I felt everything now. Pain over losing Peter and anxiety about losing my job. Emptiness when I imagined going home to that big house and my old life. I hated these feelings. I hadn't felt this weak in a long time.

"Kate, I'm going to tell you something, and I know you're not going to like it," Mindy finally said. "I think you're better off for this. You got this job because of Vincent, and even though you've worked your ass off to prove yourself—and you did—they've still kept you from your full potential."

"I don't think so," I defended. "They've helped me to grow into my full potential."

She shook her head. "One contract could make or break it all? Sounds like your boss still doesn't trust you. You deserve so much more than that. And I'm sorry if that hurts."

I frowned. I'd felt like a pawn these last few days, but what else was I going to do? Lawrence Development Company was all I'd ever known. I'd quit school at Vincent's request and taken this job. I was lucky to get a job like that without a degree and even luckier that I got promoted to my current position.

I met Vincent right after high school, and I'd never really had a serious job before that. I was grateful when Mr. Lawrence gave me a chance to be more than just a secretary. But had that kept me from growing into my full potential? Was I so grateful for the opportunity that I quit reaching for more? Vincent was still showing up at my job, almost daily, because he was friends with my boss. Maybe it was time to move on.

Being here the past couple of days had opened my eyes. There were other things I wanted to do. I wanted to live where people knew who I was. Somewhere I could make a difference. I wanted more than just Mindy as my friend. I loved her, but I needed more than just her. Laney, Frank, and Sid had showed me it was more fulfilling to have a group of people who cared about you. I wanted that.

"I can see your wheels turning, and that's good. Kate, you've been doing everything Vincent wanted you to do for so long that I don't think you've ever taken the time to figure out what you really want," Mindy said. "The man still comes around. To your job, to your house, wherever you are, he pops up."

I shivered. "Do you think he's here?"

Mindy laughed. "I wouldn't put it past him, but no. I think you're safe here."

Huh. I sat back and thought about that. I was safe here. Something I'd never felt back home. I'd never gone after what I wanted because I felt trapped. When things got bad, I just ignored it because I thought I needed to be grateful for all the opportunities he was giving me. I was naïve and dumb.

"I hate seeing you hurt, but I wish you could see this for what it is: an opportunity."

I turned to face her. "How so?"

"Well, honestly, there's a lot of good in this small town and a lot of potential. Maybe it's time we look at things a little differently. Instead of looking at what this town doesn't have, maybe look at what it can offer you? You came here thinking you needed to add something to the town, but I think you can take something away from it."

I sighed. What could this town offer me? I'd have to think about that. It seemed like a lot of things had been bringing me down since I got here. I felt like I'd been fighting an uphill battle nonstop. Maybe it was time for me to get a different perspective on things.

I rested my head on Mindy's shoulder while she found us a romantic comedy to watch on my laptop. I was so happy to have her here with me. She was the only good thing that had come out of my relationship with Vincent. I wouldn't have met her if I hadn't moved to Bellport with him. Friends like Mindy are rare, and I was glad we'd found each other. She was my other half.

I SPENT MOST OF SATURDAY morning by myself. Mindy slept in, and I didn't want to wake her. She liked to sleep as late as possible on the weekends. If I bugged her, she'd likely hit me. It was probably a good idea for me to be alone, anyway. Mindy's words from the night before were still floating around in my head.

When I woke up, I had a message from Peter apologizing for how we left things. He said he'd had to leave early in the morning to go out of town on business but wanted to have dinner when he got back. He wanted to apologize in person, and so did I. I was dying to see him again despite what happened between us.

At breakfast, Betty told me stories about the town when it was first established and how it evolved over the years. She gave me a key to Peter's house and a recipe for my apology dinner. I figured a home-cooked meal would go a long way. I just hoped he wouldn't mind that I was breaking in.

After checking the fridge and making a list of things I'd need for my dinner, I made a cup of coffee and sat down on his back porch. It was so peaceful and quiet. I could get used to something like this. I loved it here, and it pained me to think about leaving.

His bedroom was surprisingly tidy, aside from some clothes on the floor. I picked up one of his t-shirts and inhaled deeply. It smelled like pine, laundry detergent and a hint of musk. Manly, and all Peter. I imagined him wearing it for a run and then realized it was probably gross and tossed it in the hamper next to his closet.

The bathroom wasn't hard to find since it was the only other room at this end of the house. I washed my hands and then snooped around. He was neat for a bachelor. Everything was put away, either in the medicine cabinet above the sink or the drawers and cabinet below. The sink and toilet were clean. I had expected to find beard clippings in the sink and a dirty ring around the toilet.

Peter never ceased to amaze me. I missed him, and that surprised me. We didn't really know each other, and already I had deep feelings for him. It was kind of weird that he was Vincent's younger brother. A fact I forgot most of the time. He was so different from everyone else in his family. So kind and honest. He cared about people and helped them when they needed it.

Mindy texted to let me know she was awake, and I told her where I was and about my plan. She drove down to pick me up, and we met up with Sid and Frank for lunch at Sandy's. After lunch, we walked around Grand Street and Main Street, visiting shops and talking to people in town.

Mindy stopped again in front of the vacant storefront on Grand Street and peered in. It was going to be tough to convince my friend to return home. I could understand why. This place was like a little slice of heaven wrapped up in love and kindness.

It was a nice reprieve from my normal life. Sometimes I even wondered if it was real, then I'd pinch myself and still be standing on the street taking in all the shops and people milling about. Life really could be like this.

"What are you thinking about?" Mindy asked, startling me.

"Nothing."

"Peter?"

"I was actually just thinking about how hard it would be for you to go back home; I don't even want to leave here myself. I see the way you keep looking at that store. Is there something I should know?" I asked. Mindy's cheeks turned pink. I smiled. She almost never blushed.

"Nothing at all. I've just been daydreaming. You know I have my store back home. I've been generating a lot of clients. I'm in no position to move," Mindy said.

I studied her face. I could tell she was lying. I let it go, though, because honestly, I'd been doing a lot of lying lately, too. Mostly to myself.

"What's the hold-up ladies?" Frank called out.

"Nothing! Geez, can't we just stop and talk for a minute?" Mindy snapped.

"Listen here, Gingersnap, you don't always have to be so mean," Frank said, towering over her.

Mindy rolled her eyes and stuck out her hip. I bit back a laugh. The two of them were always bickering. There were feelings there that they were trying to fight. If only things were different, maybe the two of them could do something about that sexual tension. It was palpable.

But Mindy and I were leaving soon. Feelings or not, this was not our life. We'd just have to accept that and move on. It would be a lot harder for me to accept than Mindy. She still denied her attraction to Frank.

"What's the matter, Slick? Can't take it?" Mindy teased.

"Oh, I can take it. The real question is, can you be nice?"

I glanced at Mindy. There was a fire blazing in her bright green eyes, and I honestly feared for Frank.

"I know how to be nice," she said, trying to stand up taller. Frank still had her by over a foot.

She poked Frank in the chest. Caught off balance, he stumbled back a step.

"You don't deserve nice. You're an arrogant, insensitive asshole. You're whiny and used to getting your way. Let me tell you something, buddy; you will never get your way with me!" She shoved past him, her curls slapping him in the arm.

Frank cracked a smile as he watched her stomp down the street. "Aren't you going to go after little miss spitfire?" he asked me with a grin.

"On my way. See you guys later," I called out, as I hurried to catch up with Mindy.

"I hate that guy!" Mindy shouted.

She was walking so fast I could barely keep up. Of course, I was wearing heels again. When would I learn?

"He's cocky and rude. I'm so glad I'm going home tomorrow. I hope I never have to see him again."

I chose my words very carefully. I'd never met someone who could square off against Mindy. I think she and Frank would be good together if they'd stop going at each other's throats. Although that might make for some really great sex.

"Don't you think you're being a little harsh? He's just having fun."

"Not harsh enough!" she shouted. "I bet no one, especially not a woman, has ever put that man in his place." Man, was she fired up. I decided to just drop it.

I followed her through the park and back to Main Street. We stopped at Grateful Cup to get a coffee. Mindy spotted Frank through the doors and stayed outside, still stewing. Her arms were crossed, she had a scowl on her face, and her toe was tapping on the ground.

I hurried inside to order our drinks. Frank saw me, and then looked around, spotting Mindy outside. He smirked, and she flipped him off.

Mindy and I took our coffees to the grocery store just outside town. She dropped me off at Peter's so I could get ready and start dinner. My phone rang just as I set all the groceries down on the kitchen table. I couldn't fight the smile that spread across my face. It was Peter.

"Hey, are you on your way back yet?" I asked.

"I wish. I'm finishing up here, and I should be on my way home soon. Are you still okay getting together tonight?"

The sound of his deep voice sent butterflies flitting through my stomach. I couldn't wait to see him. To tell him how sorry I was and put all of this behind us. I was nervous and excited to tell him I would accept his answer for the project and put an end to this once and for all.

Earlier today, as I was walking to his house, I'd decided that my job and life back home were lonely. I was living a life I had created with Vincent, and I needed to move on. I'd already grown attached to Oak Springs and the people in it. Now I needed to figure out what was next for me.

"Mm hmm," I said, trying to hide my smile. I was terrible at keeping secrets, and I hoped he couldn't tell something was going on.

"Okay, great! I should be back to town around six. I need to go home and unload my stuff, and then I'll be all yours for the night." That last part came out a husky rasp, and it sent chills down my spine.

"Sounds great." I rolled my eyes at my response. I couldn't be seductive or flirty. I didn't even think I knew how.

I hung up the phone and got to work. Betty had given me the recipe for one of Peter's favorite dishes. I had copied it to my phone to save for the future. Just in case. I'd also brought over the little red dress I bought the other day when I went shopping with Mindy. I wanted to seduce him. It would feel awkward for me, but maybe if I opened myself up completely and gave him my heart, my words would just flow naturally.

Chapter 22

PETER

AT SIX FIFTEEN, I PULLED into town with a cramp in my leg from driving so much. I felt satisfied with my trip, and now I could put it aside and focus on Kate. I was glad she'd agreed to meet with me and let me apologize. I hated that we couldn't do it earlier, but I'd needed to see Kelly in person, and it had been worth it.

I pulled into my driveway and cut the engine. Lights were on in my house, and I wondered who the hell could be inside. No one except Aunt Betty had a key.

My foot hit the porch, and I swore I heard the low hum of music coming from inside. I slowly turned the knob; the door was unlocked. Light flooded the doorway, music danced around me, and the smell of roasting meat filled my nose. I dropped my bag and followed my nose and ears.

As I got closer to the kitchen, the music became recognizable as the rich sound of Etta James pouring from the speaker of a phone. I stopped in the doorway. Kate was standing there in bare feet and a tight red dress that hugged her in all the right places. The hem of the dress ended inches above her knees, exposing her incredible long legs. My jeans got tight as my dick swelled and tried to fight its way out of them.

I slumped against the doorway and watched her. She swayed to the music and sang along. Her voice was soft and melodic, warm and inviting. It was like magic, and I was caught in its spell. I didn't know she could sing. Add that to the ever-growing list of things I liked about her.

She turned around and jumped back against the counter, startled. "Oh."

I told myself this was supposed to be a night for apologies, that we had unfinished business, but I couldn't help myself. The urge to touch her, kiss her, and taste her was too strong. I stalked toward her. Her eyes widened as she watched me approach. Her tongue darted out and wet her bottom lip. Then she sank her top teeth into her plump bottom lip, and that was it.

All my reserve slipped, and I pulled her against me, pressing my lips to hers. She just stood there frozen, arms pinned at her side. I was moving too fast, like a freight train going off the rails. After a few seconds, she kissed me back with fury, and it only sped the train up.

Her body melded perfectly to mine, fitting there like it belonged. Her lips parted on a sigh, and I slowly pushed my tongue into her mouth. When her tongue wrapped with mine, I groaned. Bending at the knees, I ran my hands up her legs to her delectable ass. I gave it a gentle squeeze before I lifted her up and set her on the countertop.

She pushed her fingers into my hair while her lips connected with mine. This time, it was her tongue that delved into my mouth. I was losing the battle with my control. She smelled like that damn vanilla and tasted like honey. My dick strained against my jeans, begging to be free.

Kate's hands were wild, moving from my hair down my back, to my arms, and then over my chest. She tugged at the hem of my shirt, attempting to remove it. I needed to slow this back down, take back control. Even though I was just as wild for her, I needed to be sure she wanted this. I pulled away, taking a second to look at her.

She was beautiful with her flushed cheeks and swollen lips. Before I could say anything, she reached out, grabbed the back of my neck, and pulled me back in. The kiss was needy and rough. I didn't have to ask; she was as ready for this as I was.

I moved one hand up to the back of her neck to deepen the kiss, while my other hand trailed down her chest toward those gorgeous breasts that I couldn't stop thinking about. I'd had them in my mouth and in my hands once already, and I knew they were perfect.

The thin fabric of the dress did nothing to hide her hardened nipples, which meant she wasn't wearing a bra. My pulse picked up and my dick throbbed painfully against my zipper. I cupped her breast, and she moaned, pushing her breast into my hand. I flicked her nipple through the fabric while my tongue invaded her mouth. She let out a small whimper that I swallowed down.

Her hands moved to my belt, struggling to undo it. God, did I want her to undo it. I needed her to free me from the confines of my pants. They felt like a straitjacket for my junk. If I didn't get them off soon, I was going to lose all feeling down there.

Despite my desperation to get her naked, I wanted to take this slowly. To savor what was happening between us. I moved my hips back, just out of her reach, and I swear my dick groaned.

"Slow down, baby," I murmured against her lips.

"I can't," she panted.

She pulled my shirt up and over my head, and then trailed kisses and tiny bites from my neck down to my chest. I growled. My barely maintained restraint slipped. Somewhere in the back of my mind, I knew that we needed to talk, to get on even ground, but I couldn't seem to make that part of my brain work.

I grabbed her wrists and pinned them above her head against the cabinets. I cuffed them with one hand and slid my other hand up her dress. She closed her eyes as I skimmed over her hip. I paused and looked up at her.

"Look at me, Kate," I demanded, tracing her panty line with my finger.

Her eyes opened and locked with mine as I slipped my hand into her panties and cupped her. She gasped, and then pushed her hips forward, seeking more. I wanted her to give herself over to me, not just physically, though. I wanted it all.

"Open your legs for me, baby. Stay with me and don't look away."

Her legs dropped open, and I slid between them, locking them in place. I never took my eyes off hers. I needed this connection, needed to know she was right here with me. My heart was connected to hers. The pull between us consumed me, pulling me under like a strong current.

My finger moved up her slit, feeling how wet she was for me. Her legs spread wider, granting me full access. I took her mouth while I slid my finger into her tight channel and then slowly back out. I nearly came in my damn jeans. Her eyes shut, her back arched, and she gasped. I pushed in a little deeper, and she moaned a little louder.

"Open your eyes, Kate," I ground out. I wanted her eyes on me while I pleasured her, and I wanted to watch her lose control and give herself to me.

Blue eyes held my gaze. I repositioned my hand to get a better angle then watched her eyes as I pushed two fingers into her.

"Yes!" she screamed, arching her back again. Her eyes nearly rolled back in her head.

I curled my fingers and pushed in deeper while my thumb ran over that little bundle of nerves at her center. I kept up the pace until she was shaking her head back and forth, moaning and panting.

"That's it, baby, let go," I said, seeking her release.

"Oh God, yes! I'm coming!" she screamed.

Her body tensed as she pulsed around my fingers. She squeezed them almost painfully as her orgasm overtook her. Her back arched, and her mouth formed an O. Then she collapsed forward into my arms, her forehead resting against mine while she tried to regain control of her breathing. She whimpered and moaned through a few more spasms. It was the most beautiful thing I had ever seen, and I wanted to do it over and over again.

I pulled my fingers out of her, and she shuddered. Her hands dropped to hang around my neck like limp noodles when I released my hold on her wrists. I chuckled. She was still trembling, and I mentally patted myself on the back for a job well done.

I'd like to say it was my skills, but I'd be lying. It was our connection. Her body responded to me, and mine called out to hers. I'd never felt this connected to someone before. It scared the shit out of me, but I wanted more.

Grabbing her ass, I scooped her off the counter like she was a meal. I was hungry and ready for a feast. She looked so damn sexy. Her swollen lips were the perfect shade of just-kissed pink. She looked sated, and I was happy to be the one to put that look on her face. However, I wasn't done yet.

"I need to lay you down; I need to be inside you," I growled, looking for a spot to set her down. I was growing impatient.

The kitchen table was in front of me, and she'd decorated it so nicely. I really didn't want to ruin it, but I couldn't wait any longer. It was my shit anyway. With a swipe of my arm, I cleared the top, sending plates and dishes crashing to the floor. Kate looked at the mess and then back at me, her eyes wide with shock.

I laid her down on the table and shrugged. I took a step back to look at her. "God, you're beautiful."

Color flooded her cheeks again. I stepped forward and grabbed her dress, pushing it slowly up her thighs. She leaned back and lifted her arms for me. I pulled the fabric up and over her head, licking my lips as her breasts bounced free.

Leaning forward, I sucked one into my mouth while I palmed the other. Kate tipped her head back and moaned when I tugged on her nipple. Her hands moved between us, her fingers quickly undoing my belt. She lowered my zipper and shoved at my jeans in an attempt to push them down.

I stepped back, her breast falling from my mouth with a "pop," and shucked my shoes and jeans. Her teeth ran over her bottom lip as she took me in, making my dick jump. I ran a hand over myself and watched her eyes darken as she followed my movements. Damn, I wanted her pretty mouth on me.

"You're even better than I imagined. You're perfect." Her eyes trailed over my body from head to toe.

"Better than you imagined, huh? You've thought about me naked?" I asked, my voice a husky rasp.

"More than once," she said confidently. I smiled. I had pictured her naked many times, too. Some of the best material for when I was in the shower or just before bed had been of her.

She moved forward to the edge of the table and dangled her bare feet off the end. Then, she grabbed hold of me and squeezed. My eyes nearly rolled back in my head. That little amount of contact had me almost going off like a horny teenager first discovering his dick.

Her hand ran up and down my length. My eyes slammed shut, and I ground my molars together. I was about to lose it, and we still had our underwear on.

"Slow down, or this will be over too fast," I warned.

That didn't seem to stop Kate's busy hands. She jumped off the table and knelt, yanking my boxer briefs down. My cock stood at attention, saluting her. She wrapped her hand around the base, and swirled her tongue around the head, licking off the small bead of wetness at the top.

She wrapped her lips around me and took me into her mouth slowly, all the way to the back of her throat. I moaned and rocked my hips forward. She sucked hard while she pumped me with her hand. I was losing my damn mind, seeing stars. I had to stop this. I wanted to be inside her.

"Kate, stop," I begged.

She wasn't listening or slowing down. She sucked harder and drew me deeper, if that was possible, into her mouth. My balls tightened, and I felt a tingling starting at the base of my spine. I had to stop her.

I pulled her up by her arms to a standing position. I bent at the knees, lifted her and set her down on the edge of the table, positioning myself between her legs. The only thing standing between me and her warm center was her tiny black thong, which I took a second to appreciate because I was a lace man. Then I pulled it down her thighs and over her ankles, tossing it to the side.

Her head popped up as I sat down in a chair and positioned my head between her legs. "Peter, wait."

"Do you want me to stop?"

She nibbled on her bottom lip, then shook her head. "I just want you inside me."

"I will, baby. Let me taste you first. Relax your legs," I said, tapping on her thigh. She opened them, and I placed a gentle kiss over her folds.

Using my forearms to hold her thighs wide, I gently parted her and then flicked my tongue against her clit. Her legs quivered, so I did it again. She cried out and lay down so her back was resting on the table.

Her legs fell completely open. She was giving herself to me, and I got to work thanking her. Licking down her center and dipping my tongue inside, tasting the sweet nectar. She tasted like honey there, too. So damn delicious I lost myself in her.

Her fingers gripped my shoulders, her nails digging into them. She moaned loudly, but I wanted more. I wanted to make her scream. To give herself over to the pleasure. I moved my tongue in short quick strokes, then flattened it and licked from bottom to top, flicking my tongue at the top.

Her legs quivered, and she writhed beneath me. She gripped my hair and ground her hips into my face, taking what she wanted. I gave her everything and feasted on her like a dying man. She let out a scream and held my head in place while she convulsed and pulsed onto my tongue.

I lapped at her and thrust two fingers in, twisting them. It was like I'd hit a button inside of her. Her scream grew louder and she twisted around me. I stood up, dug a condom out of my wallet, and rolled it on. Just when she was about to come down, I spread her legs wide and thrust inside her.

She cried out and nearly ripped my hair from my scalp. I paused and let her adjust to me. She was so tight, I almost lost it instantly. She fit around me like a suit made just for my dick. I let out a guttural moan and counted to ten. My teeth ground together, and my jaw clenched so tight it almost snapped.

"Are you okay?" I gritted out.

"Hell yes," she said, looking up at me. When her eyes locked with mine, I knew I was a goner.

"Peter?"

"Yeah?"

"Move. Please."

She didn't need to ask me twice; I pulled out and thrust back inside her. I repeated the movement twice more, changing the angle to hit that spot I had found with my fingers. She screamed and clenched around me. I never wanted to forget this moment.

She was squeezing me tight, milking my orgasm from me, but I held out, waiting for her orgasm to stop so I could regain a little control. I wanted this to be memorable for us both. I wanted her to remember every detail from tonight. The way she felt, the way we were together. How well I fit inside her. This was so much more than just sex for me, and I hoped to God she felt it too.

I started to move again, finding my rhythm. She wrapped her legs around me and pulled me closer, pushing me deeper inside her. I growled and leaned forward, gripping the edges of the table for support, and thrust in harder. She wrapped herself tightly around me, hanging on for the ride.

"Yes, harder!" she screamed.

I moved at a furious pace. Our bodies slid together, slicked with sweat. She dug her nails into my back, and I bit her shoulder. I needed more. I lifted my head and crashed my lips against hers. One of her arms wrapped around my back, the other around the back of my head holding me in place. The kiss was so deep it ripped me in two.

My hips continued to piston into her while she held me in place. My fingers were going numb from gripping the table. Her legs shook around me. I loved the effect I had on her, how intense her orgasms were, and how many times I had been able to make her come. I'd actually lost count. She dropped her head back and screamed as she fell apart around me again. She was squeezing my dick like a vice, pulling my orgasm from me.

A roar ripped from my throat and I spilled into her with such force that I nearly blacked out. Stars floated in my vision, and I squeezed my eyes shut and fell against her. My legs nearly gave out, but I forced myself to stay standing. She grabbed onto me and pulled me down to the table with her.

Sex with Kate was like nothing I'd ever experienced. So intense, so intimate. I'd never connected to someone like that before. I wrapped my arms tightly around her and held her close. She was mine, made just for me. Now that I found her, I'd never let her go. There wouldn't ever be anyone else for me

Chapter 23

KATE

THE SETTING SUN SPILLED through the back window casting a romantic hue in the room. Sex with Peter was better than I ever could have imagined. It was unexpected, too. We were supposed to talk tonight, and I wanted to apologize for the way I had acted. Apparently, he forgave me.

Peter was still breathing heavily, sprawled out next to me, legs hanging off the side of the table. I lifted my head and looked at the place settings I had laid out so carefully, now scattered on the floor, and giggled.

"I won't ever be able to eat here again without thinking about this," he said, looking around, too.

My cheeks burned, and I threw a hand over my face. The cool air hit my naked body, and I shivered. Peeking out from under my arm, I saw his retreating form.

I propped myself up on my arms. "Where are you going?"

"To get some water. Do you want some?"

I smiled. "Water sounds great. Thanks."

He ran back over and kissed me on the forehead. "Okay. Don't move."

I studied his perfectly chiseled back muscles and ass as they flexed while he walked to the sink. I couldn't take my eyes off him. He was perfect, and no man would ever compare.

Resting my head back down on the table, I closed my eyes, feeling sated. My muscles ached, and I was ready for sleep. Emotions swirled inside me and I pushed them down. Tonight, I just wanted to enjoy his company. I wanted to bask in the happiness that Peter brought into my life and forget about everything else.

"Mmm, I know what I'm having for dessert," Peter said, bringing me out of my thoughts.

My eyes snapped open, and I craned my neck to look at him. Leaning against the wall holding two glasses of water, he looked sexy as hell. His eyes were hungry as they raked over my naked body.

If I wasn't already naked, his eyes would have undressed me. I didn't know if I had the strength to go again. I'd never orgasmed that much in my life, let alone in one night. I needed food first.

"Oh, no! Dinner!" I shouted, flying off the table.

I rushed past Peter, into the kitchen, and flung open the oven. The roast appeared to be okay. I took it out of the oven and set it on the stovetop. I'd made a glaze that still needed to be poured over the top of the roast, then it had to rest for a little longer.

"Looks delicious," Peter said, kissing me on the head. His big arms wrapped around me, and his body molded to mine. I resisted the urge to moan at the feel of his hard length pressed against my ass. "How did you know that was one of my favorite dinners?"

"It's my secret," I breathed. "It should be ready in about five minutes."

He spun me around, his hard length now pressing into my stomach. "Then we have just enough time."

He nibbled a trail from my ear down my neck, and I shivered. I wrapped my arms around his neck and let out the moan I had been holding back.

"I don't want it to get cold. I worked hard on it," I said on a whimper. His tongue trailed over my collarbone, and his lips latched onto the spot where it met my neck. "Peter, please."

He growled. "I like it when you beg. Are you begging me to continue?"

He dipped his head back down and trailed his tongue over my chest, heading straight for my breasts. I pulled his head up, stopping him. "No. It's a please let's eat the dinner I made."

He groaned. "Okay. Fine. Let's at least get some clothes on so I can enjoy it without getting distracted."

He slapped my ass before walking away. I loved this playful side to him. It was new and unexpected. I was sure not many people got to see the more relaxed version of him. He was very professional most of the time. When he wasn't all business, he was caring and nurturing. I suspected it was because he felt he needed to take care of others.

Since the table was out of the question, we ate dinner out on the back porch. Peter was wearing his jeans with the button undone. He claimed it was to give him more room for dinner, but I think it was so he could shuck them off quickly.

I couldn't concentrate on any of his questions. I couldn't take my eyes off his broad muscular chest. He had another black and gray tattoo over the left side of his chest, a lion's head. I wanted to lick it.

"What do you think?" he asked. I didn't know what he was talking about. I hadn't been listening to him.

"I think it sounds great," I lied.

He smiled. "You weren't even listening to me. What are you thinking about?"

I felt the warmth creeping into my cheeks. *Damn traitorous cheeks.* "Nothing."

"Ok, I'll let you off the hook this time. Do you want some coffee?"

I jumped up. "Yes, but I'll get it."

Peter's eyes turned dark, and a wicked grin spread across his face. I knew what that look meant. His tongue darted out and ran across his lips as his eyes raked over me, sending a shiver down my body. I wore only his t-shirt, which barely covered my ass. Now that I was standing, Peter could see it all. My nipples hardened through the fabric, giving away the effect his predatory gaze had on me.

I made a run for the door. Peter didn't hesitate and was right on my heels in two strides. I squealed as he caught me by my midsection and swung me around. Then he lifted me up and slowly lowered me down his body. My legs wrapped around his waist, and he pressed his hips up into me. My stomach did a flip as emotions flooded me. I had never wanted someone so badly before.

It was more than physical. There was such a deep emotional connection between us. We'd been fighting it since we met, but I had felt the current that passed between us that first night. The spark we had. But our personalities matched, too. He was good for me, and I liked to think I was good for him.

His hands gripped my bare ass while his lips crashed down on mine. My fingers wrapped into his hair, and he grunted when I ground my hips down onto him. I wanted him to push me against the wall. To take what he wanted from me. I'd never wanted to give myself over like that before, but I trusted Peter.

Peter carried me to his bedroom and tossed me onto the bed, keeping his eyes locked onto mine as he shucked his jeans and palmed his impressive erection. He was thick and long. He stretched and filled me in a way no other man had. I knew he'd ruined me for anyone else. No one could compare.

Desire pooled between my legs. The look in his eye made me feel so sexy, so desired. I wanted him—no, I needed him inside me.

I ran my tongue along my bottom lip and sat up onto my knees. Crossing my arms over my body, I pulled his shirt slowly up and over my head. I had never felt this confident before. Peter made me feel like a goddess. Like he wanted to worship every inch of my body. It was a feeling like no other.

He knelt on the bed in front of me. Taking his time, he looked me over. His fingers, so rough from all his hard work, gently ran up my arm to my shoulder. His eyes followed the path of his fingers, setting my skin on fire. He trailed his fingers over my shoulder, down between my breasts, across my stomach, and over the subtle curve of my hip. My body vibrated from want and need. Just his touch had me falling apart.

"You're so fucking beautiful," he groaned.

His hand dropped to his side; only his eyes stayed on me. It felt like he was touching me everywhere. My body hummed with desire, like a live current running through me.

It was my turn to touch him. I traced my fingers up his strong forearms, pausing to trace that tattoo I loved so much. Then I continued on over his impressive biceps to his broad shoulders. On a shaky inhale, I slowly trailed my fingers down his irresistible chest, resisting the urge to run my tongue over it, and down to his washboard abs.

Running my fingers over each one and feeling them flex was too much. I wrapped my hand around the base of his erection and watched his face as I squeezed him, running my fist slowly up his length. My thumb dusted over the head, spreading the wetness that was already leaking there before sliding back down to the base.

He tipped his head back, and his eyes slid closed. He growled, low and husky, and I felt it all the way to my core. I smiled, feeling powerful, and was about to repeat the motion when he grabbed my wrist, pulling my hand away.

He pushed me down onto the bed. I watched as he grabbed a condom from the bedside table, slid it down his length, and then settled between my legs.

"No more playing around. I need to be inside you."

Our lips connected, and all gentleness disappeared. I didn't want to go slow anymore. I wanted him to lose control and show me how badly he wanted me. I was dying inside with my lust for him. His mouth consumed mine while his hands roamed over my body, but it still wasn't enough.

The tip of him rested against my soaking, aching center. I wrapped my legs around his waist, trying to push him inside. He pulled back from the kiss and looked into my eyes. I froze. His bright green eyes looked so deep into my soul, it almost scared me. His hands cupped my face, and he brushed a thumb over my cheek.

My breath caught, and time stood still. Without a word, he pushed into me slowly, and I felt every inch of him as he buried himself inside me. I felt everything, especially the emotions passing between us. His eyes never left mine, and his hands still cupped my face. He moved so slowly it was almost agonizing. The intensity in his eyes was too much. It was all too much, and it scared the hell out of me.

I wanted him to lose control, to take me. This deep connection was ripping my soul open, and I felt exposed. I needed to break the connection, and fast. I pushed at him, hoping he'd take a hint. He did, and we rolled together, never breaking contact until he was on his back. Now on top, I rode him at a furious pace, chasing my orgasm.

"Kate," he said through gritted teeth.

His fingers dug into my hips, and I knew he was trying to hold back. I leaned forward and gripped the headboard to steady myself. I ground down on him before coming back up slowly while rocking my hips, finding my rhythm. His eyes snapped shut, and I could see his jaw working while he tried to remain in control.

I tried a variation on the camel pose from yoga class. I arched my back, placing my hands on his calves behind me and letting my head hang down. I moved my hips up and down. The angle felt amazing, and I cried out from the pleasure. My eyes were nearly rolling back in my head.

"Shit!" he growled.

A shudder ran through his body. I was close to my orgasm, so I kept up the pace. Peter gripped my arms and pulled me forward, locking them down next to his head. He stared into my eyes as he drove his hips up into me at a rapid pace. I screamed and dropped my head forward, my hair draping around us. His eyes bore into me, and the connection I had tried so hard to break came back stronger than ever.

He thrust up hard into me one last time, and I felt him pulse inside me with his release. His orgasm, coupled with our intense eye lock, pushed me over the edge. My body tingled everywhere, and I screamed out as my orgasm overtook me. It felt like I burst into a million tiny pieces. Energy zipped through me as my body shook and contracted around him. Squeezing him.

"Shit, that's tight," he ground out around clenched teeth.

He pushed his hips up, hitting a spot that intensified everything. I screamed again and shook harder. My body burned from head to toe as intense pleasure consumed me. I collapsed into his arms, and we melted together into the mattress. Peter wrapped his arms tightly around me and kissed my neck.

Sweat soaked my hair, and it stuck to my neck and the side of my face. Our bodies suctioned together, but I couldn't have cared less. I never wanted to leave his embrace. He broke me. This wasn't sex, it was so much more. A tear slipped down my face. I wanted to be with Peter forever, but it just wasn't possible. For many reasons. Walking away from him was going to tear me to pieces.

"I GUESS WE SHOULD PROBABLY talk about last night now, huh?" Peter asked, running his fingers gently up and down my back.

I chuckled into his chest. "Are you sure we aren't past that? I think I've forgiven you."

"Either that, or we just had some amazing hate sex."

I pinched his side, and he yelped. My whole body shook from his deep rumbling laugh.

"Let's get some ice cream, and then we can talk," he said, sliding out from under me. "I'll be right back."

He smiled at me before heading out of the room stark naked. I giggled and let out a loud sigh before snuggling under his covers. Not wanting Mindy to worry about me, I typed out a quick message to her, and then turned off my phone. Anything she had to say could wait until tomorrow. I didn't want to ruin the evening with Peter.

My head was already a cloudy mess. It felt like we were living in a fantasy bubble. I knew that once the bubble popped, we'd have to deal with reality. I still had a life that wasn't in Oak Springs. How would the two of us work, even if my job wasn't a factor?

I didn't want to think about it. It felt like bad heartburn, and I had to rub at my chest.

"You okay?" Peter asked. He stood just inside the door with two bowls of ice cream in his hands.

"Yeah. I'm fine. Just a little heartburn," I lied.

"Here, this might help." He handed me a bowl of ice cream. "Someone told me it was one of your favorites. It happens to be mine, too."

I sat up and looked down at the bowl filled with Layered Caramel Bourbon Delight and smiled. Peter settled back against the headboard, and then pulled me between his legs so my back was resting against his chest. It felt natural, like we did this all the time.

"Let's talk," he said around a bite of ice cream. He moaned. "God, this is so good."

"Okay, let's talk." I took a bite of ice cream and held in my own moan. It really was fantastic.

"I'm sorry for how I handled last night," he said. "I shouldn't have snapped at you."

"I understand. I was the one in the wrong. You were just telling me how much this place meant to you, and all I could think about was what that meant for me. It was selfish of me. After spending some time here and around town, I realized that this proposal isn't right," I said.

He set down his bowl of ice cream on his nightstand and then mine. His hands gripped my waist and spun me around so I was straddling him.

"What are you saying?"

I took a deep breath. "Most of the small towns we've developed have, in fact, been dying. We've swooped in and saved them, and now they're flourishing. Your town, however, is flourishing on its own. You don't need help from our company. In fact, if we built the condos and strip mall here, it would hurt the town instead. I don't do things unless I believe in them one hundred percent. And this is something I'm not all in on."

His smile lit up his face, and he looked so handsome. "You have no idea how happy it makes me to hear you say that."

I chewed on my lip. "Don't get too excited. I still haven't told Mr. Lawrence. I also haven't decided what I'm going to do now. I just wanted you to know that I won't push this on you anymore, and I'll accept your refusal of the development."

He kissed me deeply and then laid me back onto the bed. "Let me show you how happy this makes me." He kissed a trail down my stomach. "There is nothing standing between us anymore. Together, we can work the rest of the details out. Everything will be fine."

I wanted to believe him, but I couldn't. My life was far away from here. This time with Peter was amazing, but it wasn't my life. I was living in a dream, and it was only a matter of time before I'd have to wake up and get back to reality.

Chapter 24

KATE

MY EYES SLOWLY OPENED as a smile stretched across my face. The soreness in my muscles was a pleasant reminder of the things Peter and I had done the night before. I felt alive and refreshed for the first time in a long time. But the other side of the bed was empty and cold. Peter wasn't there. Instead, I found a note on his pillow.

Good morning, beautiful,

It was so hard to leave you, and I didn't want to wake you. I had to be in the office early. There is coffee in the kitchen; please help yourself. Meet me at my office at eleven. I have to talk to you about a few things.

See you soon,

Peter

I sat up and stretched, taking a few minutes to breathe and center myself. I slipped on Peter's t-shirt, the same one I had worn last night, and headed into the kitchen. Tucking the note away safely in my purse, I poured myself a cup of coffee and went to sit on the back porch.

This would be the last time I would ever see this view, and I added it to the growing list of memories I had of the town. It wouldn't be easy to forget this place. Leaving Peter meant I'd be leaving a piece of my heart here. I wiped a stray tear from my face and focused on the backyard and the way the sunlight spilled through the canopy of trees, lighting a path in the yard. So beautiful.

After I finished my coffee, I called Mindy for a ride. Next, I washed out my coffee mug and placed it on the drying rack beside the sink. I picked up the dishes from last night and loaded them into the dishwasher. I did a final wipe down of the counters before going in search of something to wear.

I borrowed a pair of Peter's basketball shorts and stuffed my red dress into my purse. I'd have to wear my heels, but I'd manage. With my hair piled on top of my head, I went to wait for Mindy to arrive.

A sense of emptiness pulled at me as I looked around the living room one more time. Today was the last time I'd see him. The last time we'd spend time together. Things had to end between us no matter how much we didn't want them to. My chest ached at the thought of losing him. I had finally found someone who made me happy.

We both knew this was only temporary. That we couldn't be together long-term. That's why I'd kept my distance from him. Pushed so hard to remain professional. Until last night. I was here to do a job. And now, even though I wasn't going through with it, I still had to return home and deliver the news to my boss. I had to try to fight for my job despite my failure.

Mindy pulled up in front of Peter's house and honked. I ran out barefoot with my heels in hand and dove into the back seat of her car.

"Okay, go!" I shouted.

Mindy slowly turned around and looked down at me sprawled out across the back seat and avoiding the windows. I probably looked like a lunatic; I sure felt like one.

"Whatcha doing?" She asked with a smirk.

"Everyone in town is so nosy, and I don't want them to know I stayed here last night."

Mindy nodded. "Uh huh, and you think this makes a difference?"

"Not as long as you keep sitting here, it doesn't. Will you please just go?" I asked, peeking out the window and scanning the area.

Mindy laughed as she put the car into reverse and pulled out of the driveway. My heart ached more and more the farther we got away from Peter's house. It filled me with overwhelming sadness. As much as I didn't want to leave, it was time to go home. To face my life.

Last night, things had changed between Peter and me and saying goodbye would be painful. I could feel it deep down inside. My heart was going to break.

"Do you know the old ladies have a book club that they use as a disguise for their gossip group?" Mindy asked over her cup of coffee. We were back at The B&B, and she was sitting cross-legged on my bed. Her suitcase sat on the floor next to her; she had checked out and planned to head home this afternoon.

"What?" I nearly shrieked as I spun around from my suitcase.

Mindy nodded. "Frank told me about them. It's Mrs. Anderson and her three friends, Ethel, Mary Ann, and Rose. He said they called themselves 'the reading chicks,' but they don't really do much reading, according to people around town. They mostly gossip, so the town started calling them 'the gossip hens.'"

She laughed and took another sip of her coffee like it was no big deal. I was horrified.

Ignoring me, she continued. "They're always trying to print a gossip column in the town newspaper or something, but Peter's always shutting it down. Apparently, there's an online paper already. God, I love this town."

She fell back onto my bed and sighed. Meanwhile, I was dying inside. What if someone had seen me leaving Peter's house? Or arriving there, and then leaving this morning? This could be terrible.

"What's the website?"

"What?" she asked, finally looking at me.

"The name of the website or the paper or whatever. I need to see if I'm in it."

Mindy sat up fully, "Kate, calm down. It's just for fun. Frank said they just approved a 'Daily Happenings' page, but the first one hasn't come out yet."

"What if there's a gossip blog or something?" I asked, pacing.

Mindy laughed. "That'd be awesome. I mean not for you, of course. It would just add to the town's quirkiness."

I stopped pacing. "If you're not going to help me, then get the hell out."

Mindy's eyes widened, and she pulled out her phone. After clicking around for a few minutes, she handed it over to me. I scrolled through the online paper and looked for any mention of me or Peter. Of course, Peter was in there; he was the mayor, but from what I could tell, there wasn't a link between the two of us.

I handed her phone back and plopped down on the bed with a sigh. "This is so stressful. I need to get out of here."

"Soon enough. Why don't you finish getting ready and tell me about last night?" Mindy asked.

As I got ready for my meeting with Peter, I told Mindy all about my night. Leaving out the explicit details, even though she pushed hard to get them out of me. My phone rang on the bed, and Mindy picked it up to check who it was.

"It's your boss," she said.

I shook my head, and she put the phone down. I was getting annoyed with his lack of faith and confidence in me. Even though this development wouldn't happen, it was for good reason. I had a plan for another town that we could look at already brewing in my head. I knew how to do my job, and I was damn good at it. He didn't need to keep checking up on me.

I'd call him back on my way back home after I met with Peter. I'd remind him why he'd kept me around and prep him for my new proposal for a different location altogether. He'd eventually go for it if I presented it the correct way.

"Are you sure you don't want me to stay here and follow you home? Peter could use my help another day at the store, I'm sure," Mindy said from the balcony of my room. She had been running Double Oak Furnishings the past few days since Peter had yet to hire someone.

"No, I'll be all right. I won't stay long after our meeting. I'm not pursuing this deal, so it's all pretty much a formality at this point."

"Mm hmm," Mindy mumbled.

That was an odd response, especially since it was the first time I had told her I wasn't going through with the deal. I had expected her to tell me how proud of me she was, give me some type of reaction. I walked toward the balcony.

Mindy was talking quietly to someone. When I pulled back the curtain, I saw Frank standing down below on the street. He waved up at me and pulled on the back of his neck.

"Hey, Frank," I called out.

Mindy jumped and turned around. "I was just telling him to get out of here."

She walked back into the bedroom, leaving Frank standing on the street. I waved to him as he walked away.

"Is there anything you want to tell me?" I asked as I walked back into the bedroom.

"Nope. Just... good luck," Mindy said, grabbing her suitcase. She wouldn't meet my eyes.

"Did you sleep with him?"

Mindy's head snapped up. "Hell no, I did not sleep with him. He's a flirt and he's slept with most of the town. I have to go."

I didn't have time to unpack all of what was going on. I checked the time on my phone and realized I needed to be on my way to Peter's office, anyway. I ran over and threw my arms around Mindy, pulling her in close. I waited until she dropped her suitcase and hugged me back. Sometimes it took a while for her to give in, and this was one of those times. I waited it out because I really needed it.

"Thank you." I wouldn't have gotten through this trip without her.

Mindy nodded. I could see the tears in her eyes, and then she pushed away from me. She wasn't one to show a lot of emotion and she hated hugs and sappy stuff.

"You're welcome," she whispered before walking out.

I did one more quick check around the room, making sure I packed everything before leaving.

MY FOOT BOUNCED NERVOUSLY as I sat in the waiting room at Peter's office. I thought back to the first time I arrived here; I felt the same panic in the pit of my stomach. I wasn't sure what to expect this time, and he had surprised me in his office once before.

Mr. Lawrence had already called me ten times; I had to turn off my phone. I was almost positive I was going to lose my job. Did he know I wasn't going to push this through? Of course, my first failure would be because I fell in love with the guy I needed to sell on the proposal.

My eyes shot open, and I bent over, driving my head down between my knees. I couldn't seem to catch my breath. I loved him? How could this have happened? I couldn't be in love with him. We hadn't known each other long enough.

I'd always heard rumors about love at first sight, but I thought it was a myth. I stood up and paced. It was suddenly boiling hot in here. Walking over to the water cooler, I grabbed a cup off the top and punched the button for water. I would not panic. That would be the second time I'd panicked in this office, and today of all days, I needed to keep it together.

I would not tell him, that's for sure. I'd sound like a crazy person. Professing my love for him after one night of sex? Sure, that would go over well. I guzzled down a second glass of water just as Elaine called my name. Her shocked expression told me I looked as bad as I felt. My hair was up in a ponytail now so I could air out my neck, and I had slipped off my blazer.

Ignoring her for a second, I filled up my cup once more. Then I followed her back to Peter's office. The door was closed, so Elaine knocked lightly on it. As I stood waiting, I fought off the panic attack threatening to take over. What the hell was it about this place?

I took a deep breath to center myself, closed my eyes, and shoved down my emotions. I could do this. I was a professional. I'd always been good at turning off my emotions during these types of meetings before. Whenever I was around Peter, though, everything went out the window.

"Come in," he called.

Elaine opened the door and stepped to the side, letting me walk through. Peter's eyes were trained on his computer screen while he typed. I walked in and took a seat in front of his desk. My hands were sweaty, so I wiped them on my skirt. If he looked at me, would he know?

Peter had styled his hair and wore a gray pinstripe suit that fit him like a second skin. I licked my lips as I took him all in. He was so damn attractive. My stomach flipped, this time for a whole different reason. God, I was a mess.

He looked up, but instead of looking at me, he looked to the door. Why was he acting so professional? He had just seen me naked and spent the early hours of the morning inside of me. Was this only about business with a side of sex? Did he regret everything that happened between us? I pushed my emotions further down, trying to shut them off.

"Thank you, Elaine, that will be all," he said.

I let out a breath I hadn't realized I was holding, feeling relieved. I'd had no idea Elaine was still standing at the door. The door closed, and Peter stood up. He made his way around his desk and stopped in front of me. Before I could think of what to do or say, he pulled me out of my chair and wrapped me in a tight hug. He smelled amazing, and I wanted to bury my face in his neck.

My mind went back to last night with him. The way he had held me, kissed me, and made *love* to me. It was more than sex. He poured his heart into it. It was passionate and consuming. After the second time, I had fallen asleep wrapped in his arms. It was the best sleep I'd gotten in a long time.

I didn't have a handle on my emotions again. There I was thinking about love for a second time. I needed to bury those feelings deeper. I could not let him know I was falling in love with him. Nothing could happen between us. He was my client and my ex's brother.

Peter pulled back just enough to press his lips to mine, and I melted into him, forgetting the reasons we couldn't be together. My fingers wove into his hair. I tugged a little since it drove him crazy, and he groaned into my mouth in reply. I smiled against his lips, and he pressed against me harder. My pulse picked up, and I became increasingly wet.

I wrapped one leg around his waist in an attempt to get closer. He grabbed onto my leg. His calloused fingers were deliciously rough against my bare skin. He ground into my center. My head fell back, and I moaned. He kissed down the column of my neck and stopped at the top button of my shirt.

I looked down to see why he had stopped. His green eyes were now dark and hooded with lust. I ached between my legs. Every kiss he pressed to my skin lit me on fire. He stood, and my leg dropped to the floor. I watched him adjust himself before walking away toward the door.

He flipped the lock and then stalked back over to me. My heart rate picked up, and all thoughts disappeared from my brain. The heated look in his eyes set me on fire. Grabbing my hand, he tugged me over to his desk. Then he lifted me up and placed me on top of it.

Peter unbuttoned his suit coat jacket before taking a seat in his office chair. Confidence radiated off him. It was so damn sexy that my mouth watered at the site of him between my legs. His back was straight as he rolled up his shirt sleeves.

With a cocky grin on his face, he grabbed my legs and positioned them on either side of him, my feet resting on the arms of the chair. I was spread wide open for him and it made the ache between my thighs worse.

I leaned back on his desk with my hands behind me for support and gave him my best seductress look. It must have worked because he licked his lips while his fingers worked my skirt up my thighs.

His hands trailed up my legs to the lacy thong I had worn just for him. A deep rumble of appreciation rolled through his body, and I felt it between my legs. I resisted the urge to clench my thighs together for relief.

He pulled my thong down my legs and over my feet, shoving it into his pocket. I cracked a smile that quickly faded when his mouth touched me. He kissed his way up one leg and then the other, stopping at the apex of my thighs. His eyes connected with mine, and he smiled devilishly before he thrust two fingers inside me. I dropped my head back and let out a loud moan, unable to keep it in.

"Shh," he whispered against my leg, causing goosebumps to rise on my skin.

With a feather light touch, his thumb ran over my center, and I unraveled. I never used to get off fast. Not until Peter. Now my orgasms came on fast and heavy like a speeding train. All I could do was hold on for the ride.

"Look at me, baby," he said from between my quivering legs.

I looked down and locked eyes with him. He dropped his head down and licked up my seam, parting me with his tongue. I bit back a moan. His tongue dipped into my center and he moaned against me. I clasped my hand over my mouth to keep quiet. His tongue was doing amazing things. My muscles were tensing up, and I couldn't control the shake in my legs. I was close, so deliciously close.

"Right there. Don't... stop," I panted out. "Don't fucking stop."

He looked up at me and smirked before diving back in. His tongue was magic, swirling and flicking and lapping at me. I was mewling and panting, unable to hold back.

"That's it, baby. Let go," he murmured against me.

He pushed two fingers inside me, curling them as he pumped in and out. He hit the magic spot inside that made me lose all control. One more flick of his tongue, and I tore apart. My body convulsed, and I was seeing stars.

I wanted to scream so badly. Peter placed a hand over my mouth, muffling my cries. He slowed his pace and placed gentle kisses against my center, causing mini shock waves through my body. It wasn't until I looked down that I realized my hands were around his head, smashing his face against my center.

"I'm so sorry," I said, releasing my grip on him.

He smirked. "Never apologize for that. You taking what you want from me like that is the hottest thing I've ever experienced."

I felt my cheeks burning, but before I could say anything, he gripped my hips and pulled me toward him. He wrapped me up in a hug and kissed the side of my head. My legs were still shaky, and pleasure coursed through me, spreading from the center out. I felt amazing. It was pure bliss.

"Kate, look at me," he whispered into my ear.

I opened my eyes and tilted my head to look into his gorgeous green ones. They burned with passion, but also something else I couldn't place at the moment. Eyes locked with mine, he slowly inched himself inside. I gasped as he slowly stretched me.

We moaned together as he filled me completely. I would never get tired of that feeling. I grasped his powerful arms and held on. He started moving at a slow and sensual pace.

I was already on the verge of another earth-shattering orgasm. The angle he'd found, mixed with the intense emotions between us, had me seeing stars already. I needed more, though. Leaning back on my hands, I curled my fingers around the edge of the desk for support.

Peter growled and gripped my shirt. In one swift motion he ripped it open, sending buttons flying. I didn't care. In that moment, all I could think about was having his mouth on me. Having him drive into me harder and faster. Making me come.

He pulled down the cup of my bra and sucked my breast into his mouth. I let out a scream that was cut off by his hand clapping over my mouth. I couldn't hold it in anymore. It felt too good. Peter took his hand away and quickly replaced it with his mouth. His tongue swirled with mine while he rolled my nipple between his thumb and forefinger.

With his other hand, he grabbed my leg and put it over his forearm, driving in deeper. He swallowed my cries of pleasure. I wrapped my arms around him and dug my nails into his back. He groaned. Placing my other leg over his forearm, he spread me wide. I could feel every inch of him this way, and I bit my fist to keep from screaming.

He had a sexy smirk on his face as he tilted his hips, changing the angle slightly, which allowed him to go even deeper. The pleasure was so intense I almost couldn't take it. My body convulsed, and my core clenched. I ground my teeth together to muffle the sounds of pleasure that I couldn't hold back.

"Shit!" Peter grunted.

I wrapped myself tighter around him and held on as he drove into me with all his strength. His mouth covered mine, muffling my scream. Light danced behind my eyelids, and I felt like I burst into tiny pieces. He pumped once, twice more, and then stiffened. A low, primal growl ripped from his throat.

He rested his forehead against mine. I wrapped my legs around his waist and my arms around his back. We sat there, slicked with sweat, breathing heavily, and wrapped in each other's arms. It was by far the best sex I had ever had in my life. There were so many emotions mixed with intense chemistry; nothing would ever come close.

Elaine buzzed in on the intercom. "Peter, is everything all right?"

Peter laughed into my neck. He reached around me and pushed the intercom. He was still inside me, and the movement caused me to whimper in pleasure.

"Everything is fine, Elaine; no need to worry. Why don't you take an early lunch?" No response from the woman, but I heard a door slam.

Peter laughed again, but I was mortified. She had to know what was going on in here. She couldn't get away fast enough. Peter tipped my chin up to look at him.

"Hey, what's wrong?"

"Nothing," I said, putting on a smile. "Everything is great."

He kissed me, and then stepped back and peeled the condom off, tying it before tossing it in the trash can under his desk. I dropped my legs down from the chair and hopped off the desk. My legs were wobbly, and I felt like a newborn giraffe. Peter sat down in his office chair and pulled me into his lap, placing gentle kisses down my neck. I ran my fingers through his now-wet hair.

"Shall we get down to business?" I asked him with a smile.

He chuckled. "Yeah, I guess we should. I found a way for everything to work out."

He smiled at me and ran his fingers lightly up and down my arm. I shivered.

Suddenly what he said registered, "What do you mean?" I stood up from his lap. I felt nervous and needed to pace. My giraffe legs were still wobbly and I held onto his desk for support.

"Here, let me show you." He grabbed some large papers and what looked like prints from next to his chair and spread them out on his desk. I leaned over the desk to look at them.

"This is a map of our town and all the surrounding land. Mr. Lawrence cannot build on any of the land around the town unless he goes through the proper channels."

I frowned, "What do you mean by proper channels?"

"The land is a national forest, Kate. Mr. Lawrence would need federal approval to build. Years ago, the mayor wanted to protect the town from major development. He went to great lengths to have it declared a national forest. For Mr. Lawrence to build here, he'd have to show a good enough reason to be tearing down so much of the forest. He'd also have to prove a pressing need for the condos and strip mall," Peter said, turning to face me. He wore a big smile, but I felt confused.

"How is the town able to expand, then?"

"Grand Street was already there, and the previous mayor had already gotten the approval to build the stores. The pub was something I had to seek approval for, but it was on this side of the river, so we could do with it what we wanted."

He turned to me and ran his fingers up and down my arms.

"Anyone who owns a property can build on it. We can't tear down the trees or clear forested land, though."

I felt sick to my stomach, and I was angry, so angry. Why didn't he tell me all this last night when he got home? Was that why he'd slept with me? He had his ace in his pocket. This would not save my job. It was just the opposite, in fact. It sealed my fate.

"Kate, this is a good thing. You can't lose your job because you didn't know any of this. And I won't lose my property because he'd have to jump through so many hoops that it wouldn't be worth it for one property without the other development." He reached for my arm again, but I pulled back. "What's wrong?"

"What's wrong? You went behind my back and found a way out of this. There's no way Mr. Lawrence won't fire me. I wasn't going to go through with it, anyway. I was going to accept your answer. I had a plan, but you made me look bad. There's no way I can salvage my job now."

"Kate, everything will be fine." He reached for me again, but I stepped back and walked around his desk.

"Everything will not be fine. He's been calling me for hours. Oh God, did you already send all of this to him?"

"Yes, I had Elaine fax it all over this morning. He's called me, too, but I didn't want to talk to him until I showed you. I wanted to tell you this first. I care about you. I thought you would be happy," he said, taking a step to the side.

"Happy? You slept with me after you had a smoking gun. You knew you wouldn't lose your property, and it was all over. It was okay to sleep with me because you got what you wanted. I have to go. I have to get home and explain myself. I'm about to lose everything." I picked up my bag from the ground.

Emotions flooded me, and tears ran down my face. I wanted to run. Panic quickly made its way up from the pit of my stomach, and there was no way of stopping it this time. I was crushed. How could Peter do this to me? He wanted to tell me first, but not before sending it all over to my boss. Not before making sure that he got what he wanted.

He should have given the information to me to share with my boss. It would have helped me keep my job. Instead, Peter had destroyed everything. He got what he wanted, and I guess that was all that mattered to him. He took care of himself.

Everything was an act. He didn't care about me. The sex was amazing, but that was just a bonus for him. He got to keep his house, and he got me into bed. It was a sweet deal for him. He made me sick; I couldn't even look at him.

Peter pulled me up from gathering my things and wrapped his arms around me. My back resting to his front. "Move here with me. Who cares about that asshole or that job? We can be together. I'll help you find a new job. Here."

I shook my head. I couldn't believe what he was saying. What he'd just done would crush any chance of my ever getting another job with a developer. My reputation was ruined, and worse, I looked like a fool.

Move here with him? We hardly knew each other, and after this stunt, I realized I didn't know him at all. He wasn't the man I thought he was. I twisted out of his arms and ran for the door. I unlocked it with numb fingers and flung it open, running for the stairs.

"Kate," Peter called after me from his doorway.

I didn't stop. I ran down the stairs as fast as I could without falling. I flung open the back door and ran around the building toward The B&B. I needed to get my things and get the hell out of this town as fast as possible.

Tears streamed down my face, making it hard for me to see. I stumbled and almost went down, but I regained my balance. My heels were making it hard to get away, so I kicked them off and left them in the street. I kept running as hard as I could.

I flung open the door to my room and grabbed all my things. I did a quick double check of the room, thankful I had packed before I left, and ran back downstairs. Frantically, I looked for Betty but couldn't find her. I called her name a few times. Still nothing. I went back to the front desk and started banging on the bell.

"Hold on! I'm coming, I'm coming," Betty called.

I heard her footsteps on the basement stairs. My eyes darted to the front door to make sure Peter wasn't coming. I needed to get out of there before he caught up to me.

"Kate, honey, what's going on? I thought you were leaving later tonight."

"I need to go now, Betty. Something has come up at home, and I need to get out of here," I said frantically. "Do I owe you, or did my company already pay? I have a company card. I'm really not sure how to take care of this; I just need to hurry." Tears were pouring down my cheeks again. Everything was getting blurry.

"Okay, darlin'. Did someone die?" she asked, and then shook her head "I'm sorry; I shouldn't pry. You're all set, dear. Your company paid for everything; they just wanted a receipt sent with you. Give me just a minute, and I'll print one out for you." Betty turned toward the computer and began typing. I was growing more and more anxious. I had to get out of here before a panic attack started, and then I wouldn't be able to drive. "Now if only I could remember how to print the darn invoices."

I was about ready to run. "Can you just fax it to my company?"

"Fax? Honey, we don't have a fax machine here." She put on her glasses and looked at the screen. "I mean, I guess I could print it out and take it over to Elaine and have her fax it to you. Seems like a lot of work though… there we go! Got it!"

Betty handed me the freshly printed paper, and I ran out the door. The paper was still warm; the ink hadn't even dried yet, and I was already jumping into my SUV. I felt bad for not saying bye to Betty. She was such a kind woman and had done a lot for me while I was here. I hoped she'd understand it was an emergency.

I threw my stuff into the passenger side, barely getting the door closed before I threw the car in reverse and slammed on the gas. I didn't have any shoes on; they were still in the street where I'd kicked them off. They were one of my favorite pairs, too. I peeled out of The B&B's driveway and sped down Main Street and onto Old Cedar Road.

I was going way too fast. The back of the SUV was sliding in the dirt and fishtailing around the bends, but I couldn't make myself slow down. I just prayed I wouldn't get pulled over by Frank or Sid. I needed to get away from Oak Springs fast.

Once I was safely off Old Cedar Road, I breathed a little better and slowed down to a normal speed. Mr. Lawrence and Peter were both probably trying to reach me, but I couldn't deal with it. My phone was still powered off. I tossed it into the back seat, not needing the GPS to direct me home.

I remembered how I'd gotten into town, so I'd just take the same roads back and once I got onto the highway, I'd be fine. One thing I could pride myself on was my navigational skills. When I went somewhere once, I never needed GPS again.

I usually had a plan for everything, but as I tried to think about what to do next, I came up empty. My mind was blank. I was so embarrassed, lost, and heartbroken. I had never felt so lost before, not even when Vincent had left me. Hell, it wasn't even this embarrassing or painful when things ended with him. This was so much worse.

Strange as that was, Peter had broken me far worse than Vincent. Even though Vincent was essentially stalking me at home, he was more of an annoying gnat than a problem. Losing Peter, even after only a week, was devastating. My heart was shattered.

I turned onto the highway and hit the gas. Suddenly, I knew exactly where I needed to go. The only place where no one would bother me or judge me. The only place where I could break down completely and figure out how to put the pieces back together. The one place where I could rest and figure out a new plan.

225

Chapter 25

KATE

IT WAS ALMOST MIDNIGHT when I turned down Chestnut Street in Alston, Pennsylvania and pulled into my parents' driveway. It was amazing what adrenaline did to you. I was beyond exhausted. I had never driven the eight hours from my house straight through. I always left early so I could take breaks along the way. Driving from Oak Springs was even longer and I didn't take a break. Just pushed through.

My legs were numb, my vision was blurry, and my heart was in pieces. I just needed sleep. I'd figure everything out in the morning. Luckily, I still had a key to the house. I could sneak in and up to my old room while my parents were asleep. I grabbed my suitcase and walked up the drive to the back of the house.

There were voices coming from the backyard. Some laughing and whispering. I reached the corner of the house and got the shock of my life.

"Oh my God!" I screamed. I whirled around and covered my face.

"Kate? What are you doing here?" my mom shrieked.

"Okay, we are all adults here. What your mother and I were doing is completely normal. This is our house and our backyard, and we can hot tub in the nude if we want to," my dad explained.

I heard the swishing of the water as someone got out of the tub. I wanted to crawl under the deck and die. This was officially the worst day of my life.

"I should have called. I'm so sorry. It's just that everything is falling apart, and I need you guys. I made a rash decision, which I never do, and I drove straight here. Eleven hours, to be exact. You guys haven't changed the locks, have you? I'm just going to go gouge my eyes out."

"Oh, honey, please come here," my mom said from behind me. "It's okay. You can turn around; we're decent."

I slowly turned around. My parents, wrapped in towels now, had big smiles on their faces. Well, my mom did; my dad looked concerned, and rightfully so. My mom grabbed me and pulled me in close. I melted into her embrace and sobbed. I couldn't hold it in anymore. This was exactly what I needed. They would help me figure things out and start over.

The last time I came home like this was two years ago when Vincent first walked out on me. They both told me to stick it out for a while at the house and at my job. I did, except I took Vincent back, and things were tough for a while. I still held on and stayed.

When Vincent and I broke up eight months ago, my dad drove down and helped me put the house up for sale. Again, telling me to stick it out and give life without Vincent a fair shot.

I did, and this was the end of that fair shot. It was time to pick a different path. I wanted to wash my hands of the Bradburys. The thought of losing Peter forever made my chest ache like it was caving in, and I cried harder.

"Today has been such a horrible day. I really messed up. I'm going to lose my job, if I haven't already. I fell for someone this past week, and I lost him, too. I need to start over," I cried. My mom hugged me, and my dad rubbed my back.

"Why don't we go inside and get you set up in the guest room. Tomorrow we can sit down and talk this through," my mom suggested, ushering me inside.

"Guest room?" I asked through sobs.

"Well, yes, we finally remodeled your room. We have friends that come to stay with us sometimes, and I was tired of pulling the couch out in the basement when we have a room. You haven't been home in two years, anyway."

"Did you remodel Bridget's room, too?" I asked.

My sister, Bridget, married a doctor four years ago and moved to California. We hadn't seen her since. I found out I had a new niece through a mutual friend. Bridget never returned my calls or texts. She had just ghosted us, and we didn't know why.

"We remodeled Bridget's room a year and a half ago. It's our home gym/office," my mom said.

"Katie, I'm glad you're here. Get some sleep so we can discuss everything tomorrow," my dad said, kissing me on the forehead.

He was the rational one. A logical thinker like me. He would help me formulate the best plan so everything turned out all right. I had come to the right place, and I felt slightly better. Except for the giant hole where my heart used to be. It hadn't even hurt this bad when Vincent and I had broken up.

I walked into the guest bedroom and looked around. Things hadn't changed too much. A new paint color on the walls and a new window treatment where my old pink and purple one used to hang were the most noticeable differences. My dresser was still there, but the trinkets I had left behind weren't. A full-size bed with a new, more neutral comforter had replaced my old twin bed.

There was a beautiful dark wooden bookcase filled with books along one wall. A vintage rocking chair sat next to it under the window. Family photos hung on the wall across from it in a beautifully laid out collage. The room was peaceful, and despite the changes, it still felt like home, which caused me to tear up again.

"I hope it's not too much of a change. We just wanted to give it a facelift and make it a space everyone could share. The pink and purple décor and light green walls were fine when you were little, but we thought a nice light blue would brighten up the place," my mom said, rubbing a hand over one wall.

I smiled. "I agree. It looks good. Nice job accenting it with the dark wood furniture. It adds so much warmth that it still feels like home."

My mom wrapped me up in a hug. I thought I felt a tear drop onto my shoulder. My mom wiped a hand over her eyes and walked out of the room.

"Don't pay any attention to her, she just misses you girls terribly. It's been a while, you know? Well, we'd better get ourselves changed and in bed. You need some sleep, too. Love you, kiddo," my dad said, shutting the door behind him.

Warmth spread through me. My parents' love and support filled me, replacing some of the pain from the past week. I put my suitcase down and crawled under the covers. The bed was memory foam, and I melted into it with a sigh. Exhausted beyond what any human should be, you'd think I'd fall right to sleep, but instead the sobs started again.

The myriad of emotions that overtook me caused a physical ache so deep that I didn't think it would ever go away. Was it possible to fall in love with someone in such a short period of time? It couldn't have been love.

A big part of me was missing, though, and I knew it was because I'd left it in Oak Springs. Not only with Peter, but also with Laney and Frank. With the crazy book club women who liked to spread gossip, and with Betty.

My shoulders shook with sobs as I thought about all I had run from. It was the first time in forever that I had felt like I belonged somewhere. But even though I'd love nothing more than to run back there, Peter had played me. He went behind my back to get the information that would sink the project, knowing that it would cost me my job.

When he told me what he had done and how he had already sent that information to my boss, I felt like he had stabbed me in the gut. I knew Peter was only trying to help, but he hadn't thought about what his move would cost me; he'd only thought of himself. Saving his land and his home.

Anger and regret coursed through me. I was so mad at him, but more so at myself. I was disappointed that I'd let another man—another freaking Bradbury—ruin my life. When would I ever learn? The tears kept falling. I thought they would have dried up by now. My head was starting to pound, and I knew my eyes were puffy.

Rolling onto my side, I gripped the second pillow tight, hugging it to my chest. It was comforting; my heavy eyelids closed, and the tears eventually stopped as I drifted to sleep.

LOUD BANING AND EXCESSIVE cursing woke me up. I got out of bed, took my toiletry bag out of my suitcase, and headed for the bathroom across the hall. It felt too early to be awake. I wanted to sleep longer. Actually, I wanted to sleep for the entire day before I jumped into the whole fixing my life thing. I knew my dad, though, and that wouldn't fly.

"Oh, good morning, sweetie; did we wake you?" My mom was coming up the stairs.

"Kind of. What's with the banging and profanity at… what time is it, anyway?" I asked.

"Eight o'clock. I'm sorry about that. Your dad's trying to fix the sink in the kitchen. We've been having some trouble with it, and he refuses to call the plumber. He's been banging on the pipes since six. You know how he is."

"Right. Well, good luck with that. I'm going to change and go for a run before we sit down for our little pow-wow and attempt to fix my life," I said, turning for the bathroom.

"All right, honey. Take your time."

I glanced at my reflection in the mirror and jumped back against the wall. My eyes were red and bloodshot with deep purple circles underneath them. With the pale color of my skin, my eyes almost looked like they were sinking into my face. It was a scary sight, and I ducked away from the mirror to avoid looking at myself any longer.

Tears started to fall again as I sat on the toilet. I wiped at them angrily. Crying wasn't going to solve my problems, and really, how long was I going to cry for? I'd only been in Oak Springs for a week. Irritated, I brushed my teeth a little more aggressive than I normally would. I was just so angry with myself for being so weak.

Avoiding the mirror as much as possible, I rinsed my mouth out and then brushed through the rat's nest on my head, tying it back up in a messy bun. Strands stuck out everywhere, only making my appearance worse.

After changing into my running clothes, I headed outside, stretching and taking in the neighborhood from the front porch. I took a few deep, calming breaths since I had forgotten to do that when I got out of bed. Maybe that was why I was feeling so off balance this morning. That and the fact that my stupid heart was in pieces in my chest.

My phone was still off and in the back of the rental where I had tossed it. I couldn't deal with anything or anyone before I got my shit together. So far, that wasn't going well. I needed a plan. I grabbed the phone and powered it on. Ignoring all the chiming from the messages and missed calls, I sent a text to Mindy to let her know I was okay, but staying with my parents for a little while and I'd call her later. Then I powered my phone back down and shoved it in my pocket.

I started off at a light jog. Running my old path felt nostalgic. The sun beat down, warming me. I liked to run when the sun was just starting to rise so I could avoid the morning heat. But today it just felt good to move and clear my head.

Jogging down to the end of the street, I turned and headed to the park. After running half the loop, I sat down on a nearby bench and looked around the park. I loved this park and neighborhood. A few years ago, the city had updated the play equipment and built a new structure. Some of the trees were cut down to make room for a fenced-in dog park.

I'd always pictured myself living here. Taking my kids to the park. I'd let those dreams go when I met Vincent. He promised me the same dreams in a different city, so I let him whisk me away from my family and from everything that meant something to me.

I'd almost done the same thing with his brother. And that thought shook me deep inside. Why couldn't I be strong enough to stand on my own two feet? And what was it about that family that I couldn't resist?

Enough was enough. I needed to stop following men around and living their dreams, letting all my hopes and things I want to accomplish go to make them happy. It was time to start living for me and it started with going home and facing the music.

After a few minutes, I stood and stretched. Then I continued to jog down the pathway that went around the park. If I remembered correctly, the park loop was nearly two miles. I put my heart into it and ran. I sprinted as hard as I could around the track, hoping to find the answers to all my questions. Trying to run away from Oak Springs, Peter, Vincent and the whole mess my life had been for nearly the past decade.

My head was still a mess, my feet now ached, I had a side stitch, and I still felt like there was a crater where my heart once was. I headed back to my parents' house with tears welling up in my eyes again. Why had I trusted Peter? I had just met him. The pain I felt was unlike anything I'd ever felt before, and I knew… I knew that it was love and not just a quick fling. The feelings consumed me and it was going to be hell to get over him.

I bent over and clutched my chest, letting out painful sobs. Was he hurting, too? Standing, I noticed Mrs. Fredrick staring at me in shock. She lived a few houses down from my parents, and I'd known her my whole life. She used to babysit my sister and me when we were younger.

I waved at her while wiping tears from my eyes. She picked up her tiny white dog and hurried into the house. Forcing myself to go on even though the pain was almost too much, I made it the three houses back to my parents' and then drug myself up the stairs to the bathroom where I practically fell into the tub.

I lay there for a few minutes before I finally stripped out of my clothes and turned on the water, then I collapsed back down. Tucking my knees to my chest, I cried some more. The pain and embarrassment too much to take.

When I finished pouring my sorrows into the shower drain, I got out and stood in front of the mirror. Wiping it with a towel so I could see myself, I scowled at my pathetic reflection.

"No more!" I shouted. "Enough crying; enough feeling sorry for yourself. Today is a new day. A new you, a chance at a new life. No more tears, no more panic attacks, and no more being weak!"

I almost believed the words coming out of my mouth. I really wanted to, but the panic attacks weren't just going to vanish. As much as I wanted to wake up and will myself to be different, I knew who I was deep down. But the least I could do was try.

After rustling through my bag for a change of clothes, I started down the stairs for the kitchen with new confidence. My feet stilled on the steps when I heard my mom and dad arguing.

"Bill, just call the plumber," my mom said in an exasperated tone. My dad *had* been at this for hours already.

"I'm not calling a plumber, June!" my dad shouted back.

I laughed. This was how it always was with them. I pictured my mom sitting at the table with a coffee cup in her hand watching my stubborn dad trying to fix the sink. It was a familiar and comforting image.

"Good morning," I said cheerfully, as I walked into the kitchen.

My dad had his head under the sink, and my mom stood off to the side with a mug in one hand and tools in the other.

"Coffee?" Mom asked.

"Yes, please."

"There's a fresh pot brewing right now. Maybe if your dad would take a break, we could all sit down for breakfast and chat," my mom suggested a little louder than necessary while she leaned toward the sink. I could just see my dad rolling his eyes at her.

"All right, all right. You win. I'll take a break, but I'm not calling a plumber," Dad huffed as he pulled his head out from under the sink. I smiled around the mug of coffee my mom handed me.

Chapter 26

KATE

AFTER AN HOUR OF TALKING with my parents, I got into the SUV and headed home. I'd always run home and had my parents help me fix things, but it was time to do things differently and that started with facing my problems head-on. Fixing them myself.

The "talk" with them went about as well as I had expected it to go. My mom suggested I move back home while I got on my feet, while my dad suggested I move into an apartment or with my "tiny" friend and keep moving forward on my own. He felt that if I came home, I'd never leave. There was some truth to that.

The real truth was that I'd let them fix my life and then I'd move into an apartment near them and curl into myself. I'd get a job that was easy and just enough to make ends meet, and I'd lose myself to a routine that was safe.

I didn't want that. I wanted to stand on my own. I wanted to build the life that I wanted and work the job that I wanted to work. To do something I loved that got me up in the morning. I didn't want to live a life dictated by a man or a life that was safe so I'd never get hurt.

Even though the pain was strong and the worst I'd ever felt, worse than the car accident, I still wanted to go through it. To come out on the other side stronger. To grow and use it as something to learn from. My dad respected that, and my mom came to terms with it.

Plus, I really didn't want to accidentally walk in on any more nude hot-tub days or nights. Mindy had offered me a job at her art gallery numerous times. I knew that she'd hire me, no questions asked if I needed it. There were a lot of options at home, and as soon I talked to Mr. Lawrence, I'd go home and start looking for places to live.

My mom was sad to see me go, but she was also okay with it. She was always so relaxed about everything. She wasn't a realist or logical thinker like my dad. My mom was a hippie. "Wherever the wind blows you," was what she would always tell us. It didn't matter how many times the wind blew or in what direction, my mom would always tell us it was okay, and the wind of change would blow again. My dad hated it.

He helped me load my car and made sure there was air in the tires and the oil was okay, even though it wasn't my car and they do that before they rent it out to you. It gave him peace of mind, so I let him go through his checks.

My mom sent me off with homemade banana nut muffins, which were made with whole wheat flour, flax seed, and whatever other healthy things she could throw in there. Luckily, my dad snuck in a few of his processed cake snacks that he wouldn't give up. We said goodbye and shed some tears, mostly my mom and I, and I was on my way back to Bellport.

I arrived back late in the afternoon and headed straight to work. I needed to return the company vehicle, but first I needed to figure out what was going on with my job. My cell phone was still off, and I hadn't listened to any messages from Mr. Lawrence. I didn't want to.

After swiping my badge on the pad beside the door, I ran into the door when it didn't open. I tried again and still nothing. I turned on my cell phone and waited. The phone buzzed for what felt like forever as text messages, voicemails and e-mails flooded it. Once I was able to get past all the crap, I scrolled through my contacts for the office number.

Bonnie answered on the second ring, "Lawrence Development Company, how may I help you?"

"Bonnie, it's Kate. I need you to let me in," I said, looking up at my office window.

"Kate, where have you been? Mr. Lawrence is furious. He cleaned out your office. Sent all of your stuff with Vincent. Something strange went down between them, too."

I frowned. I did not have time to deal with whatever strange things were happening with Vincent. That would have to be dealt with another time.

"Bonnie, I need to get in there and talk to him. I deserve to tell my side."

"I agree. I think you should get to defend yourself. I'll be down there in a jiff."

The call ended, and I waited, checking the street for any signs of Vincent. I hadn't thought about him coming back here to wait for me to return. That man was a pain in my ass. After a few minutes, the door opened, and Bonnie poked her head out.

"Come in," she said holding the door so I could walk through. "I don't know how much he's going to let you get in. He's furious, Kate. I've never seen him so mad."

The elevator doors opened, and we stepped inside. "I understand that. I'm not happy either. The project was not at all what I expected, and I got the short end of the deal."

She looked at me, her expression sad. "Kate, something feels fishy with this one. The way he's acting. How angry he is. I've seen him lose out on property before, and he just moves on to something bigger and better. This seems personal."

I nodded. "It does feel that way, doesn't it? I'm just not sure why."

She shrugged. We'd soon find out. The elevator doors opened. Quincy was walking by. His eyes widened, and he dropped a folder that was in his hand. Instead of picking it up, he ran down the hall. Not a good sign.

I walked past my empty office and headed straight for Mr. Lawrence's. His door was open, and he was on the phone yelling at someone for something they hadn't done correctly. I walked straight in with my shoulders back and my head held high and closed the door behind me.

The click of the door startled him, and he whirled around to face me. His eyes narrowed when they landed on me.

"Jim, I've got to go. I'll call you later," he barked into the phone. He slammed it down and leaned forward onto his fists, resting them on his desk. "What the hell are you doing here?"

I sat down in the chair in front of his desk and crossed my jeans-clad legs. "We need to talk."

"The hell we do. I told you if you didn't close this, you'd be fired. Now get the hell out of my building before I call security."

I laughed. "You're not even going to let me explain? After years of working for you and bringing in how much money?" I waited for him to respond. His jaw ticked as he stared at me, but he said nothing. "I deserve to tell my side of things."

He sat down in his chair and let out a chilling laugh. He tented his hands over his belly as he leaned back in the chair and looked at me. "Your side of things? You mean falling for the town and the client, having fun with your friend and shopping on the office dime and clock, and allowing your client to steamroll you? Have I missed anything?"

My mouth opened and closed a few times before I could formulate a response. I had done all of those things, but not the way he said them. "First of all, I spent my money on off hours, to get to know the town. Second, I did not fall for the client or allow him to steamroll me. He surprised me because it wasn't a good deal to begin with. Whoever you had scout this town failed. It was a lockout from the start because you couldn't develop on the land from the beginning."

His eyes narrowed into slits, and he leaned forward on his desk. "It doesn't matter what you think. You failed, so you're fired."

I crossed my arms over my chest. "I don't want to work here anyway, and I'm not fired; I quit. I just want answers. Who scouted the town?

Conveniently there wasn't any documentation on that. Who talked to the mayor with the first proposal? Who checked the land and made sure there weren't any issues with it? Who took pictures and measurements, and where is the documentation of it all? The whole thing was a mess from the beginning, and I deserve to know why I am losing my job when things weren't done right from the start."

"You don't deserve shit! I don't pay you to look into things. I pay you to get stuff done. You have one job. To get the client to sign on the dotted line. It doesn't matter what the hell happens before you get there; you just force their hand. You didn't do that, and that's why you're losing your job! I do not accept your resignation because I already fired you. The paperwork has already gone through as of yesterday when you didn't return my thousands of calls, voicemails, texts, and e-mails and then didn't show up. Now get the hell out of my office and building before I call security and then the police."

I sighed. "This didn't have to go this way. I had a plan for a nearby town that really did need our help. A place where you could build all the things you wanted in Oak Springs and then some. I was going to show it all to you and send the scouts in to look things over and make sure I wasn't missing anything. Instead, you put everything into this project, but why? The town wasn't dying. It was flourishing. Why did you need to develop there so badly?"

He stood up and buttoned his suit jacket. Picking up his phone, he held the receiver down and glared at me. "It is none of your damn business why I pick the towns I do or why I need to develop there. It was your job to make me money, and you failed. This job cost us billions. Billions!" he shouted. "I could sue you for damages, but instead I'm allowing you to leave here with your dignity intact."

I laughed as I stood up. "You wouldn't win even if you did sue me."

The expression on his face turned sinister. "How would you like to go up against your ex in court?"

I froze.

"Vincent is the company's lawyer. I'm not sure if you knew that."

I shook my head.

He smiled. A sick, twisted smile that sent chills down my spine. "For a long time now. He has a lot of say here. You should really think long and hard about going after me."

I lifted my chin. "I don't need to go after you. One day you'll sink yourself. And if Vincent really is your lawyer, you've already been sunk. He's in debt up to his eyeballs and he skirts the system. If you're entangled with him, you'll get what's coming to you."

I turned to go, but not before he got the last word in, "Kate, you'll get what's coming to you as well. It's already begun. You'll never work for another development company as long as I live. If I had it my way, we'd be in court."

If he had it his way? What did that mean? He wasn't going to take me to court because someone stopped him? I didn't have the energy to sort through this mess. The more I tried to figure it out, the deeper I stepped in the shit.

I was proud of how I handled everything and without a panic attack. Maybe my pep talk in the mirror really worked. Or maybe it was the fact that I was cutting another string that connected me to Vincent. Either way, I was happy to be leaving. This place stunk of dirty deals and dirty money.

Chapter 27

KATE

IT WAS LATE IN THE EVENING when I arrived home. I returned the SUV and got an Uber instead of calling Mindy for a ride. I loved her to death, but I couldn't deal with her energy. She'd be angry about the situation, and I knew that it would be too much to handle.

I walked up the front steps and unlocked the door. All the lights were off, which was strange. Mindy had been checking in on the place before she went to Oak Springs. I'd finally listened to all my messages in the Uber—another reason I was beat; the messages were brutal— and her last message said that she'd stopped by the house last night and brought the mail in. I would've thought she'd have left a small light on in the living room for me.

Looking up, I noticed the front porch light wasn't on either. I froze in the house's entryway. Something felt wrong. Standing as still as possible, I tried to listen through the silence, which seemed deafening. I couldn't hear a thing. Maybe I was just nervous about returning to the house. Even though I was trying to stop panicking, it was my first response to stress, and that was a tough habit to break.

I reached over for the light switch next to the door and flipped it. Nothing. The lights weren't working. Did I lose power? I thought I had paid the electric bill while I was gone. My feet were silent on the carpet as I walked farther into the house.

The large six-paned window in the living room let in some light from the moon. Not enough for me to see anything, though. I used the flashlight feature on my cell phone to illuminate the room. I took a step and froze in my tracks. In the archway that opened to the kitchen, I thought I saw something move.

With a shaky hand, I shined the light into the doorway. Nothing there. My heart beat out of my chest. My keys were still in my hand, and I remembered from a self-defense video I'd watched that you could use your keys as a weapon. So I put them between my fingers like I had seen in the video and hoped it would work.

Something was definitely wrong. Why was I still standing in the dark house? I needed to find out whether the power outage extended to my neighbors. If not, then someone had cut power to my house. I shivered and turned to run back out the door. I made it three steps before someone grabbed me from behind. I screamed and twisted, trying to free myself.

My assailant swung me around and tossed me back into the living room. My head almost hit the stone coffee table I hated. I landed upright in front of it facing the kitchen and my attacker.

Darkness covered the room like a blanket. The sliver of moonlight that had shone through the large open windows was now gone. I kept my eyes locked on the dark figure instead of turning to see whether the moon had slipped behind a cloud. I wasn't stupid. I'd watched a lot of horror films.

My hands moved across the carpet in search of my phone. A small slice of light shone from across the room. It was my phone, flashlight side down. I tried to crawl for it but stopped when a dark shape loomed over me.

My attacker was dressed in all black and wearing a mask; only their eyes were visible. Judging by the height and build, I'd say it was a male.

Had I interrupted a robbery when I came home? I lunged for my phone, but before my fingers could connect with it, he picked it up and threw it across the room. I heard it hit the wall behind me and winced. Did it break? Please don't let it be broken.

"Katherine, you've been a very bad girl. Messing around on vacation, and I'm not happy about it," a deep, nasally voice said. My stomach dropped. I recognized that voice. It was Vincent.

Anger and fear coursed through me. Anger at the fact that he thought he owned me, and fear because I didn't know what he would do to me. I attempted to crawl again, but he pushed me down. His weight came down on top of me, pressing me further into the ground. My face smashed into the carpet, and I struggled to breathe.

I tried wiggling so I could turn over to see him, but he was pushing so hard. His knee dug into my back. I started to scream, but a gloved hand covered my mouth, muffling the sound.

"Oh, that's not nice. I'm just trying to talk to you. If you stay calm and quiet, nothing will happen. We can talk and work this out," he said.

I stayed still and tried to figure out what to do. How was I going to get out of this? I moved my hand and touched something. Grabbing onto it, I realized it was my keys. I curled my fingers around them, pushing two keys between my first and second fingers.

With one quick motion, I jabbed the keys into Vincent's face. He screamed and rolled off me. I scrambled to my feet and made a run for the front door. He grabbed my foot, and I pitched forward, screaming as I went down again. My face narrowly missed the small step between my living room and the entryway.

"No," I sobbed as I lifted my head. My phone was just out of reach in front of me. My fingers inched toward it, but Vincent yanked me backward.

"That won't work, sweetheart. I knocked out the cell service in the house. I had a lot of time on my hands since I waited three days for you to come home. Nice try with the keys, by the way. Hand them over," he said, holding onto my legs and crawling up my body.

"No, Vincent. Let me go. Stop this!"

"Ah, so you know it's me. Then you know why I'm here, too. Give me the keys, Katherine," he demanded, reaching for them.

I rolled underneath him and drove my palm up into his nose. He grabbed his face and shouted, "You bitch! Peter broke my nose two weeks ago. Damn it!"

Scrambling, I got to my feet and ran for the kitchen. I made the classic mistake of looking behind me instead of running straight for the garage and locking myself in there. I was relieved to see he wasn't there. But when I looked back in front of me, my heart stopped, and my feet froze. Vincent stood there with a menacing look on his face.

He had removed the mask, and the moonlight that now trickled through the French doors to my left illuminated his face. The same French doors I sat in front of enjoying a cup of coffee at my small dining room table, staring out into the large backyard, and dreaming of barbecues and get-togethers. I'd never be able to look at this house the same way.

Vincent's eyes were dark, and his smile was twisted. Blood dripped from his nose. He looked like a real-life villain. I'd never feared him more than I did tonight. This was worse than that night at his grandmother's memorial service. I didn't know what he'd do to me, and the look in his eyes right now terrified me. If I made it out alive, that look would haunt me.

The kitchen was very large and used to be my favorite room in the house. It was now the room I feared the most because of all the knives in it. I kept my back to the counters along the wall by the French doors and moved slowly past the sink until the large island was in front of me.

Vincent stayed put, only shifting his body and following my movements with his eyes. For some reason, that scared me more. It was like watching a horror film. The villain not speaking or moving, just staring and waiting. My heart rate increased, and my hands shook as I slid them gently along the edge of the counter behind me while I shuffled along it.

As long as I was on the opposite side of the island, I'd be okay. He lunged for me, and I screamed, pressing myself back against my countertops. My eyes darted around the room looking for a knife or something I could use to defend myself. Where the hell was the knife block I kept on the counter?

Vincent moved to the left, and I moved right. He moved the other way, and I did the same. He moved to the left again, I moved right, and he lunged over the island and grabbed my arm. He held on tightly while he walked around to me.

"Now you've really pissed me off. You thought you could sneak around with my brother, and I wouldn't find out?" he spat out. His breath was sour, and it turned my stomach.

He pulled his fist back and punched me in the face before I had a chance to block it. My head snapped back. Pain reverberated through my cheekbone. I was pretty sure he'd shattered it. I hung my head and lifted my free hand to my face.

The pain was unbearable, and I wanted to scream, but I wouldn't give him that. I would remain tough even if it killed me. He would not win without a fight.

His grip tightened on my arm, his fingers digging in. I knew there would be bruising. The pain in my face was so intense I was on the verge of blacking out or throwing up. Before I could do either of those, he threw me across the room toward the living room again. My body hit the wall between the two rooms, and pain shot through my back as I fell to the floor.

A sob escaped me, and I sucked air in, trying to fill my lungs back up. Vincent stood over top of me and kicked me in the side. I screamed and fell onto my stomach, curling into a fetal position. I clutched my side.

"Get up!" he screamed.

I was in too much pain to move. Was this how I would die?

He began to pace. "I'm so sick of giving to people, and this is what I get. I was so nice to you. I gave you this house. I moved back so we could reconnect. I got you a job, and you lost it! Did you think I wouldn't find out where you went? You thought you could sleep with my brother and I wouldn't find out?"

He threw photos at me. One fluttered to the floor, landing in front of me. It was a photo of me running from Peter's house in his clothes. How the hell did Vincent get those pictures?

Vincent kicked me in my side again, and I almost threw up from the pain. I curled into a tighter ball, trying to protect my side. He reached down and pulled me to a standing position by my arms. My shoulders were rounded, and I still clutched my side; it hurt too much to stand up straight. He ducked down so he could look at me. His eyes were wild, and rage rolled off him in waves.

I tried to speak, but it came out as a whisper. "Vincent, stop."

Without a word, he punched me again, this time connecting with my mouth. I cried out in pain and fell forward, holding onto my face with my other hand. Blood trickled out of my mouth and into my hands.

I looked up at him and spit the blood onto the floor at his feet. If he was going to kill me, then I wanted him to know how much I hated him. I dug deep, trying to find the courage and strength to run. My whole body was in pain, though, and I felt dizzy.

"Do you honestly think Peter can support you? He doesn't have any money, and that house of his is a joke. A strong wind would knock it over. I doubt he makes much as the mayor of that pitiful town. Our family had a good laugh when we found that out."

I spit again and looked up at him. "I don't need someone to take care of me. I have a job, and I take care of myself."

He laughed, sounding like a hyena. "You *had* a job. One that I got you."

"And I got myself the promotion," I gritted out.

He laughed again and took a step back, crossing his arms over his chest. "You got that promotion thanks to me."

"No, I earned it. I worked hard for it."

"Katherine, did you really think Trent would allow a woman to work that close to the top? He called me the day before and asked me to lunch.

You got the promotion thanks to me. I did it as a favor to you. I did it for us."

He was lying. He had to be lying.

He put his hands together at his chest and looked at me like I was a child and he was going to explain the meaning of life to me. "I can see you don't understand. Let me see if I can simplify it for you. Trent only gave you the job because of me. You worked hard, and it paid off for us both."

Vincent leaned forward, and his eyes filled with hate. "Then you lost it and sullied both our reputations," he gritted out.

"Sullied your reputation? How did I do that? You don't even work there."

"That deal was for me! I needed to sink that damn town to bulldoze it and build a casino. The strip mall was a bargaining chip because they seemed to want some proof we were doing it for the good of the town. Once I found out my brother was the mayor, I had to move forward. Taking everything out from under him and leaving him with nothing was going to be so damn sweet. Then you slept with him and lost everything because you didn't see him coming."

He let out a laugh, "I don't know what was better, seeing him betray you like the Bradbury he is or seeing the pain on your face when you didn't see it coming."

"You were there?"

He shook his head. "I have my ways of finding things out, Katherine."

He threw another set of photos at me. I picked one up off the ground. It was a picture of me running from Peter's store. Tears running down my face. The anguish in my expression hit me again in my chest, and I held back the tears. The pain I felt that day came back in a rush.

"That company you work for belongs to me. I bought into the company just before we broke up. I owned you and your boss. Except you had to go and ruin it all. Everything that was going to make me money."

I laughed and spit more blood at his feet. "Now you have nothing. You bought into the company using your mommy's money, didn't you? You hoped you'd be able to make money to clear some of your ever-growing debt. This deal was a way for you to wipe it clean and end up in the black for the first time in your life, wasn't it?"

He stepped into me, and I backed up against the wall, "When are you going to learn where your place is? How hard is it to just shut the hell up and do what you're told? On your knees, Katherine."

My eyes widened. "No."

He punched me in the eye and then in the stomach, and I doubled over in pain. His fingers dug into my shoulders as he forced me into a kneeling position.

"Your place is here. I provide for you; I am the only one who gets you. You belong to me. Maybe if you do a good job—." He paused and ran a thumb over my now puffy bottom lip. "If you show me you know where your place is, I might consider forgiving you."

He unbuttoned his cargo pants and started to slide his hand into them, and my eyes widened in horror. Without hesitation, I punched him in the crotch, and he fell to his knees.

"You bitch!" he screamed.

I scrambled to my feet and turned for the door. Before I could even take a step, he grabbed onto my hair, whipping me around, and then tossing me into the living room. I landed against the stone coffee table. Pain shot through my back and radiated out to other parts of my body. A tingling and numbing feeling spread quickly.

I was fading. There was a metallic taste in my mouth, and I could only see out of one eye since the other was already swelling shut. The good eye wasn't that great either thanks to the swelling of my cheekbone.

Vincent stood over me with something in his hand. He turned slightly, and whatever it was glinted in the moonlight. Was it a knife? Pain bit into my stomach, and I realized he'd stabbed me.

He pulled his arm back, and I grabbed onto it as the knife came down over me again. I put both hands onto his arm and pushed against him. Reached deep down inside to find my inner strength. I would not die here. Not like this, and not at his hands.

Leaning forward, he put all his weight onto me, pressing his knee into the wound. I screamed, too weak to push him off me. He pressed his knee in harder and placed his other hand on top of the arm I was pushing against. This allowed him to push his arm down, bringing the blade close to my throat. I couldn't breathe, and my arms shook from trying to push him away.

I rolled to the side, and the tip of the knife pierced my shoulder. I let out a muffled cry. He pulled back just enough to look at me. I dropped my arms to the side in defeat and stared up into his eyes. Tears spilled down my cheeks as I realized Vincent's was the last face I was ever going to see.

"If I can't have you, Katherine, no one can!"

He pulled his arm back and hit me over the head. Everything went black.

I OPENED MY EYES, and Mindy was standing over me. She was talking, but her voice sounded muffled, and I couldn't understand what she was saying. A bright light was shining in my face; I winced. I could only see out of one eye and only partially from that one. My entire body throbbed with pain so intense that I threw up. I would have aspirated on my vomit if someone hadn't helped me turn my head to the side. I was too weak even to do that. Where was I? What was going on? I was so confused.

"Kate, please don't die," someone said.

I tried to cry out for help, but my swollen lips wouldn't allow it. The pain was becoming too much, and everything faded into black again.

MY EYES FLUTTERED OPEN, and I looked around. My heart pounded loudly in my ears. Lots of people moved around me. I tried to speak, but my mouth was dry, and my lips were too puffy. Tears ran down my face.

"Don't cry, sweetie; you're safe now. You're safe," a nurse said, patting my arm.

I turned my head and saw Mindy through a crack in the curtain. She was crying and looked panicked. One hand was over her mouth; the other on her stomach. I wanted her in here with me. I wanted her to hold my hand and tell me I'd be okay.

Big arms wrapped around her, and she fell against someone's chest. I couldn't see who it was; the curtain blocked my view. A man barked out orders, drawing my attention back to the tiny room.

"It will be all right. We've got you now," the doctor said softly. "Nurse, let's give her something for the pain while we look her over."

The nurse stuck something in my IV. "There you go, honey."

Everything started getting fuzzy, and I panicked a little. What if he came back? Could he get me here? The voices sounded far away. My eyelids got heavy, and my body relaxed as I faded again.

Chapter 28

KATE

A QUIET AND STEADY BEEPING noise grew louder as I started to wake up. I looked around out of a slit of one eye. I wanted to reach up and touch my face, but I couldn't will my arms to move. Pain radiated through my body. Slowly, painfully, I turned my head.

Peter was asleep in a chair next to my bed. *He came for me.* A tear escaped my eye and slid down my cheek.

"Hey, you're awake," Mindy said.

I rolled my head, wincing with the pain. She walked over with two cups in her hands and set them down on the tray beside my bed. Her smile was warm, but her eyes looked worried. I couldn't talk or smile. There was a tube down my throat; my lips were stretched around it and cracked. It took everything in me not to panic.

"How are you feeling?" Peter asked, sitting up and leaning toward the bed. He shook his head. "Sorry; dumb question. I'm glad you're okay. I was so worried."

He reached down and slid his hand underneath mine. Just his touch helped me to focus less on the tube. It was soothing, and I needed it. I wanted so badly to tell them who did this to me, but I couldn't speak. Another tear escaped my eye and rolled down my cheek.

"It's okay, Kate. We're here for you. I'm just happy you're okay. Your parents are on their way," Mindy said, brushing the tear off my cheek.

I lifted my hand and winced at the pain that shot through my arm. I mimed writing with what little movement I had in my fingers. Mindy looked around frantically and then dug through her purse. She handed me a receipt and a pen. I wrote the question I was dying to have answered, then handed it to Mindy.

"Did they catch him?" she read out loud. "No, honey, they didn't. It was just a random break in, and you came home at the wrong time. The person, or people, trashed the house. The police are still sweeping the area and dusting the house for prints."

He got away? I tried to shake my head, but it barely moved. The pain felt like shock waves reverberating through it. I wiggled my fingers in a "gimme" motion, and Mindy handed the paper back to me. I wrote Vincent's name, underlined it, and then shoved the paper back at Mindy. Peter looked over Mindy's shoulder, and his face hardened. His hand twitched against mine, and a tic started near his jaw. It was the same look he'd had the night he hit Vincent in the nose.

"Are you sure?" Mindy asked.

"If he did this to you, I'll kill him!" Peter growled. "I don't care if he is my brother."

I squeezed his hand as best I could, trying to calm him down. There was nothing he could do, and I was too afraid for them to leave me here alone. Vincent was still out there, which meant I was still in danger.

"I'm sorry. Let's focus on getting you better first. Are you sure it was him?" Mindy asked.

My head barely moved when I tried to nod. I was frustrated with the failure, but Mindy nodded back. She understood.

"Let's let her rest," she whispered to Peter.

My hand latched onto Mindy's arm as she turned away from me. There was no way I was closing my eyes again. Not while Vincent was still out there. If he knew I was alive and in the hospital, he could show up here and try to cover his tracks. Especially if he thought he'd gotten away with it. I couldn't speak with the tube down my throat, and I panicked. My breathing rate increased and so did the beep on the monitor that read my heart rate.

"Hey, I'm right here. Don't freak out. The tube will come out. Relax. Look at me, Kate." Peter leaned over me and looked into my eyes. His hand gently caressed the side of my face. "Calm down. You're okay. Mindy went to get a nurse."

I kept my eyes locked on Peter's, breathing in sync with him. A few minutes later, a nurse hurried into the room and checked my vitals.

"We'll get that taken out, okay?" she cooed.

After a while, a doctor came in. He checked me over and talked with the nurse before coming over to pull the tube. I gagged and choked, then panicked, gasping for breath like a fish. I was about to die. After all that, I was going to die because I couldn't breathe.

"Kate, breathe. You can take a deep breath. Breathe with me," Peter said from beside me. I met his gaze and copied him. After a few minutes, the panic started to subside, and I was breathing normally on my own again.

"That's it," he said stroking my hand.

"We'll let you rest. You're not due for pain meds for another few hours," the doctor said after checking me over again.

"How did you find me?" I whispered. My lips were puffy, and my throat felt scratchy from the tube.

"It was late, and you said you'd call when you got in," Mindy said. "I hadn't heard from you, so I called your phone. It kept saying you were unavailable, and I got worried. I rushed over as fast as I could. When I pulled up in the driveway, something seemed off. I saw someone run out of the house and over behind the neighbor's house. I ran inside and called out for you. It was so dark, and you didn't answer me. I turned on my cell phone flashlight, and that's when I found you lying in a pool of blood." Tears formed in Mindy's eyes and ran down her cheeks.

"Oh God, Kate, I thought you were dead. I was so scared. I tried to call the police, but my phone service wouldn't work. I ran out front and into the street where I finally got service and called 9-1-1. They searched the block but came up empty-handed."

I couldn't believe Vincent had gotten away. I needed to speak to the police. To give them his name. Maybe they would find the knife or his fingerprints in my house. My stomach churned the more I thought about it. Tears fell from my eyes.

Peter leaned down and pressed a kiss to my forehead. His soothing voice eased my worry. "Try to rest, baby. I'm not going anywhere."

What was he doing here, and why was he being so nice to me? Things between us were strange. We needed to talk about what had happened, but it would have to wait. I needed sleep. Peter sat down in the same chair he'd been in earlier and held my hand until I fell asleep.

PAIN SHOT THROUGH MY BODY, waking me. I cried out—although it came out as more of a whimper—and opened my one good eye. The room was empty.

"Help!" I screamed. No one came. "Is anyone there?"

Peter walked in carrying a Styrofoam cup. He took one look at my face and ran over. "Kate, don't cry. What's wrong? Are you in pain?"

"The room was empty when I woke up and it scared me." My voice was louder, and my lips didn't feel as swollen.

"I'm so sorry. I went down to the cafeteria for a snack and some coffee. I thought you would still be sleeping. I shouldn't have left you. Are you in pain? I can call a nurse," Peter said, pushing the hair away from my face.

Before I could answer, a nurse came in carrying a clipboard, "All right, Miss Miller, it's time for your next dose of medicine, and I need to check your vitals."

I recognized her voice from when I had first arrived here. Peter stepped aside so the nurse could scoot in. He took another step and was closer to the door. Where was he going? I didn't want him to leave me alone.

As if he could read my thoughts, he said, "I'm right here. I'm not leaving."

"I'm so glad to see you up and talking," the nurse said. "Things could have been a lot worse for you. How's the pain? Are you nauseous?" The cuff squeezed my arm as she took my blood pressure.

"The pain is bad. No nausea."

"Okay, we'll give you something for the pain, but I think you should try to eat something first. Maybe your boyfriend could run down and get you some crackers while I finish checking you out, and then he can order you something from the menu," the nurse said.

Just as I was about to tell her that Peter wasn't my boyfriend, he nodded and slipped out of the room. I guess I'd worry about what was going on with us later.

The nurse lifted my gown and checked the dressing on my stomach. Mindy came in while she was finishing up, carrying a few board games and a frozen fruit drink.

"I'm going to check on another patient. As soon as your boyfriend returns with those crackers, eat them so I can come back and give you your pain medication."

I nodded, and she left the room.

Mindy's eyes widened, and she smirked. "Your boyfriend?"

I waved her off. "Who's the drink for?"

"You. It's your favorite, blue raspberry. I thought it might feel good on your throat and go down easy." She shook the cup in front of me, and I could hear it sloshing around. My mouth watered.

255

"Thank you. I really don't know what I would do without you," I said, taking a sip of the blue goodness. It was cold, and Mindy was right; it felt amazing against my dry throat.

Peter came in with a handful of crackers. He opened a pack and handed one to me.

"What can I do?" Mindy asked.

"The nurse said to order food. She needs something in her stomach for the medication. I was thinking maybe soup and some Jell-O." Peter handed Mindy the menu.

"On it. You can take off if you want," Mindy said.

Peter shook his head. "Thanks, but I don't think I'm going very far. I'll just go down to the cafeteria. Make some calls and check my e-mails."

"Peter, go to the hotel. Get some sleep, take a shower, and get something to eat. I'm here. I won't leave until you get back. I promise," Mindy assured him. "Kate's parents will be here soon. They got stuck in some traffic and are about an hour out."

"Okay. Maybe I will. Kate, I promise I'll be back." He bent down and kissed me on the head and then left the room.

"He really cares about you. You should have seen him, Kate. He was a wreck." Mindy sat down beside the bed. "Do you want to talk about what's going on with you guys? Might be a nice distraction."

I sighed. "I'm so confused. I like him, but how could a relationship ever work between us? I've lived in Vincent's shadow for so long. I finally felt independent and like I had my life together when I met Peter. But instead of being a strong, independent woman, I fell right back into being the girl who panics all the time and can't be on her own."

I took a sip of the slush before continuing. "When everything fell apart a few days ago, and I went to my parents, I really had to reevaluate my life. I gave myself a pep talk. I promised myself I was going to be strong and stand up to fear. Then I ended up here. I need to heal, Min, and learn how to stand on my own two feet before I can even think of giving myself to someone else. I don't want to follow a man again. I want to know that I'm strong enough to be on my own."

"You could always move to Oak Springs and start over. Take things slow with Peter. He'd understand and respect that," Mindy said.

"Yeah, but then I'd be jumping into another relationship. With another Bradbury. How do I know I wouldn't just fall into the same habits? I'm afraid I'd try to become everything I thought he wanted me to be and lose sight of myself again. I don't want to give up my dreams and live life on someone else's terms."

"Peter wouldn't do that to you. He'd support you in your decisions. You wouldn't be the same person you were with Vincent, Kate."

I shook my head. "Before you got to Oak Springs, I was timid and had two major panic attacks. I was a mess around Peter. A poor animal in need of rescuing. Just like Mrs. Anderson's damn cat."

"Do I even want to know about the cat?" she asked.

I waved her off. "The point is, I don't want to be that person anymore. Now's my chance to change my life. To create the life *I* want. Mindy, I want to start my own event planning company. Plan parties and meet people. Get an apartment on my own, maybe take some online business classes. Make money because I earned it, not because someone else got me a job. Vincent told me he had bought into the company before we broke up. Everything I thought I worked for on my own was a lie. It was all because of him. He owned me, and I just didn't know it. I don't want any more ties with the Bradbury family. Unfortunately, that includes Peter."

"I'm here for you, and I'll help you however I can. I love you, Kate, and I want what's best for you. If you think you need to be alone for a while and take your life in a new direction, then I'll support you. I might be able to help you out with starting your own business, too. You could host some events at the gallery for me. Once word gets out, you should be able to build clientele up in no time," Mindy said, squeezing my hand. "I think you need to talk to Peter, though. Give him a chance. Don't shut him out because of his family name. He doesn't deserve that. Plus, you two are good together."

"Min, he acted just like his family. First chance he got, he stabbed me in the back because he was looking out for himself. He may be a good man, but the Bradbury hold on him is strong, and you can't fight the way you were raised. It has had some effect on him, and unfortunately, I got hurt in the process."

She shook her head. "I don't think that's the case."

I lifted one brow. "You've talked to him. You believe him." I wasn't asking. The fact that Mindy was defending him told me enough.

"Yes, we talked, and I will stand behind you as your friend with whatever you choose, but Peter is a good guy deep down. He was doing what he felt was right and he wanted *you*. I think he hoped that if your boss had all the facts, he'd spare your job. No one could have predicted it would go the way that it did."

I sighed. "I'll talk to him, but it doesn't change things. I need to do this for me."

I closed my eyes. First, I needed to rest and heal. Then I could think about what to say to Peter. In my heart I felt like taking some time for myself was the right decision, even if it meant losing him. There were a million reasons why we'd never work out. Besides, the betrayal hurt. The words Vincent said to me rang through my head, *"I don't know what was better, seeing him betray you like the Bradbury he is or seeing the pain on your face when you didn't see it coming."* I was such a fool.

Chapter 29

KATE

IT HAD BEEN TWO WEEKS since the accident, and I was finally able to go home. Except home wasn't where I wanted to go. The sale of the house was on hold. The police didn't want anyone in there yet, and there was blood that had to be cleaned up.

Peter had stayed the entire time I was in the hospital. My parents, Mindy, and Peter were allowed into the house once to get things from my bedroom. Nothing from the main floor could be touched or moved. Mindy was letting me stay on her couch until I was better and until my house sold, which could take a while. I needed the money to get a new house or an apartment.

My clothes were in a portable closet in Mindy's living room. Mindy lived in a studio apartment with one of those dividers that looked like it came from a Japanese restaurant separating the living area from her bedroom. We shared the tiny bathroom and petite kitchen. The apartment suited her, and she loved it.

I liked that it was small and nothing like what I had lived in for the last five years or so. It felt more like home to me than my house did, and I was thankful that Mindy was willing to share it with me for a little while. My mom tried to insist I come back home, but that was not an option. My parents wanted to take care of me, but I stood firm on my decision to move in with Mindy.

They had a tough time understanding my decision. They supported me, but it was hard for them to leave me in such a broken state. I could understand where they were coming from; it would be hard for any parent to leave their child who was hurting and physically broken. My mom wanted me to move home and start over, build a life back in my hometown.

I loved my parents very much, but I also liked the independence I had here in Bellport. The possibilities here were endless, and I wanted to stay. Mindy was like a sister to me, and I couldn't see myself leaving her either.

A knock on the door startled me out of my thoughts. I shifted into a seated position on the couch, wincing at the pain that I felt everywhere. It was worse than the car accident, but I'd get through this, too.

Mindy ran from the bathroom to the door, wrapped in a towel. She whipped open the door without looking through the peephole first. Peter was standing in the door, a look of shock on his face as his eyes took in the five-foot-tall redhead dressed in a white towel.

He cleared his throat. "Um, can I come in?"

"Sure," Mindy said, aiming her smile my way. She sauntered back into the bathroom and closed the door. That was the only privacy we'd get.

Peter walked in and stood in the middle of the room, looking around. He'd helped me settle in two days ago, but the visit was brief since I was in so much pain and needed to sleep it off. He ran a hand over the back of his head as he studied my bedroom/living room.

"How are you feeling?" he asked when his eyes met mine.

"I'm okay. Slowly getting better each day." It wasn't a total lie. Each day was an improvement; some days it was harder to see that than others.

He nodded. "Kate, I'm so sorry this happened to you."

"It's okay."

He fell down in front of me and crumpled into my lap. Shocked at his reaction, my hand hovered over his head before I ran my fingers through his hair in a soothing manner.

"It's not okay, and this should have never happened. I shouldn't have let you go the way that I did. We shouldn't have fought like that. We should have worked it out together."

A tear ran down my cheek. I wanted so badly to wrap my arms around him and pull him against me. To crawl into his lap and let him hold me, tell me everything would be okay, and make me forget about the pain and Vincent. But I couldn't bring myself to do that. I needed to stand on my own. To heal on my own.

I couldn't run back to him like that. Especially now that I didn't have a job. I was a broken woman, both physically and emotionally. I didn't want to depend on Peter. I wanted to support myself and live the life that I wanted for once. Choose a path for myself instead of one that someone else carved out for me. It was best for us to be apart, and deep down, I think he knew that, too.

"Peter, will you please look at me?"

He lifted his head. His eyes glistened, and it cracked my chest open more. The pain sliced through my heart like a sharp blade. I closed my eyes for a split second to break the connection between our gazes. When I opened them, I plunged ahead.

"I want you to know that the week we spent together was one of the best weeks of my life. Oak Springs is a wonderful place, and you've done an amazing job as mayor. You're a very special man, and even though you went behind my back, I don't believe it came from a malicious place."

That last part was easier for me to say than I thought. The last few days, I'd thought about Peter's actions the day I ran from him, and I really did believe that deep down, he was doing it because he cared for me. He wasn't doing it to gain something. He might have been trying to keep his house, but I thought he was also trying to protect me and my job. It just didn't work out that way.

"All that aside, we still can't be together."

"Kate," he started, but I cut him off.

"You're an amazing guy and this is hard for me. I want nothing more than to be with you, but I can't. I've lived in your brother's shadow for the last six years. That's a very long time, and I lost sight of who I was. I did everything for him and because of him. My job that I worked so hard for was a lie. I was promoted because of Vincent."

He sat back on his heels, his face hardening. "I am not my brother."

"I know you're not. You are nothing like him. I just meant I can't follow you like I followed him."

"I would never make you do that."

"I know you wouldn't. This is so hard for me to explain." I looked down at my hands, twisting them in my lap. "Peter, I can't be with you. I need to stand on my own. My life is such a wreck right now. I have to heal, and then I can start focusing on what I want to do for once in my life. It's not about you. It has everything to do with me and how I'm feeling."

He sighed and stood up. I watched as he paced back and forth without saying a word. He was deep in thought, and I wanted to give him time to absorb what I was saying. He stopped in front of me.

"Kate, I care about you. More than I've cared for any other woman."

My heart flipped in my chest, and I willed it to stop. I needed to do this. We couldn't be together.

"I just want you to be happy, and I hoped that it would be with me, in Oak Springs. The people there love you, and you fit so well in the town. You could do whatever your heart desired, and you wouldn't have to live with me. You could get your own place. We wouldn't even have to jump into a relationship right away; we could date and take it slow. I just don't want to lose you."

His gorgeous green eyes pleaded with me, and I almost broke.

"I'm sorry. I can't," I whispered.

He dropped to his knees in front of me again, and my heart shattered. Tears leaked down my face. His eyes glistened with unshed tears. The look on his face was one of utter defeat, and if I wasn't already sitting, it would have brought me to my knees.

"Please don't let this be the end of us," he begged.

I looked away and took a deep breath. "You ended things when you betrayed me."

I couldn't look at his face. I couldn't bring myself to see how my words hurt him. I needed him to walk away, and I couldn't listen to him beg anymore. The only way I knew how to get him to leave was to hurt him.

Without a word, he stood up and walked out the door. The door shut quietly, but I felt it in my chest as my heart shattered and my chest caved in. Loud sobs ripped from my throat as I fell apart on the couch. The pain would be temporary, just like the physical pain I was experiencing. I had to keep telling myself that to move forward, this was necessary.

Mindy ran out of the bathroom, still wrapped in her towel. She scooped me up and cradled me in her arms. She didn't say a word, just held me and let me fall apart. It was what I needed to get it all out so I could put it all back together. Alone.

It was the only way I'd become stronger and independent. To achieve the things I wanted in life without a handout from someone. Without help from a man. It wasn't about feminism, it was about breaking free of the chains that had held me back for so long. About not being the weak woman I once was, afraid of her own shadow and afraid of the world. I leaned on Vincent as a crutch, and after a while it was comfortable.

Now was my chance to do this on my own, and I was taking it. No matter how badly I hurt myself or Peter in the process. In time we'd both heal, and he'd find that he was better off without me. I'd only drag him down if I didn't learn to live life on my own. I'd cling to him, and that wasn't the life that either one of us deserved.

Chapter 30

PETER

LEAVING KATE HAD BEEN one of the hardest things I'd ever done. Next to seeing her lying in a hospital bed with a tube down her throat. That shit would haunt me for a long time. Her face had been black and blue, and one eye was swollen shut. Her lips were puffy, and the cheek below her good eye was the size of a golf ball. All at the hand of my brother.

I'd thought she looked bad after her car accident, but this was so much worse. It tore me in two. If I ever got my hands on my fucking brother, I was going to rip him apart. They wouldn't be able to take him to jail because there would be nothing left of him.

I wanted to find him, but he'd hidden himself well. I'd called everyone I knew in search of him. My brother, Thomas, was ready to kill him, too, when I told him what Vincent had done. He said he'd keep an eye out, and if Vincent crawled back home like a sick puppy, he'd let me know. But not before hurting him first.

I had connections to some people I knew could take care of Vincent for good, through Kelly and a few old friends who had turned bad. The only thing stopping me from making those calls was Kate. I didn't think she'd ever forgive me if she found out. She was good-hearted and would consider justice served if Vincent was rotting in a jail cell. The only way I'd consider it justice was if he was six feet under in an unmarked grave where no one would ever find him. Rotting away alone.

I rubbed at my chest. It hurt. Every day for the last two months, my heart hurt. I couldn't eat, couldn't sleep, and couldn't concentrate at work. Kate had pushed me away. I'd stayed for two weeks at a hotel and run up a hefty bill that would set me back a little on starting the build for my house. It ended up being all for nothing.

She couldn't be with me. She needed to stand on her own two feet. I understood, but it hurt like hell. It hurt worse knowing I did this to us. I acted like my family without even realizing it and betrayed her. I went behind her back and got what I needed to save my house and my life and caused her to lose everything in the process.

I didn't mean for it to happen. It wasn't my intent. Hell, I wanted her to forget about everything and move in with me. I was so head over heels for her that I couldn't think straight. Once Kelly called with that information, I ran with it. I was so happy that they couldn't build in Oak Springs and that I didn't have to deal with Lawrence Development Company anymore that I just went all in.

It wasn't like I did it for myself. I did it for Kate, too. It wasn't her fault that her boss was trying to develop somewhere he couldn't. She had no idea. I figured that information would help her boss to move on from our town but also help Kate keep her job.

I was going to figure out a way to persuade her to move to Oak Springs and give up her job, anyway. Those few nights with her were some of the best of my life. She was a light in my life that I didn't realize I needed, and I fell hard for her.

We didn't just have sex, we made love. Every stroke of my cock inside her, every kiss, every touch, it was all writing our love story. Showing her how much I needed her, how much I cared for her, how much she meant to me. It was so much deeper than sex, and part of me thought she ran because it scared her.

It would be easy to assume I acted maliciously and that everything was a win for me, including her. It would be a lot harder to admit that we had something beautiful and lasting. Something deeper and bigger than we imagined.

The fact that it wasn't just a fling was what made it hurt like hell. I'd never felt this kind of lasting pain in my life, and I didn't know how to make it go away. I wanted Kate. I wanted to give up my life here and follow her, not the other way around. It didn't matter what I did with my life as long as she was in it. But she wasn't willing to say that we were enough. To give up her life to be with me.

I understood her need for independence, but it made me feel like shit that she cared more about that than she did about me. Maybe everything I had been feeling was all one-sided. Maybe she didn't feel that way about me at all.

Thankfully, a loud _thwack_ as Frank hit his golf ball off the tee interrupted my thoughts. He'd made solid contact, and the ball sailed straight down the fairway. There was minimal wind, and the sun wasn't too hot. It was perfect weather for a round of golf.

"You're up, man," Sid said, nudging me with his arm.

I rubbed the back of my neck. "Thanks."

"So, have you heard from her?" Frank asked.

I set my ball on the tee, grabbed my driver, and took a few practice swings. Despite the perfect conditions, I wasn't really in the mood for golf. At least I could pretend I was hitting Vincent's head each time I struck the ball. It was actually helping my game.

"No," I said, stepping up to the tee. I swung with everything I had, picturing Vincent's nose under the driver, and watched the ball sail. Sid whistled, and Frank cussed. The ball dropped on the green, and I smirked. Not bad. Not bad at all.

"Damn it!" Frank yelled. "How the hell are you playing this well?"

I walked over and put my club back in my bag with a smug smile. I picked up my beer from the cart and took a sip as I sat down. Sid was up last.

"Seriously, how?" Frank asked, taking a seat next to me.

"I keep picturing my brother's head instead of the ball. The rest is just pure luck."

Frank scoffed.

"Have you—"

"No," he said, cutting me off. "I would tell you if I'd heard anything. I've got my ear to the ground. I'm not sure where he went, but he's hiding pretty damn well."

I kicked the ground with the toe of my golf shoe. This was bullshit.

"Let's go," Sid called out to us.

Sid and I wanted to play just the back nine, but Frank insisted we play the whole eighteen. We'd been out here since eight in the morning, and I was hungry and tired and thoroughly pissed off. I wasn't good company, and I didn't give a damn about the fucking game.

We finally made it to the last hole. Frank was pissed off. He was in last place by a lot, and there was no way he'd make it up. I was leading with almost ten fewer strokes. Sid was hanging out in the middle; he'd played well. Surprisingly, this was the best damn game I'd ever played.

Frank set up his ball on the tee, took a few practice swings, and then let it fly. Right into the water. He cursed and flung his club down the fairway. I shook my head and sighed. He waded into the pond and tried to fish his ball out of the water.

"Hey man, just—"

I placed a hand on Sid's shoulder and shook my head. "Let him go."

I set my ball up on the tee, took a few practice swings, and let out a deep breath before stepping up to the ball. I pictured my brother's head on the ball again, and then I saw Kate's face in the hospital. The bruises, the pain she had endured at his hand. I hit the ball with everything I had, letting out a shout as I swung through. The ball sailed down the fairway, dropping just before the green.

Sid patted me on the back, and I blinked a few times. I stood frozen in my swing, chest heaving, staring down at the ball. The only thing I saw was the bastard's face. My arms felt like lead when they dropped to my side. Tired, I drug myself over to the golf cart and collapsed down into the seat. I grabbed the bottle of liquor Frank had stashed in his bag and took a big gulp.

Frank came out of the water with his hand held high. He was soaked from the waist down but smiling proudly. I chuckled and took another swig of liquor. The burn felt nice, so I took a few more. Frank waited for Sid to play his ball, which he hit nice and straight down the fairway. Frank flipped him off, and Sid laughed.

We headed to the clubhouse to grab a late lunch after we finished that hole. It was one o'clock, and I was exhausted and really drunk thanks to Frank's liquor. I'd finished the bottle on the way back to the clubhouse and almost fallen out of the golf cart while Frank drove. Now I was nursing a beer.

"I can't believe you beat me by that much," Frank said, shoving fries in his mouth.

"That was an impressive game, man," Sid agreed, tipping his beer back.

I grunted.

"We should get you home," Sid said.

"He's fine. He'll sober up." Frank stuffed more of his burger in his mouth.

"He's drinking beer," Sid pointed out.

"Oh. Oops." Frank pulled my beer over in front of him and placed a glass of water in front of me. "Here you go, buddy. Drink up."

"I'm not that drunk, you asshole," I grumbled.

Frank laughed. "Yeah, you are. You're drooling on your burger."

I looked down, and sure enough, there was a small wet spot on the bun. I wiped my mouth and leaned back in my chair, almost tipping it over. Sid grabbed hold of it and sat me back up.

"All right, time to go. I'll get us some takeout containers before we get kicked out of here," Sid said, standing up.

"This is the shitty one. They won't kick us out. I once got a waitress to take off her top and serve tables here for half an hour before her manager even noticed. It was a good night. She made a lot of money," Frank said.

I let out a deep rumbling laugh. "That was hillarous. Thought she was gon home wif you too."

"Is he slurring his words?" Frank asked, pointing a fry at me.

"Yes. Get the check. We need to go before he passes out and we have to carry him out."

"Too late," Frank said from far away as my eyes closed and all my weight dropped downward. Everything was black and shutting down. It felt really good to shut down.

LOUD CHOMPING AND OBNOXIOUS laughter rattled through my head as I woke up from a deep sleep. I opened one eye and saw Frank reclined back in my chair popping chips into his mouth. He let out another loud peal of laughter at something on the TV. Rolling over, I scrubbed a hand down my face. My head throbbed. How the hell did I get home?

"Morning, sleeping beauty. Do you want your burger now? It might have some drool on it." Frank sat up in the chair. The familiar squeak sounded five times louder than usual and reverberated through my skull. I groaned.

"What the hell happened?"

"You drank too much and passed out at Tiny's."

I rolled my eyes. "Remind me again why we play there? The name is stupid, and the course isn't that nice, either."

"The beer is cheap, they don't give a shit if you drink on the course, and they serve you until you pass out or die," Frank ticked off on his fingers.

I lifted my hand from my face and looked at him.

"What?" he asked with a shrug.

"There is something seriously wrong with you if you think those are all good things," I pointed out.

"Well, not the last part, but the first two are good. Plus, Tiny makes great burgers."

Frank jumped up and ran to the kitchen. I heard the buttons on the microwave, and then he was back with a plate of food and a bottle of my favorite power drink. He handed them both to me and helped prop me up. We ate in silence and watched some game show on TV where people were playing some type of mini golf course and doing a bunch of crazy things to win money.

"I want to play poker tonight," I said with a mouthful of burger. They were great burgers even reheated.

Frank lifted an eyebrow at me. "Are you sure?"

"Are you afraid I'll take your money?"

"Are you still drunk?" he asked.

"No, but I want to be."

He nodded and pulled out his phone.

Four hours later we were all seated around Tom's poker table in my living room.

"Dude, you gonna be okay?" Frank asked. He was sitting across the table from me.

"I'm fine. Now shut up and play," I snapped, and threw chips onto the table.

"All right fine. I fold. And you are full of shit!" Frank shouted, throwing his cards down.

"Ladies, can we not do this?" Sid asked, throwing his chips onto the pile. "Show me what you got."

We all laid our cards down at the same time. Sid won. I slammed my hand down on the table. I was off my game and losing money in my own damn house. Worse than that, Frank wouldn't let me drink anymore. Asshole could get shit-faced for months without me saying anything, but the minute I wanted to, and for good reason, he stopped me.

I shoved my chair back and stood up. "I need another beer. If that's okay with you, *mom*."

Without waiting for Frank to respond, I walked into the kitchen, grabbed a beer out of the fridge, and slammed the door shut. I twisted off the cap and threw it into the sink, listening to it ping off the dirty dishes that were piling up.

"You sure you're okay?" Frank asked, coming into the kitchen. He reached into the fridge and grabbed another beer.

"I'll be fine," I retorted and took a long pull of my beer.

"Call her," Frank said, leaning against the counter.

"I can't call her, Frank. She made it pretty damn clear she's done with me. The minute Mindy called me, I dropped everything and ran. I stayed for weeks and worked remotely, trying to hold it all together here and there. I paid out a fortune for the damn hotel room and now I'm delayed on starting the house. Then I found out my own brother was the one who did that to her. I want to hunt him down and beat the shit out of him, but no one can find him. Where the hell is he?" I shouted.

"I don't know," Frank muttered.

"I went with Mindy to get her clothes from the house. I saw the pool of blood where they found her. There was blood on the walls. So much fucking blood, Frank." I scrubbed a hand down my face.

"I stayed a few more days after getting her settled into Mindy's. Checked in with the police to make sure they had security detail on her until they caught Vincent, and do you know what happened?"

Frank said nothing. I waited. He looked at me and shrugged.

"She told me to get lost anyway. She doesn't think she's good enough. She's not strong enough to be with me. She said she needs to stand on her own. I tried to tell her I'd take things slow. Tried to tell her we could work it all out together, but she threw me away anyway. Told me she followed my dumb-ass brother for far too long. That she couldn't jump into a relationship and lose sight of herself again. She honestly thought I'd want her to change. To be someone else. I'm nothing like my fucking brother." I spat out.

"No, you're not like him or any of them. I'm sorry, man. It sounds like she's made the choice for you, and now you've got to move on."

"Yeah, no shit. Easier said than done."

Frank stepped away from me.

"Sorry. You'll tell me when they catch him, though, right?" I asked for probably the hundredth time.

"Yes. I have a friend who works at the precinct in Bellport. I called him the minute you told me. He's keeping tabs on the situation, and he'll call me. Don't worry, they'll get him."

"If they don't, I will, and then no one's ever going to find him." I slammed my hand on the counter.

Frank rubbed the back of his neck. "Jesus, you really think it will come to that?"

I turned to face him. "I should have done it already. He doesn't deserve to live."

"I know."

"You don't. You didn't see her, Frank. You didn't see what he did to her. He tried to kill her! I barely recognized her," I shouted.

Sid popped his head into the kitchen. "Everything okay in here?"

"Fine," Frank and I yelled at the same time.

We made our way back to the living room and took our seats. I didn't give a shit about the game anymore. The only thing I cared about was my brother's head on a platter.

Chapter 31

KATE

TWO MONTHS HAD PASSED since I got home from the hospital. It had been just as long since I last saw Peter. I felt terrible about the things I said to him. Especially the last part about how he was the one that ruined it between us. That wasn't true, and I forgave him for what he had done. I only said that because I needed him to leave. To stop begging me before I gave in.

I needed to do this, and I only hoped that in time he'd understand that. My heart hurt every day, and I cried myself to sleep almost every night. My life was a mess, and it was taking all my strength to put it back together.

The police finally let me back into the house a month ago, and I threw up just outside the door as I shook with fear. There was no way in hell I'd be able to enter the house, let alone get my things out so I could sell it.

Mindy called my parents, and they came down the following weekend and helped her drag everything out of the house and into a storage unit. Mindy and I had spent a lot of late nights over the last week and half going through things. Donating some of it and tossing the rest. That part felt really good. It was like therapy to get rid of the things that linked me to Vincent.

"I think you should put a business plan together," Mindy suggested.

"That's a good idea. Did my laptop make it here?"

"On the kitchen table. You sure you'll be okay here for the day?" she asked.

"I'll be fine. I'm feeling much better. You were at my checkup yesterday. My stomach looks good and has healed well. I'm still going to physical therapy, and my PT said I was improving quickly. My ribs don't hurt when I stretch anymore, either. See?" I said, showing Mindy that I could stretch my arm above my head without wincing.

Vincent had caused so many injuries. A fractured cheekbone, a broken eye socket—I was lucky that hadn't damaged my eye—one fractured vertebra, a busted upper lip, a concussion, and a massive stab wound on my side. He'd also broken three ribs when he kicked me in the side. I had a lot of cuts, scrapes, and bruises that were fading now. The healing process was slow, but it was moving a lot faster than the doctors had expected.

I'd meant the promise I made to myself in the mirror at my parents' house. Panic and fear were not going to control me any longer. I would not let Vincent be the reason I gave up on life. And my injuries wouldn't stop me from going after my dreams. I would fight to get better and fight for what I wanted in life. It was *my* life, and it was time to take it back.

Losing Peter was still painful, but the pain lessened every day along with my injuries. I loved him, but I just wasn't sure if I was actually in love with Peter the man, or with the life I imagined I could have with him. I'd fallen so hard and fast for him, and it felt too familiar. To cope with the gaping hole where my heart once was, I'd channeled all my energy into other things. Like figuring out what I wanted to do for work and going for it.

I'd spent the last week writing down different options, and I kept coming back to starting an event planning business. Mindy and I had lots of ideas, and the business aspect was really starting to take shape. I was excited, and focusing on my future plans kept me distracted from the pain—from my injuries and from losing Peter.

"There's a uniformed officer outside. I'm safe," I assured Mindy, placing my hand on her arm.

Peter had wanted an officer on me until they found Vincent. At first it was every day, and then it lessened. They didn't have the manpower to babysit me forever. There was only an officer on me today because the police had a lead on Vincent's whereabouts and were concerned he'd look for me. And Vincent knew where Mindy lived.

"Okay. I've got to get to the gallery. Call me if you need me. Or stop by if you get bored. Whenever you're ready, I have work for you," Mindy said, heading out the door.

I had worked with Mindy before and helped for free. She'd offered to pay me this time until I got on my feet and my new business could take off. I was happy to earn the money since I was still waiting to get the house back on the market. It was taking longer than I'd liked.

The house was mostly ready now. We had a cleaning crew in last weekend. I was waiting on final inspection before it could be listed again. As soon as it sold, I could put that money toward my business and getting a place of my own. It was so close I could feel it.

I stood up slowly and made my way over to the kitchen table. I needed to type out a business plan and come up with a good name for my company. After staring at a blank document for twenty minutes, I got up and brewed another pot of coffee. I needed the extra caffeine to be creative. Another ten minutes ticked by, and I sat back in my chair frustrated. I needed to call in a favor.

"Hello?" a cheerful voice answered. I almost teared up at the sound.

"Laney?"

"Kate?" Laney's voice rose an octave, and I had to pull the phone away from my ear. "Oh my gosh, how are you?"

"I'm all right. Slowly getting better."

"That's so good to hear. When Frank told us what happened, I wanted to rush there to help you. He said that we should all just wish you the best from here and give you some space to get better. Are you? Getting better? Do you need anything?"

I smiled. It was good to know that people in Oak Springs cared about me. Despite everything, I cared about them, too. I itched to ask about Peter but thought better of it. I needed to give him space to get over me; it wouldn't be fair if he found out I'd been asking around about him. I didn't want to risk hearing he'd moved on, either.

"I'm healing quickly. Thanks for the basket of fruits, chocolates, and ice cream. The card was beautiful. Mindy was so happy when she opened the box that she screamed," I said with a laugh. It felt good to laugh.

Laney chuckled. "That's good. She called and asked me to send more."

"Sounds like something she'd do. Listen, I actually called because I need a favor."

"Sure, anything," she said.

"I'm starting a business, but I need help getting started."

Laney laughed. "Girl, that's the hardest part. What do you need help with?"

"Writing a business plan, marketing, and coming up with a name," I said, chewing on my thumbnail.

"I can help you with all of that. How much time do you have?" she asked.

"Loads."

"Right. Well, let's get started then."

After hanging up with Laney, I felt good. She gave me some great advice, and we came up with a name. I wrote out bullet points highlighting the things I wanted in my business proposal and she explained the structure I needed for it.

When Mindy got home, I went over it with her and told her Laney said hello. Mindy's face lit up and then fell flat. I knew she missed Oak

Springs, and part of me wondered whether I was holding her back. She wanted that store on Grand Street, and I wanted her to have it.

"Are you sure it's okay that I stay here?" I asked.

"Of course. Are you kidding me? I wouldn't have it any other way," Mindy said.

I wrapped my arms around her and pulled her close, wincing into her neck. My body was sore since I'd spent most of the day at the kitchen table. Even though I was feeling a lot better, I still had a long way to go. Healing both emotionally and physically would take time.

IT WAS ANOTHER MONTH before the police finally caught Vincent. Another month of nightmares, of feeling eyes on me everywhere I went, of living in fear that he would come back for me. When Officer Wright, who'd been handling my case this whole time, called and told me they had caught him hiding out in Violet's guest house, relief washed over me. It was finally done.

I could finally move forward with my life. The house had sold a few weeks ago, which was another weight lifted off my shoulders. The realtor was respectful and understood I couldn't do a walk-through with him. I received an offer over the asking price, and the family was eager to move in. Since I was eager to sell, I accepted and signed on the dotted line. Mindy and I celebrated with margaritas and junk food.

My new business cards had arrived in the mail a few days ago with my company name, *Moments Worth Celebrating*, in beautiful, elegant lettering across the top. Life can be so unpleasant sometimes. I wanted to celebrate the moments that shine through the darkness. The moments that make you remember why you're alive.

The celebrations for achievements, life and love. Moments that you wanted to capture and hold onto. Moments that you could relive when you're feeling down. That's why I wanted to do this. I wanted to help make life beautiful. Especially after all I'd been through.

I knew a few places in the area needed a wedding and event coordinator, so I mailed some packets to them. I had a few meetings set up for next month. I was slowly making progress, and it felt fantastic. Mindy had a meet and greet event with potential clients lined up for me at her gallery, and I couldn't wait. The event wasn't for a few more weeks, so I spent most of my days working at Mindy's gallery and the nights working on the event.

My phone rang on the table, and I held my breath as I answered it. "Kate Miller."

"Hi Kate, this is Officer Wright. I wanted to call and let you know that Vincent took a plea deal. He's going away for fifteen years with possibility of parole. There was a lot of evidence stacked against him, and he knew it. He still tried to wiggle his way out of things and pled not guilty. But we found the knife, Kate. It was a match to the sample we collected from you. The prosecutors offered a deal, and he took it."

"A deal? Why would they offer him a deal when he could have gone away for life?" My heart was pounding in my chest.

Officer Wright sighed. "He had information on another case we were chasing. So in exchange for his information, they lessened the sentence."

"That means in fifteen years he can come after me again." My voice shook.

"That won't happen. You'll be notified in the future when he's eligible for parole. Kate, he's going to be stuck in there for fifteen years. He's either not going to make it, or he'll turn his life around. Guys like him push women around because they think they can get away with it. But in there, it's a different world."

I nodded. "I'm still afraid."

"Are you getting help? Talking to someone?"

"No."

"You should be. You went through something traumatic. I'll text you a few numbers of some great trauma counselors who can help you get through this. In time the fear will lessen, and you'll be able to face him in the future."

I chewed on my lip and thought it over. I wanted to be stronger. To face this fear and what happened to me. Part of getting stronger was facing things head-on. "Okay. I'd like the numbers."

"Great. I'll send them right over. Kate, this is a good thing. No testifying. No trial. This part is over. Now you can work on healing."

"Thank you for everything," I said.

"You're welcome. If there is anything else you need, call me."

I let out a sigh of relief. Though I was still nervous about the future, I was happy Vincent was behind bars. My phone buzzed in my hand almost immediately with a message from Officer Wright. The numbers for a few counselors. It was time to start healing inside, too.

Chapter 32

PETER

THE CRISP AIR BLEW MY HAIR in all directions. It had been a God-awful summer with the heat index regularly reaching 100 degrees. Fall was here, even though it was late, and it was promising. There was only a small window before winter started, but I was making good progress on the house, and I was confident I could get a lot accomplished. Things were coming along nicely.

We broke ground for the house two months ago. It was bittersweet to tear down my grandfather's house. I kept most of the wood so I could use it for building materials. That way the new house would have pieces of the old house. I dropped off a few pieces to Laney so she could make signs for the house, too.

Overall, I felt good, despite the ache in my heart. I missed Kate every day. I wished she would have been here when we tore the house down, when we broke ground for the new house, and when the town re-elected me as mayor a few weeks ago.

I wanted to call her. But I had tried to call, and text, and e-mail for a month after I left her at Mindy's and she never responded. So much time had passed now. Six months was a long time to hang on to someone who wasn't interested.

It was time to let it go. I needed to put Kate behind me and just move on. We hadn't even known each other that long. It was crazy, and I wished I could stop the longing and the ache in my chest. I wished I could erase her from my memory.

"Hey, idiot!" a woman yelled from behind me.

"Excuse me?" I growled, turning around.

Mindy Clark stood in my driveway, hands on her hips and fire red hair blazing in the sun. I swallowed hard. Was *she* here?

"She's not with me. I'm flying solo," she said, reading my mind.

"What do you want?"

"I want you to go get our girl." She took a step toward me.

I sighed. "It's been months of radio silence. She doesn't want to see me. I gave up two months ago when she ignored the formal invitation I sent her to my re-election ceremony. That was the final blow."

"Go get her," Mindy said, approaching me. I instinctively took a step back. She was small, but terrifying.

"What?" I asked.

"Kate's been moping around for months. She misses you. She acts tough, like she has it all together, but that's a lie. She's sad. She lost everything, Peter. Then she was assaulted in her own home—a home she didn't feel was hers to begin with—by a man she trusted for many years. She was fired from her job. A job she worked her ass off at to get promoted only to find out it was because of Vincent."

She took another step toward me. I stood still.

"Kate's slowly finding her footing, working for me, going to physical therapy and working on her new business. She just wants to prove to herself that she can stand on her own, that she's living her own life and not the one someone else wanted for her. She's lived in Vincent's shadow for so long, doing everything he asked and wanted. For a long time, she lost sight of who she was. The week we were here, and she was with you, I saw the old Kate I used to know coming back. But she was so afraid she'd wind up living in your shadow if she moved here and pursued a relationship with you. She needed to find her own way."

"I am not my fucking brother!" I shouted.

"I know you're not, and Kate knows it, too. It's not even about you. It's about her. She needed to find her backbone. To be strong and independent. It just wasn't something she felt she could do while starting something with you."

"You came all this way to tell me this?" I ground out. It was painful to hear it again. Kate had already given me a similar lecture when she tore my heart out.

"Don't flatter yourself. You and Frank both, I swear," she said, throwing her hands in the air. "I came all this way to look at my new store."

"New store? Where?"

"Down on Grand Street. I spotted it when I was here with Kate, and it's taken this long for me to work out all the details. I'm selling my store in Bellport and moving here. I have an offer in on a house on Grand Street not too far from the store. Kate won't come with me, though. You need to go get her before she buys her own place and plants roots in Bellport."

I sighed. "I don't think so, Mindy. I laid myself out there several times. Over text message, over e-mails, over voice mail. She never once responded. I know things are over. I just need to move on. She'll plant roots and figure out who she is. She'll move on, and she'll do well. Leave me out of it."

She took a step forward, and I took a step back. Her green eyes narrowed. "Wow, I thought Frank was bad, but you take the cake. He's just dumb; you're stubborn, and I think that's almost worse. I'm telling you; Kate loves you. She needs you. You need her, too. So let's go."

"Why didn't you drag her here with you? You could have made things easy by telling her she needed to come look at a new location with you. Why make me go to her?" I asked.

I crossed my arms over my chest and readied myself for battle. I wasn't just going to leave everything behind for who knows how long to go chase after someone who wanted nothing to do with me. Also, I was pissed. I gave Kate everything, pouring my heart out, and she gave me nothing but a broken heart in return. She should have known I wouldn't try to control her. I wasn't my damn brother. I just wanted to be a part of her life and have her be a part of mine. I loved her for who she was, panic attacks and all.

Wait, I loved her? When did that happen? It made sense with how much pain I was feeling without her. But was it even possible for two people to fall in love so quickly?

"Why did I think this would be easy? I think you should just come with me and then everything else will make sense." Mindy tugged on my arm.

I shook her off. "Mindy, I can't. She doesn't want me, and I'm building a house. I'm involved in the building and all the plans. I have mayoral duties and my store to deal with, too. I can't just drive three hours to go see someone who wants to forget me. Thanks for trying, but just go."

"Fine, but you're really dumb if you think she just forgot you. She thinks about you all the time. I catch her staring off into space, and when I ask what she's thinking about, she says nothing. But there are tears in her eyes, and I know it's you. I think you need to get your head out of your ass and go get her. If you want to live alone in that big house you're building, then go ahead, but if you're the man I think you are, then you want to fill it with love, and a family, and Kate. Don't be stupid, Peter. Only stubborn fools refuse to change their minds."

I turned around. "What did you just say?"

"Only stubborn fools refuse to change their minds," she repeated.

"That's something my Aunt Betty says. Did she send you here with that?"

"Maybe," she wiggled her eyebrows. "Did it work?"

I grinned and looked away. "Maybe. Where is Kate staying? And I'll think about it."

Mindy gave me the address of her gallery back in Bellport. She was ready to hand me the keys when I stopped her. "Let me think about this. I don't want to scare her by barging in with a key. You make a very compelling argument. Has anyone told you that you should be a lawyer?"

"Many times. Not my style," she said, flipping her long red curls. She turned and walked away.

I laughed and shook my head. Mindy was a force to be reckoned with, and whoever ended up with her would have their hands full. I wiped my hands off on a towel and told the guys I was taking a break.

I'd been staying at The B&B while my house was being finished. Aunt Betty saw me come in the front door and smiled from the kitchen. She never said a word. I knew she was in on the idea of me going to get Kate, and I shook my head at her while I headed up the stairs.

Collapsing down onto the bed, I stared at the ceiling and thought about everything. What would I say to Kate? *"We haven't spoken in six months, but I'm in love with you."* Yeah, that would not go over well.

She was so dead set on her plan that I doubted she'd listen to a word I said, even if she was miserable. She believed so deeply that she needed to stand on her own and be strong that she didn't care if she lost everyone in the process. It would be hard to convince her of anything.

But Mindy was right, even though I hated to admit it. My house would not be the same without Kate. I'd already pictured her in the house. Every time I looked at the plans or talked about a room in the house. Hell, even stepping into the bones of the house, I pictured her there.

I loved Kate, and I needed her in my life. If I went to her now, maybe I could persuade her to come back and finish the house with me. It would be ours and she could put her stamp on it, too. I missed her so much it hurt. I knew what I had to do.

"Bye, Aunt Betty. Thanks!" I said, running into the kitchen and kissing her on the cheek.

She smiled and patted my cheek. "Go get our girl."

"I'll try."

Thank you so much for reading *Dare You to Love* This book has been in my head for so long. It started on paper over a decade ago. The story has changed a lot, but the characters remained the same. Originally, I wrote the story to take place in Bellport and it was written to be a standalone. As I went through the first rewrite years later, Oak Springs was born. I can't wait for you to read more about the town and fall in love with the people like I did when I was writing it.

Thank you so much for purchasing this book and for meeting Kate, Peter and the residents of Oak Springs. If you enjoyed it, please consider leaving a review or recommending it to a friend.

Thank you again for all of your support!

Mina Cole

Acknowledgments

Writing this book took a lot of dedication and a lot of love. I pushed hard in 2020 during a crazy time to get my dream to take off. I couldn't have done it without the help of some exceptional people.

To my amazing husband, Tony, my rock and support system. Without your love and encouragement, and your help at home so I could write, I wouldn't have been able to make this possible.

To Sarah, my cheerleader, supporter, encourager, and sounding board. Thank you for being there for me from the start. You've loved my books from idea form and pushed me to get them out there for everyone to read.

To the RWR Facebook Group. Thank you for all of your support and encouragement. It made getting my words out into the world less scary. My dream took off after I joined the group and saw that it was possible.

To Beth, Sarah, Breanna and Sax for taking time to beta read and provide suggestions and encouragement. The feedback you provided helped shape the story into what it is now.

To my amazing editor, Kelly. I appreciate all you did for this book. All the revisions and plot holes that you helped me to correct. This book wouldn't be what it is today without your help. It was such a pleasure to work with you and I look forward to working together on future books.

Thank you, Beth, for proofreading the book to catch all those last-minute mistakes. Your feedback and suggestions have helped me tremendously. I appreciate your friendship and support. Your encouraging words have always helped to lift me up when I needed it most. Sometimes we just need someone to lend an ear and you are always willing to do that.

The cover to this book is amazing, thanks to the skillful design of Kate at Y'all. That Graphic. It was exactly what I had hoped for and more. Thank you for making my vision come to life, for putting up with all my questions and being so open to answer all of them, even non cover related ones.

To my author friends that helped provide information and help with formatting. The support in the community has been amazing.

Last but not least, to my readers. I hope you enjoyed reading about Oak Springs and the residents as much as I enjoyed writing about them. Thank you for supporting me and joining me in my journey.

About the Author

Mina Cole is a contemporary romance author who writes swoony heroes, loveable, sassy heroines and steamy heartwarming stories with a guaranteed happily ever after. She loves giving her readers a place to escape and characters that will capture their hearts.

She survives on coffee, her Kindle, and a healthy dose of sarcasm. When Mina is not writing, you can find her lounging with her nose in a book, or enjoying time with her family outdoors. She resides in Michigan with her husband, sons, and two fur babies.

Hang out with Mina in her reader group, Mina Cole's Chatter Room!

Connect with Mina:

Website: www.minacoleauthor.com

Instagram: www.instagram.com/minacoleauthor/

TikTok: www.tiktok.com/@minacolebooks

Facebook: www.facebook.com/minacoleauthor/

Goodreads:www.goodreads.com/minacoleauthor

BookBub:www.bookbub.com/authors/mina-cole